Waiting for the Mahatma

Waiting

for the

Mahatma

R. K. NARAYAN

MICHIGAN STATE UNIVERSITY PRESS

1955

Copyright 1955

The Michigan State University Press

Library of Congress Catalog Number: 55-11689

MANUFACTURED IN THE UNITED STATES OF AMERICA

A GLOSSARY OF INDIAN TERMS

Ahimsa.   Kindness. Nonviolence. A Hindu ethical ideal.

Almirah.   A cabinet, or cupboard.

Babu.   A title like Mr., or Esquire.

Badam Halwa.   A sweet made of almonds, sugar and ghee.

Banian.   A loose woolen jacket or vest.

Beeda.   Betel leaf, folded and ready for chewing.

Beedi.   Popular Indian cigarette, with the tobacco wrapped
   in a leaf.

Bhai.   Brother.

Bhajan.   Collective prayer, song.

Bharji.   A sweet made of sugar and milk.

Bidi.   Cheap tobacco.

Bonda.   A fried, hot food.

Budmash.   A ne'er-do-well, a good-for-nothing, scoundrel.

Bund.   Embankment.

Chalak.   Captain of a volunteer corps.

Chappati.   Wheat-flour pancake.

Charka.   Spinning wheel.

Cholam.   Indian corn.

Chutney.   A spicy condiment, a sauce.

Coir.   Coconut-husk fiber.

Deepavali.   Hindu festival, accompanied by fireworks.

Devata.   Celestial being, friendly to man.

Dhobi.   Washerman, sometimes laundry.

Dhoti.   Cloth worn around the body below the waist.

Dorai.   "King," used in referring to Europeans.

Dosai.   Rice-and-black-gram-flour pancake. (South India.)

Ghee.   A butter-product, from milk of the buffalo.

Gita.   Usual way of referring to the Bhagavad-Gita.

Goonda.   Hooligan.

Gram.   A grain, or dried-bean food.

Guru.   Teacher, spiritual guide.

Himsa.   The contrary to *Ahimsa;* cruelty, unkindness.

Hindi.   The official language of the Indian Republic, and of a great part of North India.

Idli.   Popular steamed cake of South India.

Jaggery.   Sugar, sweets.

-ji.   Honorific suffix, as in Gandhiji, Mahatma-ji.

Jibba.   Shirtlike Indian garment.

Jilebi.   Popular sweet of North India.

Jutka.   A light carriage, a cart.

Karma.   Hindu theological idea meaning desert, or destiny; doctrine that one's actions continue to have their effects in another incarnation.

Khaddar, Khadi.   Homespun cloth popularized by Mahatma Gandhi.

Kara sev.   Fried savory.

-ki-jai.   Victory to ——.

Lathi   A heavy stick, often bamboo, bound with iron.

Lavani.   An ode, memorial poem.

Mahatma.   Great Soul.

Mantra.   Sacred verse.

Mull.   Thin, translucent cloth.

Namaste.   A greeting: "I bow before you."

Peepul.   The *peepul* tree *(ficus religiosa)*, considered sacred by the Hindus.

Puja.   Worship.

Pulav.   Islamic dish of rice, meat. (Pilaf.)

Purdah.   A veil, a sheltered woman.

Pyol.   Elevated, roofed veranda in front of a house.

Raghupati Raghava, etc.   Devotional couplet mentioning the name and attributes of Rama.

Ramayana. Hindu epic, the adventures of Rama.

Ram Dhun or *Ram Nam.* Chanting of the name of the Hindu *avatar,* Sri Rama.

Sadhu. Religious mendicant.

Salaam. A profound obeisance.

Sambhar. South-Indian vegetable curry.

Sari. Hindu woman's dress.

Satyagraha. The Mahatma's program.

Satyagrahi. A dedicated follower of the Mahatma.

Sevak Sangh. Social service association.

Shastras. Sacred Scriptures.

Sircar. The Government, the local authority.

Subadhar. Revenue official of preBritish days. Noncommissioned officer in the British Army.

Swaraj. Home Rule.

Thali. Sacred marriage-badge tied by the husband around his wife's neck at wedding. Symbol of wifehood.

Tonga. Horsedrawn vehicle.

Vadai. A food delicacy.

Zamindar. Big landowner.

Zigomar. Popular name for highwaymen, robber, rogue.

Waiting for the Mahatma

Part One

HIS MOTHER who died delivering him, and his father who was killed in Mesopotamia, might have been figures in a legend as far as Sriram was concerned. He had, however, concrete evidence of his mother in a framed photograph which for years hung too high on the wall for him to see; when he grew tall enough to study the dim picture, he didn't feel pleased with her appearance; he wished she looked like that portrait of a European queen with apple cheeks and wavy coiffure hanging in the little shop opposite his house, where he often went to buy peppermints with the daily money given him by his granny. Of his father, at least, there were recurring reminders. On the first of every month the postman brought a brown, oblong cover, addressed to his granny. Invariably granny wept when the envelope came to her hand. It made his childish mind wonder what could be there in that envelope to sting the tears out of her eyes. It was only years later he understood that his granny had been receiving a military pension meant for him. When the envelope came she invariably remarked: "I don't have to spend your pension in order to maintain you. God has left us enough to live on," and took it to the fourth house in their row which was known as the "Fund Office," (what it meant, he never understood) and came back to say: "There is nothing so fleeting as untethered cash. You can do what you like with it when you are old enough."

That portrait in the opposite shop fascinated his adolescent mind. The shopman was known as Kanni, a parched, cantankerous, formidable man, who sat on his haunches all day briskly handing out goods to his customers. Until eleven at night, when he closed the shop, his hollow voice could be heard haranguing someone, or arguing, or cowing his credit-demanding clientele: "What do you think I am! How dare you come again without cash? You think you can do me in? You are mistaken. I can swallow ten of you at the same time, remember." The only softening influence in this shop of cigars, *beedies*, explosive aerated drinks, and hard words, was the portrait of the lady with apple cheeks, curls falling down the brim of her coronet, and large, dark eyes. "Those eyes look at me," Sriram often thought. For the pleasure of returning that look, he went, again and again, to buy something or other at the shop. "Whose is that picture?" he asked once, pausing between sips of a colored drink.

"How should I know?" Kanni said, "It's probably some queen, probably Queen Victoria," although he might with equal justification have claimed her to be Maria Theresa or Anne Boleyn.

"What did you pay for it?"

"Why do you want to know all that?" said Kanni, mildy irritated. If it had been anyone else, he would have shouted, "If you have finished your business, begone. Don't stand there and ask a dozen questions."

But Sriram occupied a unique position. He was a good customer, paid down a lot of cash every day, and deserved respect for his bank balance. He asked, "Where did you get that picture?"

Kanni was in a jovial mood and answered, "You know that man, the revenue inspector in Pillaiah Street. He owed me a lot of money. I had waited long enough, so one day I walked in and brought away this picture hanging in his room. Something, at least, for my dues."

4

"If there is any chance," said Sriram with timid hesitation, "of your giving it away, tell me its price."

"Oh, oh!" said Kanni, laughing. He was in a fine mood. "I know you can buy up the queen herself, master *zamindar*. But I won't part with it. It has brought me luck. Ever since I hung the picture there, my business has multiplied ten-fold."

One evening his grandmother asked: "Do you know what star it will be tomorrow?"

"No. How should I?" he asked, comfortably reclining on the cold cement window-sill, and watching the street. He had sat there, morning to night, ever since he could remember. When he was a year old his grandmother put him down there and showed him the various diversions passing outside: bullock-carts, horse-carriages, and the first few motor cars of the age, honking away and rattling down the road. He would not be fed unless he was allowed to watch the goings on of the street. She held a spoonful of rice and curd to his lips and exclaimed: "Oh, see that great motor car. Shall our little Ram travel in it?" And when he blinked at the mention of his name and opened his mouth, she thrust in the rice. This window became such a habit with him that when he grew up he sought no other diversion except to sit there, sometimes with a book, and watch the street. His grandmother often reproached him for it. She asked:

"Why don't you go out and mix with others of your age?"

"I am quite happy where I am," he answered briefly.

"If you left that seat, you would have many things to see and learn," said the old lady sharply. "Do you know at your age your father could read the almanac upside down, and could say at a moment's notice what star was reigning over which particular day?"

5

"He was probably a very wise man," ventured Sriram.

"He *was* very wise. Don't say 'probably,' " corrected his grandmother. "And your grandfather, you know how clever he was! They say that the grandfather's reincarnation is in his grandson. You have the same shaped nose as he had and the same eyebrows. His fingers were also long just like yours. But there it stops. I very much wish you had not inherited any of it, but only his brain."

"I wish you had kept a portrait of him for me to see, granny," Sriram said. "Then I could have worshipped it and become just as clever as he."

The old lady was pleased with this, and said: "I'll teach you how you could improve yourself." She dragged him by the hand to the little circle of light under the hall lamp. She took out the brown-paper-covered almanac from under a tile of their sloping roof. She sat down on the floor, clamored for her glasses till they were fetched, and forced Sriram to open the almanac and go through it at a particular page. It was full of minute bewildering symbols in intricate columns. She pushed his face close to the page.

"What is it you are trying to do?" he pleaded pathetically. She put her finger on a letter and asked: "What is this?" "*Sa—*" he read.

"It means *Sadhaya*. That's your star." She drew her finger along the line and pointed at the morrow's date. "To-morrow is this date, which means it's your birth star. It's going to be your twentieth birthday, although you behave as if you are half that. I am going to celebrate it. Would you like to call up any of your friends?"

"No, never," said Sriram positively.

So all alone next day he celebrated his twentieth birthday.

His guest as well as hostess was his grandmother. No one outside could have guessed what an important occasion was being celebrated in that house in Kabir Street bearing number "14." The house was over two hundred years old and looked it. It was the last house in the street or "the first house" as his great-grandfather used to say at the time he built it. From here one saw the backs of market buildings and heard night and day the babble of the big crowd moving on the market road. Next door to Sriram's house was a small printing press which groaned away all day and next to it another two-hundred-year-old house in which six noisy families lived, and beyond that was the Fund Office, where granny kept her grandson's money. A crooked street ran in front of these houses; their closeness to the market and to a Higher Elementary Town School, the Local Fund Dispensary, and above all to the half dozen benches around the market fountain, was said to give these houses in Kabir Street a unique value.

These houses were all alike—a large single roof sloping down to slender rosewood pillars with carvings and brass-decorations on them, and a *pyol,* an open brick platform under the windows, on which the household slept in summer. The walls were two feet thick and the doors were made of century-old teak planks with bronze knobs, and the tiles were of burnt mud, which had weathered the storms and rains of centuries. All these houses were alike; you could see end to end the slender pillars and tiles sloping down as if all of them belonged to a single house. Many changes had occurred since the houses were built two centuries ago. Many of them had changed hands, the original owners having been lost in the toils of litigation; some of the houses were rented out to tradesmen, such as the Sun Press, and the Butter Factory or the Fund Office, while their owners retired to villages or built themselves modern villas in Lawley Exten-

7

sion. But there were still one or two houses which maintained a continuity, a link with the past. Number 14 was one such. There the family lineage began centuries ago, and continued still, though reduced to just two members—Sriram and his grandmother.

Granny had somewhere secured a yard-long sugar cane for the celebration, although it was not the season. She said: "No birthday is truly celebrated unless and until a sugar cane is seen in the house. It's auspicious." She strung mango leaves across the doorway, decorated the threshold with colored rice powder. A neighbor passing down the road stopped to ask:

"What's the celebration? Shall we blow out the ovens in our house and come for the feast in yours?"

"Yes, by all means. Most welcome," said the old lady courteously, and added as if to neutralize the invitation, "You are always welcome." She felt sorry at not being able to call in the neighbors, but that recluse grandson of hers had forbidden her to invite anyone. Left to herself she would have engaged pipes and drums and processions for this particular birthday was a thing she had been planning all along. This twentieth birthday when she would hand over the Savings Pass Book to her grandson, and relinquish the trust.

It was an adventure accompanying granny to the Fund Office, four doors off. She seemed to shrink in stature under an open sky—she who dominated the landscape under the roof of Number 14—lost her stature completely in the open.

Sriram couldn't help remarking, "You look like a baby, granny."

Granny half-closed her eyes in the glare and whispered, "Hush! Don't talk aloud, others may hear."

"Hear what?"

"Whatever it may be. What happens behind one's door, must be known only to the folk concerned. Others had better shut up."

As if confirming her worst suspicion, Kanni cried breezily from his shop: "Oho, grandmother and her pet on an outing! A fine sight! The young gentleman is shooting up, madam!"

Sriram felt proud of this compliment; he was seized with a feeling of towering height, and he pursed his lips in a determined manner. He gripped in his right hand the brown calico-bound passbook presented to him with a somewhat dramatic gesture by his grandmother a moment ago.

"Oh, the young *subadhar* is going to the right school with the right book," Kanni remarked. "He must live to be as great as his father and grandfather put together."

Granny muttered, quickening her steps, "Don't stand and talk to that man; he will plague us with his remarks; that's why I never wanted your grandfather to sell that opposite site, but he was an obstinate man, such an obstinate man! He was also fond of this Kanni, who was then a young fellow."

"Was grandfather also buying plantains?"

"Not only plantains," she muttered, with a shudder, recollecting his habit of buying cheroots in Kanni's shop. She had thought it degrading for any person to be seen smoking a cheroot, "like a baby sucking a candy stick!," she was wont to remark, disturbing the even tenor of their married life. She had always blamed Kanni for encouraging her husband to smoke and never got over a slight grudge on that account. Before reaching the Fund Office they had interruptions from other neighbors who peeped out of their doorways and demanded to be told what extraordinary thing made the old lady go out in the company of her grandson. They could understand her going out all alone on the first of the month in the direction of the Fund Office, that was understandable. Now what made the lady go out in the company of the young fellow, who was an unusual sight—holding on to a bank book?

"What!" cried a lady who was a privileged friend of granny's. "Does it mean that this urchin is going to have an independent account?"

"He is no longer an urchin," cried the old woman. "He's old enough to take charge of his own affairs. How long should I look after him! I'm not an immortal. Each responsibility should be shaken off as and when occasion arises to push off each responsibility."

This was a somewhat involved sentiment expressed in a roundabout manner, but her friend seemed to understand it at once, and she cried, coming down the steps of her house, "How wisely you speak! The girls of these days should learn from you how to conduct themselves," which pleased granny so much that she stopped to whisper in her ear:

"I was only a trustee of his money. From today he will take care of his own money."

"Wisely done, wisely done," the other cried and asked, "How much in all?"

"That you will never know," said granny and walked off.

Sriram who had gone ahead asked: "How is it, granny, you stop and talk to everyone! What were you telling her?"

"Nothing," she replied, "and you follow the same rule and you will be a happier man. Your grandfather ruined himself by talking. Anything that happened to him, good or bad, was bound to be known to everyone in the town within ten minutes; otherwise his soul felt restless."

"Why should anything be concealed from anyone?" asked the boy.

"Because it's better so, that's all," said the lady. All these interruptions on the way delayed her arrival at the bank. The clock struck four as she showed her face at the counter.

"Must you be on the last second, madam?" the manager asked. "Is there any reason why you could not come a little earlier?"

"No, none," she said, "except that I'm not a young creature who can frisk along."

The manager, used to her ways, got down from his high seat, opened a side door, and without a word, let her in.

Sriram was being initiated into the mysteries of banking. The bank manager opened the last page of his passbook and said: "What figure do you see here?"

Sriram wondered for a moment if he was testing him in arithmetic, a most terrible memory of his early school days. He became wary and ventured to say: "Thirty-eight thousand, five hundred rupees, seven annas, and six pies."

"Quite right!" cried granny. She appeared to be surprised at the intelligence he exhibited.

Sriram asked petulantly, "What did you take me for, granny? Did you think I would not be good enough even for this?"

"Yes," she said quietly. "How should I think otherwise, considering how well you have fared in your studies!"

The manager, a suave and peace-loving man, steered them out of these dangerous zones by changing the subject: "You see, this is your savings deposit. You may draw two hundred and fifty rupees a week, not more than that; here is the withdrawal form. See that you don't lose it, and that nobody gets at it."

"Why? Would it be possible for anyone else to get at my money with that form?"

"Usually not, but it's our duty to take all possible precautions in money matters," said the manager.

Granny for some reason felt upset at Sriram's questions, "Why do you ask so much? If the manager says, 'Do this,' or 'Do that,' it's your duty to obey, that is all."

"I always like to know what I am doing," said Sriram, and added, "There's nothing wrong in that."

Granny turned to the manager and said with pride, "You see the present generation! They are not like us. How many years have you been seeing me here? Have you ever heard me asking why or how and why not at any time?"

The manager made indistinct noises, not wishing to displease either his old customer or the new one. He placed before the old lady a letter, tapped the bottom of the page with his finger, and said, "May I have your signature here? It's the new authorization, and you won't be bothered to come here as often as before."

"After twenty years, relief!" granny cried. She had the triumphant expression of one who had run hard and reached the winning line.

Sriram did not fully realize what it all meant, but took it quite casually. He simply said, "If I had been you I wouldn't have taken all this trouble to accumulate the money."

"You are not me, and that's just as well. Don't say such things before this man who has watched and guarded your property all these years!"

Sriram wanted to test how far the magic toy put into his hands would work. He seized the penholder, stabbed it into the inkwell and wrote off a withdrawal for two hundred and fifty rupees, tore off the page and pushed it before the manager with an air of challenge: "Let us see if I am really the owner of this money!"

The manager was taken aback by the speed of his activity. He smiled and said: "But my dear fellow, you know we close at four, and cash closes at two every day. If you want cash, you must be here before two on any working day. Change the date, and you can come and collect it the first thing tomorrow. Are you sure you want all that sum urgently for the first draw?"

"Yes, I am positive," said Sriram. "I would have taken more if you had permitted more than two hundred and fifty at a time."

"May I know why you need all this amount?" asked granny.

"Is it or is it not my money?" asked Sriram.

"It is and it is not," said granny in a mystifying manner. "Remember, I don't have to ask you what you do with your own funds. It's your own business. You are old enough to know what you do. I don't have to bother myself at all about it. It's purely your own business. But I want to ask you— just to know things, that is all—why do you want two hundred and fifty rupees now? It's your business, I know, but remember one thing. One is always better off with money unspent. It's always safer to have one's bank balance undamaged."

"Quite right, quite right," echoed the bank manager. "Great words of wisdom. I tell you, young man. Come tomorrow morning," he said picking up the form in his hand.

Granny cried: "Give it here," and she snatched the paper from his hand, and said, "Correct it to fifty. You need only fifty rupees now and not two hundred and fifty. I'd have torn up this but for the fact that it is your first withdrawal form and I don't want to commit any inauspicious act."

"Ah! That's a good idea," said the manager. "It's better

you carry less cash on you nowadays with pickpockets about."
He dipped the pen in the ink and passed it to Sriram: "Write
your signature in full on all the corrections."

Sriram obeyed, muttering, "See! This is just what I suspected! I'm supposed to be the master of this money, but I
cannot draw what I want! A nice situation!"

The manager took the form back and said: "Come at ten-
thirty tomorrow morning for your cash."

"I hope you won't expect me to come again with my grandmother!" Sriram said with heavy cynicism.

Next day Sriram stood at Kanni's shop and ordered colored
drinks and plantains. "How much?" he asked after he was
satisfied.

"Four annas," said Kanni.

Sriram drew from his pocket several rolls of notes, and
pulled one out for Kanni. It was a veritable display of wealth.

Kanni was duly impressed. He immediately became defer-
ential. "Have you examined your pockets to see if there may
not be some small change lying somewhere there?"

"If I had small change, would I be holding this out to
you?" asked Sriram grandly.

"All right, all right." Kanni received the amount and
transferred it immediately to his cash chest. Sriram waited
for change. Kanni attended to other customers.

Sriram said, "Where is my change?"

Kanni said: "Please wait. I have something to tell you.
You see—" An itinerant tea vendor just then came up with
his stove and kettle to ask for a packet of cigarettes. And then
there were four other customers. The place was crowded and
Kanni's customers had to stand on the road below his plat-

form and hold out their hands like supplicants. All the while Sriram stood gazing at the portrait of the rosy-cheeked queen who stared at the world through the plantain bunches suspended from the ceiling. School children came in and clamored for peppermints in bottles. Kanni served everyone like a machine. When everybody was gone Sriram asked, "How long do you want me to wait for my change?"

"Don't be angry, master," Kanni said. He pulled out a long notebook, blew the dust off its cover, turned an ancient page, and pointed at a figure and asked, "Do you see this?"

"Yes," said Sriram, wondering why everybody was asking him to read figures these days. He read out: "Nine rupees, twelve annas."

"It's a debt from your grandfather, which is several years old. I'm sure he'd have paid it if he had lived—but, one doesn't know when death comes: I used to get him special cheroots from Singapore, you know."

"Why didn't you ask Granny?"

"Granny! Not I. He wouldn't have liked it at all. I knew someday you would come and pay."

"Oh," Sriram said generously. "Take it, by all means," and turned to go.

"That's a worthy grandson," muttered Kanni. "Now the old man's soul will rest in peace."

"But where will the soul be waiting? Don't you think he will have been re-born somewhere?" said Sriram. Kanni did not wish to be involved in speculations on post-mortem existence, and turned his attention to the other customers waiting there. Before going away Sriram said, "I can buy that picture from you whenever you can sell it, remember."

"Surely, surely. When I wind up this shop, I will remember to give it to you, not till then: it's a talisman for me."

"If the lady's husband turns up and demands the picture,

what will you do?" Sriram asked, which made Kanni pause
and reflect for a moment what his line of action should be.

Sriram walked down the street, not having any definite
aim. He felt like a man with a highpowered talisman in his
pocket, something that would enable him to fly or go anywhere he pleased. He thrust his fingers into his *jibba* pocket
and went on twirling the notes. He wished he had asked the
manager to give him new notes: he had given him what
appeared to be second-hand notes: probably the Fund-Office
Manager reserved good notes for big men. Who was a big
man anyway? Anyone was a big man. Himself not excluded.
He had money, but people still seemed to think he was a
little boy tied to the apron strings of his grandmother. His
grandmother was very good no doubt, but she ought to leave
him alone. She did not treat him as a grown-up person. It
was exasperating to be treated like a kid all the time. Why
wouldn't she let him draw two hundred fifty instead of fifty,
if he wanted it? It would be his business in the future, and
she ought to allow him to do what he pleased. Anyway it
was a good thing he had only fifty to display before Kanni.
If he had shown two hundred he might have claimed half of
it as his grandfather's debt. Sriram was, for a moment, seized
with the problem of life on earth: was one born and tended
and brought up to the twentieth year just in order to pay off
a cheroot bill? This philosophical trend he immediately
checked with the thought: "I shall probably know all this
philosophy when I grow a little older, not now. . . ." He
dismissed his thought with: "I am an adult with my own
money, going home, just when I please. Granny can't ask
me what I have been doing. . . ." He walked round and

round the Market Road, gazing on shops, and wondering if there was anything he could buy. The money in his pocket clamored to be spent. But yet there seemed to be nothing worth buying in the shops. He halted for a moment reflecting how hard it was to relieve oneself of one's cash. A man who wore a cotton vest and a tucked-up *dhoti* held up to him a canvas folding chair, "Going cheap, do you want it?" Sriram examined it. This seemed to be something worth having in one's house. It had a red striped canvas seat and could be folded up. There was not a single piece of furniture at home. "Ten rupees sir, best teakwood." Sriram examined it keenly, although he could not see the difference between rosewood and teak or any other wood. "Is this real teak?" he asked.

"Guaranteed, Mempi Hill teak, sir, that is why it costs ten rupees: if it were ordinary jungle wood, you could have got it for four."

"I will give seven rupees," said Sriram with an air of finality, looking away. He pretended to have no further interest in the transaction. The man came down to eight rupees. Sriram offered him an extra half rupee if he would carry it to his door. Granny opened the door and asked in surprise, "What is this?" Sriram set up the canvas chair right in the middle of the hall and said, "This is a present for you, granny."

"What! For me!" She examined the canvas and said, "It's no use for me. This is some kind of leather, probably cowhide, and I can't pollute myself by sitting on it. I wish you had told me before going out to buy."

Sriram examined the seat keenly, dusted it, tapped it with his palm and said, "This is not leather, granny, it is only canvas."

"What is canvas made of?" she asked. Sriram said, "I have no idea," and she completed the answer with, "Canvas is only another name for leather. I don't want it. You sleep on it if you like."

He followed this advice to the letter. All day he lounged on this canvas seat and looked at the ceiling or read a tattered novel borrowed from the municipal library. When evening came he visited The Bombay Anand Bhavan and ordered a lot of sweets and delicacies, and washed them down with coffee. After that he picked up a *beeda* covered with colored coconut gratings, chewed it with great contentment, and went for a stroll along the river or saw the latest Tamil film in the Regal Picture Palace. It was an unruffled, quiet existence, which went on without a break for the next four years, the passing of time being hardly noticed in this scheme— except when one or the other of the festivals of the season turned up and his granny wanted him to bring something from the market. "Another Dasara!" Or "Another *Deepavali!*" "It looks as though I lighted crackers only yesterday!" he would cry, surprised at the passage of time.

It was April. The summer sun shone like a ruthless arc lamp—and all the water in the well evaporated and the road dust became bleached and weightless and flew about like flour spraying off the grinding wheels. Granny said as Sriram was starting out for the evening, "Why don't you fetch some good *jaggery* for tomorrow, and some jasmine for the *puja*?" He had planned to go towards Lawley Extension today and not to the Market, and he felt reluctant to oblige Granny. But she was insistent. She said, "Tomorrow is New Year's Day."

"Already another New Year!" he cried. "It seems as though we celebrated one yesterday."

"Whether yesterday or the day before, it's a New Year's Day. I want certain things for its celebration. If you are not going, I'll go myself. It's not for me! It's only to make some sweet stuff for you." Grumbling a great deal, he got up, dressed himself, and started out. When he arrived at the Market he was pleased that his granny had forced him to go there.

As he approached the Market Fountain a pretty girl came up and stopped him. "Your contribution?" she asked shaking a sealed tin collection box. Sriram's throat went dry and no sound came. He had never been spoken to by any girl before; she was slender and young, with eyes that sparkled with happiness. He wanted to ask, "How old are you? What caste are you? Where is your horoscope? Are you free to marry me?" She looked so different from the beauty in Kanni's shop; his critical faculties were at once alert, and he realized how shallow was the other beauty, the European queen, and he wondered that he had ever given her a thought. He wouldn't look at the picture again even if Kanni should give it to him free. The girl rattled the money box and the sound brought him back from his reverie, and he said, "Yes, Yes," and fumbled in his *jibba* side pocket for loose change and brought out an eight-anna silver coin and dropped it into the slot. The girl smiled at him in return and went away, she seemed to be moving with the lightest of steps; her movement was like that of a dancer. Sriram had a wild hope that the girl would let him touch her hand, but she moved off and disappeared into the market crowd. "What a dangerous thing for such a beauty to be about!" he thought. It was a busy hour with cycles, horse-carriages and motor cars passing down the road, and a jostling crowd was moving in and out of the arched gateway of the market. People were carrying vegetables, rolls of banana leaves and all kinds of

New Year purchases. Young urchins were hanging about with baskets on their heads soliciting, "Coolie, sir? Coolie?" She had disappeared into the market like a bird gliding on its wings. He felt he wanted to sing a song for her. But she was gone. He realized he hadn't even asked what the contribution was for. He wished he hadn't given just a nickel but thrust a ten-rupee note into her collection box (he could afford it), and that would have given her a better impression of him, and possibly have made her stand and talk to him. He should have asked her where she lived. What a fool not to have held her up! He ought to have emptied all his money into her money box. She had vanished through the market arch. He vaguely followed this trail, hoping that he would be able to catch a glimpse of her. If ever he saw her again he would take charge of the money box and make the collection for her, whatever it might be for. He looked over the crowd for a glimpse again of the white sari, over the shoulders of the jostling crowd, around the vegetable stalls. . . . But it was a hopeless quest, not a chance of seeing her again. Who could she be and where did she come from? Could it be that she was the daughter of a judge or might she be another worldly creature who had come suddenly to meet him and whom he did not know how to treat? What a fool he was! He felt how sadly he lacked the necessary polish for such courtesies. That was why it was urged on him to go to a college and pass his B.A. Those who went to colleges and gained their B.A. were certainly people who knew how to conduct themselves before girls. He passed into the market arch in the direction she took. He said tentatively at the fly-ridden *jaggery* shop: "A lot of people are about collecting money for all sorts of things." The *jaggery* merchant said sourly, "Who will not collect money if there are people to give?" "I saw a girl jingling a money box. Even girls have taken to it," Sriram said, holding his breath, hoping to hear something.

"Oh, that," the other said, "I, too, had to give some cash. We have to. We can't refuse."

"Who is she?" Sriram asked, unable to carry on diplomatically any further. The *jaggery* merchant threw a swift look at him which seemed slightly sneering, and said: "She has something to do with Mahatma Gandhi and is collecting a fund. You know the Mahatma is coming." And Sriram suddenly came out of an age-old somnolence, and woke to the fact that Malgudi was about to have the honor of receiving Mahatma Gandhi.

In that huge gathering sitting on the sands of Sarayu, awaiting the arrival of Mahatma Gandhi, Sriram was a tiny speck. There were a lot of volunteers clad in white *khaddar,* moving around the dais. The chromium stand of the microphone gleamed in the sun. Police stood about here and there. Busybodies were going about asking people to remain calm and silent. People obeyed them. Sriram envied these volunteers and busybodies their importance, and wondered if he could do anything to attain the same status. The sands were warm; the sun was severe. The crowd sat on the ground uncomplainingly.

The river flowed, the leaves of the huge banyan and *peepul* trees on the banks rustled; the waiting crowd kept up a steady babble, constantly punctuated by the pop of sodawater bottles; longitudinal cucumber slices, crescent-shaped, and brushed up with the peel of a lime dipped in salt, were disappearing from the wooden tray of a vendor who was announcing in a subdued tone (as a concession to the coming of a great man), "Cucumber for thirst, the best for thirst." He had wound a green Turkish towel around his head as a protection from the sun. Sriram felt parched, and looked at the tray longingly. He wished he could go up and buy a crescent. The thought of biting into its cool succulence was tantalizing. He was at a distance and if he left his seat he'd have no chance of getting back to it. He watched a lot of others giving their cash and working their teeth into the crescent. "Waiting for the Mahatma makes one very thirsty," he thought.

Every ten minutes someone was starting a canard that the great man had arrived, and it created a stir in the crowd. It became a joke, something to relieve the tedium of waiting. Any person, a microphone fitter or a volunteer, who dared to cross the dais was greeted with laughter and booing from a hundred thousand throats. A lot of familiar characters, such as an old teacher of his, and the pawnbroker in Market Road, made themselves unrecognizable by wearing white *khaddar* caps. They felt it was the right dress to wear on this occasion. "That *khaddar* store off the Market Fountain must have done a roaring business in white caps today," Sriram thought. Far off, pulled obscurely to the side was a police van with a number of men peering through the safety grill.

There was a sudden lull when Gandhi arrived on the platform and took his seat. "That's Mahadev Desai," someone whispered into Sriram's ears. "Who is the man behind Gandhiji?"

"That's Mr. Natesh, our Municipal Chairman." Someone sneered at the mention of his name. "Some people conveniently adopt patriotism when Mahatmaji arrives." "Otherwise how can they have a ride in the big procession and a seat on the dais?" Over the talk the amplifiers burst out, "Please, please be silent."

Mahatma Gandhi stood on the dais, with his palms brought together in a salute. A mighty cry rang out, "Mahatma Gandhi-ki Jai!" Then he raised his arm, and instantly a silence fell on the gathering. He clapped his hands rhythmically and said: "I want you all to keep this up, this beating for a while." People were halfhearted. And the voice in the amplifier boomed, "No good. Not enough. I like to see more vigor in your arms, more rhythm, more spirit. It must be like the drum-beats of the nonviolent soldiers marching on to cut the chains that bind Mother India. I want to hear the great beat. I like to see all arms upraised, and clapping. There is nothing to be ashamed of in it. I want to see unity in it. I want you all to do it with a single mind." And at once, every man, woman, and child, raised their arms and clapped over their heads.

Sriram wondered for a moment if it would be necessary for him to add his quota to this voluminous noise. He was hesitant. "I see someone in that corner not quite willing to join us. Come on, you will be proud of this preparation." Sriram felt he had been found out, and followed the lead. Now a mighty choral chant began: *"Raghupathi Raghava Raja Ram, Pathitha Pavana Seetha Ram,"* to a simple tune, led by a girl at the microphone. It went on and on, then ceased, when Mahatmaji began his speech. Natesh interpreted in Tamil what Gandhi said in Hindi. At the outset Mahatma Gandhi explained that he'd speak only in Hindi as a matter of principle. "I will not address you in English. It's the language of our rulers. It has enslaved us. I very much wish I could speak to you in your own sweet language, Tamil; but alas, I am too hard-pressed for time to master it now, although I hope if God in his infinite mercy grants me the longevity due to me, that is one hundred and twenty-five years, I shall be able next time to speak to you in Tamil without troubling our friend Natesh."

"Natesh has a knack of acquiring good certificates," someone murmured in an aggrieved tone. "Runs with the hare and hunts with the hounds," said a schoolmaster.

"He knows all of them inside out. Don't imagine the old

gentleman does not know whom he is dealing with." "I notice two men there talking," boomed Gandhiji's voice. "It's not good to talk now, when perhaps the one next to you is anxious to listen. If you disturb his hearing, it is one form of *himsa*." And at once the commentators lowered their heads and became silent. People were afraid to stir or speak. Mahatma Gandhi said: "I see before me a vast army. Everyone of you has certain good points and certain defects, and you must all strive to discipline yourselves, before we can hope to attain freedom for our country. An army is always in training and keeps itself in good shape by regular drill and discipline. We the citizens of this country are all soldiers of a nonviolent army, but even such an army has to practice a few things daily in order to keep itself in proper condition: we do not have to bask in the sun and cry 'Left' or 'Right.' But we have a system of our own to follow: that's *Ram Dhun*; spinning on the *charka* and the practice of absolute Truth and nonviolence."

At the next evening's meeting Sriram secured a nearer seat. He now understood the technique of attending these gatherings. If he hesitated and looked timid, people pushed him back and down. But if he looked like one who owned the place, everyone stood aside to let him pass. He wore a pair of large dark glasses, which gave him, he felt, an authoritative look. He strode through the crowd. The place was cut up into sectors with stockades of bamboo, so that people were penned in groups. He assumed a tone of bluster which carried him through the various obstacles and brought him to the first row right below the dais. It took him farther away from the sellers of cucumber and aerated water, who operated on the fringe of the vast crowd. But there was another advantage in this place: He found himself beside the enclosure where the women were assembled. Most of them were without ornaments, knowing Gandhiji's aversion to all show and luxury. Even then they were an attractive lot, in their saris of varied colors, and Sriram sat unashamedly staring at the gathering, his favorite hobby for the moment being to speculate what type he would prefer for a wife. He fancied himself the center of attraction if any woman happened to look in his direction. "Oh, she is impressed with my glasses—takes me to be a big fellow, I suppose." He recollected Gandhiji's suggestion on the previous day: "All women are your sisters and mothers. Never look at them with thoughts of lust. If you are troubled by such thoughts, this is the remedy: walk with your head down, looking at the ground during the day, and with your eyes up, looking at the stars at night." He had said this in answering a question that someone from the audience had put to him. Sriram felt uncomfortable at the recollection. "He will probably read my thoughts." It seemed to be a risky business sitting so near the dais. Gandhi seemed to be a man who spotted disturbers and cross-thinkers however far away they sat. He was sure to catch him the moment he arrived on the platform, and say, "You there! Come up and make a clean breast of it. Tell this assembly what your thoughts were. Don't look in the direction of the girls at all if you cannot control your thoughts." Sriram resolutely looked away in another direction, where men were seated. "A most uninteresting and boring collection of human faces; wherever I turn I see only some shopkeeper or a schoolmaster. What is the use of spending one's life looking at them?" Very soon, unconsciously, he turned again towards the women, telling himself, "So many sisters and mothers! I wish they would let me speak to them. Of course I have no evil thoughts in my mind at the moment."

Presently Mahatmaji ascended the platform and Sriram hastily took his eyes off the ladies and joined in the hand-clapping with well-timed devotion and then in the singing of *Raghupathi Raghava Raja Ram*. After that Gandhi spoke on nonviolence, and explained how it could be practiced in daily life. "It is a perfectly simple procedure, provided you have faith in it. If you watch yourself, you will avoid all actions, big or small, and all thoughts however obscure, which may cause pain to another. If you are watchful, it will come to you naturally," he said. "When someone has wronged you or has done something which appears to you to be evil, just pray for the destruction of that evil. Cultivate an extra affection for the person and you will find that you are able to bring about a change in him. Two thousand years ago, Jesus Christ meant the same thing when he said, 'Turn the other cheek.'"

Thus he went on. Sometimes Sriram felt it impossible to follow his words. He could not grasp what he was saying, but he looked rapt, he tried to concentrate and understand. This was the first time he felt the need to try and follow something, the first time that he found himself at a disadvantage. Until now he had a conviction, especially after he began to operate his own bank account, that he understood everything in life. This was the first time he was assailed by doubts of his own prowess and understanding. When Mahatmaji spoke of untouchability and caste, Sriram reflected parallelly, "There must be a great deal in what he says. We always think we are superior people. How granny bullies that ragged scavenger who comes to our house every day to sweep the backyard!" Granny was so orthodox that she would not let the scavenger approach nearer than ten yards, and habitually adopted a tone of bullying while addressing him. Sriram also took a devilish pleasure in joining the baiting and finding fault with the scavenger's work, although he never paid the slightest attention to their comments. He simply went about his business, driving his broom vigorously and interrupting himself only to ask, "When will master give me an old shirt promised so long ago?"

He suddenly noticed on the dais the girl who had jingled a money box in his face a few days ago, at the Market. She was clad in a sari of *khaddar,* white homespun, and he noticed how well it suited her. Before he had felt that the wearing of *khaddar* was a fad, that it was an apparel fit only for cranks, but now he realized it could be the loveliest stuff. He paused for a moment to consider whether it was the wearer who was enriching the cloth or whether the material was good in itself. But he had to put off the whole problem. It was no time for abstract considerations. There she stood, like a vision beside the microphone, on the high dais, commanding the whole scene, a person who was worthy of standing beside Mahatmaji's microphone. How confidently she faced the crowd! He wished he could go about announcing, "I know who that is beside the microphone into which Mahatmaji is speaking." The only trouble was that if they turned and asked him, "What is her name?" he would feel lost. It would be awkward to say, "I don't know; she came jingling a collection box the other day at the market. I wish I could say where she lives. I should be grateful for any information."

At this moment applause rang out, and he joined in it. Gandhiji held up his hand to say, "It is not enough for you to clap your hands and show your appreciation of me. I am not prepared to accept it all so easily. I want you really to make sure of a change in your hearts before you ever think of asking the British to leave the shores of India. It's all very well for you to take up the cry and create an uproar. But that's not enough. I want you to clear your hearts and mind and make certain that only love resides there, and there is no residue of bitterness for past history. Only then can you

27

say to the British, 'Please leave this country to be managed or mismanaged by us, that's purely our own business, and come back any time you like, as our friend and distinguished guest, not as our rulers,' and you will find John Bull packing his suitcase. But be sure you have in your heart love and not bitterness." Sriram told himself looking at the vision beside the microphone, "Definitely it's not bitterness. I love her." "But," Mahatmaji was saying, "if I have the slightest suspicion that your heart is not pure or that there is bitterness there, I'd rather have the British stay on. It's the lesser of two evils." Sriram thought: "Oh, revered Mahatmaji, have no doubt that my heart is pure and without bitterness. How can I have any bitterness in my heart for a creature who looks so divine?"

She was at a great height on the platform, and her features were not very clear in the afternoon sun which seemed to set her face ablaze. She might be quite dark and yet wear a temporarily fair face illumined by the sun or she might really be fair. If she were dark, without a doubt his grandmother would not approve of him marrying her. In any case it was unlikely that they would have her blessing, since she had other plans for his marriage, a brother's granddaughter brought up in Kumbum, a most horrible, countrified girl who would guard his cash. If grandmother was so solicitous of his money she was welcome to take all of it and hand it to the Kumbum girl. That would be the lesser of the two evils, but he would not marry the Kumbum girl, an unsightly creature with a tight oily braid falling on her nape and dressed in a gaudy village sari, when the thing to do was to wear *khaddar*. He would refuse to look at anyone who did not wear *khadi*; *khadi* alone was going to save the nation from ruin and get the English out of India, as explained untiringly by that venerable saint, Mahatmaji. He felt sad

28

and depressed at the thought that in the twentieth century there were still people like the Kumbum girl, whom he had seen many many years ago when his uncle came down to engage a lawyer for a civil suit in the village. Sriram wanted to go and assure the girl on the grandstand that he fully and without the slightest reservation approved of her outlook and habits. It was imperative that he should approach her and tell her that. He seized a chance for himself at the end of the meeting.

Mahatmaji started to descend from the platform. There was a general rush forward, and a number of volunteers began pushing back the crowd, imploring people not to choke the space around the platform. Mahatmaji himself seemed to be oblivious of all the turmoil going on around him. Sriram found a gap in the cordon made by the volunteers and slipped through. The heat of the sun hit him on the nape, the huge trees on the river's edge rustled above the din of the crowd, birds were creating a furore in the branches, being unaccustomed to so much noise below. The crowd was so great that Sriram for a moment forgot where he was, which part of the town he was in, and but for the noise of the birds he would not have remembered he was on the banks of the Sarayu. "If that girl can be with Mahatmaji I can also be there," he told himself indignantly as he threaded his way through the crowd. There was a plethora of white-capped young men, volunteers who cleared a way for Mahatmaji to move in. Sriram felt that it would have been so much better if he had not made himself so conspicuously different with his half-arm shirt and *mull-dhoti,* probably products of the hated mills. He feared that any moment someone might discover him and put him out. If they chal-lenged and asked, "Who are you?" he felt he wouldn't be able to answer coherently, or he might just retort, "Who do you think you are talking to? That girl supporting the Mahatma is familiar to me. I am going to know her, but don't ask me her name. She came with a collection box one day at the market . . ."

But no such occasion arose. No one questioned him and he was soon mixed up with a group of people walking behind Mahatmaji in the lane made by the volunteers, as crowds lined the sides. He decided to keep going till he was stopped. If someone stopped him he could always turn round and go home. They would not kill him for it anyway. Killing! He was amused at the word: no word could be more incongruous in the vicinity of one who would not hurt even the British. One might be confident he would not let a would-be follower be slaughtered by his volunteers. Presently Sriram found himself in such a position of vantage that he lost all fear of being taken for an intruder and walked along with a jaunty and familiar air, so that people lining the route looked on him with interest. He heard his name called. "Sriram!" An old man who used to be his teacher years before was calling him. Even in his present situation Sriram could not easily break away from the call of a teacher: it was almost a reflex: he hesitated for a moment wondering whether he would not do well to run away without appearing to notice the call, but almost as if reading his mind, his teacher called again, "A moment! Sriram." He stopped to have a word with his master, an old man who had wrapped himself in a colored shawl and looked like an apostle with a slight beard growing on his chin. He griped Sriram's elbow eagerly and asked, "Have you joined them?"

"Whom?"

"Them—" said the teacher pointing away. Sriram hesitated for a moment wondering what he should reply, and mumbled, "I mean to . . ."

"Very good, very good," said the master, "In spite of your marks I always knew that you would go far, smart fellow. You are not dull but only lazy. If you worked well you could always score first-class marks like anyone else, but you were always lazy, I remember how you stammered when asked the capital of England. Ho! Ho!" he laughed at the memory. Sriram became restive and wriggled in his grip. The teacher said, "I am proud to see you here, my boy. Join the Congress. Work for the country. You will go far, God bless you . . ."

"I am glad you think so, sir," said Sriram and turned to dash away. The teacher put his face close to his and asked in a whisper, "What will Mahatmaji do now after going in there?"

"Where?" Sriram asked not knowing where Gandhi was going, although he was following him.

"Into his hut," replied the teacher.

"He will probably rest," answered Sriram, resolutely preparing to dash off. If he allowed too great a distance to develop between himself and the group they might not admit him at all. A little boy thrust himself forward and asked, "Can you get me Mahatma's autograph?" "Certainly not," replied Sriram, gently struggling to release himself from his teacher's hold. His teacher whispered in his ear, "Whatever happens, don't let down our country."

"No, sir, never, I promise," replied Sriram, gently pushing away his old master and running after the group who were fast disappearing from his view. They were approaching a wicket gate made of thorns and bamboo. He saw the girl going ahead to open the gate. He sprinted forward as the crowd watched. He had an added assurance in his steps now he felt that he belonged to the Congress. The teacher had put a new idea into his head and he almost felt he was a veteran of the party. He soon joined the group and he had

mustered enough pluck to step up beside the girl. It was a
proud moment for him. He looked at her. She did not seem
to notice his presence. He sweated all over with excitement
and panted for breath, and could not make out the details
of her personality, complexion or features. However, he
noted with satisfaction that she was not very tall, himself
being of medium height. Gandhi was saying something to
her and she was nodding and smiling. He did not understand
what they were saying, but he also smiled out of sympathetic
respect. He wanted to look as much like them as possible,
and cursed himself for the hundredth time that day for being
dressed in mill cloth.

The Mahatma entered his hut. This was one of the dozen
huts belonging to the city sweepers who lived on the banks of
the river. It was probably the worst area in the town; it was
an exaggeration even to call them huts; they were just hovels,
put together with rags, tin-sheets, and coconut-matting, all
crowded in anyhow, with scratchy fowl cackling about,
and children growing in the street dust; the municipal services were neither extended here nor missed although the
people living in the hovels were employed by the municipality
for scavenging work in the town. They were paid ten rupees
a month per head, and since they worked in families of four
or five, each had a considerable income by Malgudi standards.
They hardly ever lived in their huts, spending all their time
around the municipal building, or at the toddy shop, run
by the government nearby, which absorbed all their earnings. These men spent less than a tenth of their income on
food or clothing, always depending upon mendicancy in their
off hours for survival. Deep into the night their voices could
be heard clamoring for alms, in all the semi-dark streets of
Malgudi. Troublesome children were silenced at the sound
of their approach. Their possessions were few; if a cow or a

calf died in the city they were called in to carry off the carcass and then the colony at the river's edge brightened up for they held a feast on the flesh of the dead animal and made money out of its hide. Reformers looked on with wrath and horror, but did little else, since as an untouchable class they lived outside the town limits, beyond Nallappa's Grove, where nobody went, and they used only a part of the river on its downward course. This was the background to the life of the people in whose camp Gandhi had elected to stay during his visit to Malgudi. It had come as a thunderbolt on the Municipal Chairman, Mr. Natesh, who had been for weeks preparing his palatial house, "Neel Bagh," in the aristocratic Lawley Extension for receiving Ghandi. His arguments as to why he alone should be Mahatmaji's host seemed unassailable, "I have spent two lakhs on the building, my garden and lawns alone have cost me twenty-five thousand rupees so far. What do you think I have done it for? I am a simple man, sir, my needs are very simple. I don't need any luxury. I can live in a hut, but the reason why I have built it on this scale is that I should be able for at least once in my lifetime, to receive a great soul like Mahatmaji. This is the only house in which he can stay comfortably when he comes to this town. Let me say without appearing to be boastful that it is the biggest and the best-furnished house in Malgudi, and we as people of Malgudi have a responsibility to give him our very best; how can we house him in any lesser place?"

The Reception Committee applauded his speech. The District Collector, who was the head of the district and the District Superintendent of Police, who was next to him in authority, attended the meeting as ex-officio members. A dissenting voice said, "Why not give the Circuit House for Mahatmaji?" The Circuit House on the edge of the town was an old East India Company building standing on an acre of land, on the Trunk Road. Robert Clive was supposed to have halted there, while marching to relieve the siege of Trichinopoly. The citizens of Malgudi were very proud of this building and never missed an opportunity to show it off to anyone visiting the town and it always housed the distinguished visitors who came this way. It was a matter of prestige for the governors to be put up there. Even in this remote spot they had arranged to have all their conveniences undiminished, with resplendent sanitary fittings in the bathrooms. It was also known as the Glass House, by virtue of a glass-fronted bay room from which the distinguished guests could watch the wild animals that were supposed to stray near the building at night in those times. The dissenting voice in the Reception Committee said, "Is it the privilege of the ruling race alone to be given the Circuit House? Is our Mahatmaji unworthy of it?"

The Collector who was the custodian of British prestige rose to a point of order and administered a gentle reproof to the man who spoke, "It is not good to go beyond the relevant facts at the moment; if we have considered the Circuit House as unsuitable it is because we have no time to rig it up for receiving Mr. Gandhi." It was a point of professional honor for him to say *Mr.* Gandhi and not *Mahatma,* and but for the fact that as the Collector he could close the entire meeting and put all the members behind bars under the Defense of India Act, many would have protested and walked out, but they held their peace and he drove home the point. "Since Mr. Gandhi's arrival has been a sudden decision, we are naturally unable to get the building ready for him; if I may say so our chairman's house seems to suit the purpose and we must be grateful to him for so kindly obliging us."

"And I am arranging to move to the Glass House, leaving my house for Mahatmaji's occupation."

That seemed to decide it. His partisans cheered loudly, and it was resolved by ten votes to one that Mahatmaji should stay in "Neel Bagh," and the chairman left the meeting with a heavy, serious look. He wrote to Gandhiji's secretary and received a reply, which he read at the next meeting, "Mahatma Gandhi wishes that no particular trouble should be taken about his lodging, and that the matter may be conveniently left over till he is actually there." The council debated the meaning of the communication and finally concluded that it only meant that though the Mahatma was unwilling to be committed to anything he would not refuse to occupy "Neel Bagh." The dissenting voice said, "How do you know that he does not mean something else?" But he was soon overwhelmed by the gentle reprimand of the Collector. The communication was finally understood to mean, "I know Mahatmaji's mind, he does not want to trouble anyone if it is a trouble."

"He probably does not know that it is no trouble for us at all."

"Quite so, quite so," said another soothsayer. And they were all pleased at this interpretation. A further flattering comparison was raised by someone who wanted to create a pleasant impression on the Chairman: "Let us not forget that Mahatmaji takes up his residence at Birla House at Delhi and Calcutta. I am sure he will have no objection to staying in a palatial building like the one our Chairman has built." The dissenting voice said, "Had we better not write and ask if we have understood him right, and get his confirmation?" He was not allowed to complete his sentence but was hissed down, and the District Superintendent of Police added slowly, "Even for security arrangements any other place would present difficulties." For this sentiment he received an appreciative nod from his superior, the District Collector.

When Gandhi arrived, he was ceremoniously received, all the bigwigs of Malgudi and the local gentry being introduced to him one by one by the Chairman of the municipality. The police attempted to control the crowd, which was constantly shouting, "Mahatma Gandhi Ki Jai." When the Chairman read his address of welcome at the elaborately constructed archway outside the railway station he could hardly be heard, much to his chagrin. He had spent a whole week composing the text of the address with the help of a local journalist, adding whatever would show off either his patriotism or the eminent position Malgudi occupied in the country's life. The Collector had taken the trouble to go through the address before it was sent for printing in order to make sure that it contained no insult to the British Empire, that it did not hinder the war effort, and that it in no way betrayed military secrets. He had to censor it in several places: where the Chairman compared Malgudi to Switzerland (the Collector scored this out because he felt it might embarrass a neutral state): a reference to the hosiery trade (since the Censor felt this was a blatant advertisement for the Chairman's goods and in any case he did not want enemy planes to come looking for this institution thinking it was a camouflage for the manufacture of war material); and all those passages which hinted at the work done by Gandhiji in the political field. The picture of him as a social reformer was left intact and even enlarged; anyone who read the address would conclude that politics were the last thing that Mahatmaji was interested in. In any case, in view of the reception, the collector might well have left the whole thing alone since cries of 'Mahatmaji Ki Jai' and 'Down with the Municipal Chairman' made the speech inaudible. The crowd was so noisy that Mahatmaji had to remonstrate once or twice. When he held up his hand the crowd subsided and waited to listen to him. He said quietly, "This is sheer lack of order, which I cannot commend. Your Chairman is reading something and I am in courtesy bound to know what he is saying. You must all keep quiet. Let him proceed."

"No," cried the crowd. "We want to hear Mahatmaji and not the Municipal Chairman."

"Yes," replied Mahatmaji. "You will soon hear me, in about an hour on the banks of your Sarayu River. That is the program as framed."

"By whom?"

"Never mind by whom. It has my approval. That is how it stands. On the sands of Sarayu in about an hour. Your Chairman has agreed to let me off without a reply to his very kind address. You will have to listen to what he has to say because I very much wish to . . ." This quietened the mob somewhat and the Chairman continued his reading of the address, although he looked intimidated by the exchanges. The Collector looked slightly displeased and fidgety, feeling he ought to have taken into custody the dissenting member, who had perhaps started all this trouble in the crowd. He leaned over and whispered to the Chairman, "Don't bother, read on leisurely. You don't have to rush through," but the Chairman only wished to come to the end of his reading; he was anxious to be done with the address before the crowd burst out again. He did not complete his message a second too soon as presently the crowd broke into a tremendous uproar, which forced the Police Superintendent hastily to go down and to see what was the matter, an action which had to be taken with a lot of discretion since Gandhi disliked all police arrangements.

Through archways and ringing cries of "Gandhi Ki Jai" Gandhi drove in the huge Bentley which the Chairman had left at his disposal. People sat on trees and house tops all along the way and cheered Gandhiji as he passed. The police had cordoned off various side streets that led off from the Market Road, so the passage was clear from the little Malgudi station to Lawley Extension. There were police everywhere although the District Superintendent of Police felt that the security arrangements had not been satisfactory. All shops had been closed and all schools, and the whole town had gone into festivity on this occasion. School children felt delighted at the thought of Gandhi. Office-goers were happy, and even banks were closed. They waited in the sun for hours, saw him pass in his Bentley, a white-clad figure, fair-skinned and radiant, with his palms pressed together in a salute.

When they entered "Neel Bagh," whose massive gates were of cast iron patterned after the gates of Buckingham Palace, the Chairman, who was seated in the front seat, waited to be asked: "Whose house is this?" But Gandhiji did not seem to notice anything. They passed through the drive with hedges trimmed, and flower pots putting forth exotic blooms, and lawns stretching away on either side, and he kept his ears alert to catch any remark that Gandhiji might let fall, but still he said nothing. He was busy looking through some papers which his secretary had passed to him. The thought that Gandhiji was actually within his gates sent a thrill of joy up and down the Chairman's spine. He had arranged everything nicely. All his own things for a few days had been sent off to the Circuit House (which the Collector had given him on condition that he limewash its walls and repaint its wooden doors and shutters). He felt a thrill at the thought of his own sacrifice. Some years before he could never have thought of forsaking his own air-conditioned suite and choosing to reside at the Circuit House, for anybody's sake. The Chairman had now surrendered his whole house to Gandhiji. No doubt the house was big enough to accommodate his own family without interfering with his venerable guest and his party (a miscellaneous gathering of men and women, dressed in white *khaddar,* who attended on Mahatmaji in various capacities, who all looked alike and whose names he could never clearly grasp); but he did not like to stay on because it seemed impossible to live under the same roof with such a distinguished man, and moreover it seemed to take away a little from the sense of patriotic sacrifice that his action entailed, and hence he decided to transfer himself to the Circuit House. He had effected a few alterations in his house, such as substituting *khaddar* hangings for the gaudy chintz that had adorned his doorways and windows, and he had taken down the pictures of hunting gentry, vague gods and kings, and he had even the temerity to remove the picture of George V's wedding, and substitute pictures of Maulana Azad, Jawaharlal Nehru, Sarojini Naidu, and Motilal Nehru, C. Rajagopalachari and Annie Besant. He had ordered his works manager to secure within a given time "all the available portraits of our national leaders," it was a wholesale order, satisfactorily executed; and all the other pictures were taken down and sent off to the basement room. He had also discreetly managed to get a picture of Krishna discoursing to Arjuna on Bhagavad-Gita, knowing well Gandhi's bias towards Bhagavad-Gita. He had kept on the window-sill and in a few other places a few specimens of *charka* (spinning wheel). No film decorator sought to create atmosphere with greater deliberation. He had worked all the previous night to attain this effect, and he had also secured for himself a *khaddar jibba* and a white Gandhi cap and for his wife a white *khaddar* sari, and for his son a complete outfit in *khaddar;* his car drove nearly a hundred miles within the city in order to search for a white *khaddar* cap to fit his six-year-old son's dolichocephalic head, and on his shirt front he had embroidered the tricolor and a spinning wheel.

Now he hoped as he approached the main building that his wife and son would emerge in their proper make-up to meet Gandhi: he hoped his wife would have had the good sense to take away the diamond studs not only in her ears but also in their son's. He had forgotten to caution them about it. The moment the car stopped in the decorated porch of the house, the Chairman jumped down and held the door open and helped Mahatmaji to alight.

"You are most welcome to this humble abode of mine, great sire," said the Chairman in confusion, unable to talk coherently. Mahatmaji got down from the car and looked at the house.

"Is this your house?" he asked.

"Yes, sir, by the grace of God, I built it four years ago," the chairman said, his throat going dry. He led Gandhi up the veranda steps. He had placed a divan in the veranda, covered with *khaddar* printed cloth. He seated Gandhi on it and asked his secretary in a whisper: "May I give Mahatmaji a glassful of orange juice? The oranges are from my own estates in Mempi." A number of visitors and a miscellaneous crowd of people were passing in and out. It seemed to the Chairman that Mahatmaji's presence had the effect of knocking down the walls of a house, and converting it into a public place—but that was the price one had to pay for having the great man there. People were squatting on the lawns and the Chairman saw helplessly that some were plucking flowers in his annual bed, which had been tended by his municipal overseers. Gandhi turned in his direction and asked: "What were you saying?" His secretary communicated the offer of oranges. Gandhi said: "Yes, most welcome. I shall be happy to look at the oranges grown in your own gardens."

The Chairman ran excitedly about and returned bearing a large tray filled with uniform, golden oranges. He was panting with the effort. He had gone so far in self-abnegation that he would not accept the services of his usual attendants. He placed the tray in front of Mahatmaji: "My humble offering to a great man: these are from my own orchards on the Mempi hills," he said. "They were plucked just this morning," and then he asked, "May I have the honor of giving you a glass of orange juice? You must have had a tiring day."

The Mahatma declined, explaining that it was not his hour for taking anything. He picked up one fruit and examined it with appreciative comments, turning it slowly between his fingers. The Chairman felt as happy as if he himself were being scrutinized and approved. On the edge of the crowd, standing below on the drive, Mahatmaji noticed a little boy and beckoned to him to come nearer. The boy hesitated. Mahatmaji said: *"Av, Av—"* in Hindi. When it made no impression on the boy, he said in the little Tamil he had picked up for this part of the country, *"Inge Va."* Others pushed the boy forward; he came up haltingly. Gandhi offered him a seat on his divan, and gave him an orange. This acted as a signal. Presently the divan was swarming with children. When the tray was empty, the Mahatma asked the Chairman: "Have you some more?" The Chairman went in and brought a further supply in a basket and all the children threw off their reserve, became clamorous and soon the basket was empty. "There are some flowers and garlands in the car," Gandhi whispered to his secretary. These had been presented to him on his arrival and all along the way by various associations. The place was fragrant with roses and jasmine. These he distributed to all the little girls he saw in the gathering. The Chairman felt chagrined at the thought that the event was developing into a children's party. After the

41

oranges and flowers he hoped that the children would leave, but he found them still there. "They are probably waiting for apples, now, I suppose!" he reflected bitterly. Gandhi had completely relaxed. His secretary was telling him: "In fifteen minutes the deputation from . . . will be here . . . and after that—" He was reading from an engagement pad. The Chairman regretted that both the District Superintendent of Police and the Collector had turned away at his Buckingham Palace gate after escorting the procession that far as an act of official courtesy: if they were here now, they would have managed the crowd. For a moment he wondered with real anxiety whether the crowd proposed to stay there all night. But his problem was unexpectedly solved for him. Mahatmaji saw one child standing apart from the rest—a small dark fellow with a protruding belly and wearing nothing over his body except a cast-off knitted vest, adult size, full of holes, which reached down to his ankles. The boy stood aloof from the rest, on the very edge of the crowd. His face was covered with mud, his feet were dirty, he had stuck his fingers into his mouth, and was watching the proceedings on the veranda keenly, his eyes bulging with wonder and desire. He had not dared to come up the steps, though attracted by the oranges. He was trying to edge his way through. Mahatma's eyes travelled over the crowd and rested on this boy—following his gaze, the Chairman was bewildered. He had a feeling of uneasiness. Mahatmaji beckoned to the young fellow. One of his men went and brought him along. The Chairman's blood boiled. Of course people must like poor people and so on, but why bring in such a dirty boy, an untouchable, up the steps and make him so important? For a moment he felt a little annoyed with Mahatmaji himself, but soon suppressed it as a sinful emotion. He felt the need to detach himself sufficiently from his surroundings to watch

42

without perturbation the happenings around him. Mahatmaji had the young urchin hoisted beside him on the divan. "Oh, Lord, all the world's gutters are on this boy, and he is going to leave a permanent stain on that Kashmir counterpane." The boy was making himself comfortable on the divan, having accepted the hospitality offered him by the Mahatma. He nestled close to the Mahatma, who was smoothing out his matted hair with his fingers, and was engaged in an earnest conversation with him. The Chairman was unable to catch the trend of their talk. He stepped nearer, trying to listen with all reverence. The reward he got for it was a smile from the Mahatma himself. The boy was saying: "My father sweeps the streets."

"With a long broom or a short broom?" the Mahatma asked.

The boy explained, "He has both a long broom and a short broom." He was spitting out the seeds of an orange. The Mahatma turned to someone and explained: "It means that he is both a municipal sweeper and that he has scavenging work to do in private houses also. The long broom ought to be the municipal emblem."

"Where is your father at the moment?"

"He is working at the Market. He will take me home when he has finished his work."

"And how have you managed to come here?"

"I was sitting on the road waiting for my father and I came along with the crowd. No one stopped me when I entered the gates."

"That's a very clever boy," Mahatmaji said. "I'm very happy to see you. But you must not spit those pips all over the place, in fact you must never spit at all. It's very unclean to do so, and may cause others a lot of trouble. When you eat an orange, others must not notice it at all. The place

43

must be absolutely tidy even if you have polished off six at a time." He laughed happily at his own quip, and then he taught the boy what to do with the pips, how to hide the skin, and what to do with all the superfluous bits packed within an orange. The boy laughed with joy. All the men around watched the proceedings with respectful attention. And then Gandhi asked: "Where do you live?"

The boy threw up his arms to indicate a far distance: "There at the end of the river—"

"Will you let me come to your house?"

The boy hesitated and said, "Not now—because, because it's so far away."

"Don't bother about that. I've a motor car there given to me, you see, by this very rich man. I can be there in a moment. I'll take you along in the motor car, too, if you will show me your house."

"It is not a house like this," said the boy, "but made of bamboo or something."

"Is that so!" said the Mahatma. "Then I'll like it all the more. I'll be very happy there." He had a brief session with a delegation which had come to see him by appointment; when it left, he dictated some notes, wrote something, and then picking up his staff said to the Chairman, "Let us go to this young man's house. I'm sure you will also like it."

"Now?" asked the Chairman in great consternation. He mumbled, "Shall we not go there tomorrow?"

"No, I've offered to take this child home. I must not disappoint him. I'd like to see his father, too, if he can be met anywhere on the way."

Mahatmaji gave his forefinger to the young boy to clutch and allowed himself to be led down the veranda's steps. The Chairman asked dolefully, "Won't you come in and have a look round my humble home?"

"I know how it will be. It must be very grand. But would you not rather spare an old man like me the bother of walking through those vast spaces? I'm a tired old man. You are very hospitable. Anyway, come along with us to this little man's home. If I feel like it, you will let me stay there."

The Chairman mumbled, "I hoped—" But Gandhiji swept him aside with a smile: "You will come along with me, too. Let me invite you to come and stay with me in a hut." Unable to say anything more, the Chairman merely replied, "All right, sir, I obey."

The warmth of Mahatma's invitation made him forget his problems as a Chairman and his own responsibilities. Otherwise he would not have become oblivious of the fact that the sweepers' colony was anything but a showpiece. Not till the Collector later sought him out and arraigned him for his lapse did it occur to him what a blunder he had committed. The Collector said, "Have you so little sense, Chairman, that you could not have delayed Mr. Gandhi's visit at least by two hours, time to give the people a chance to sweep and clean up that awful place? You know as well as I do, what it is like!" All of which the Chairman took in without a word. He was gloating over the words spoken to him by Mahatmaji. Not till his wife later attacked him, did he remember his omission in another direction. She said in a tone full of wrath, "There I was waiting, dressed as you wanted, with that boy, and you simply went away without even calling us!"

"Why couldn't you have come out?" he asked idiotically.

"How could I, when you had said I must wait for your call?" She sobbed "With the great man at our house, I'd not the good fortune even to go before him. And that child—what a disappointment for him!"

When they got over their initial surprise, the authorities

45

did everything to transform the place. All the stench mysteriously vanished; all the garbage and offal that lay about, and flesh and hide put out to sun-dry on the roofs, disappeared. All that night municipal and other employees kept working, with the aid of petrol lamps: light there was such a rarity that the children kept dancing all night around the lamps. Gandhiji noticed the hectic activity, but out of a sense of charity refrained from commenting on it. Only when it was all over did he say, "Now one can believe that the true cleaners of the city live here." The men of the colony tied round their heads their whitest turbans and the women wore their best saris, dragged their children to the river and scrubbed them till they yelled, and decorated their coiffures with yellow chrysanthemum flowers. The men left off fighting, did their best to keep away from the drink shops, and even the few confirmed topers had their drinks on the sly, and suppressed their impulse to beat their wives or break their household pots. The whole place looked bright with lamps and green mango leaves tied across lampposts and tree branches.

Gandhi occupied a hut which had a low entrance. He didn't like to oust anyone from his hut, but chose one facing the river sand, after making certain that it had been vacant, the occupant of the hut having gone elsewhere. The Chairman brought in a low divan and covered the floor with a coarse rush mat, for Gandhi's visitor to sit on. Sriram lowered himself unobtrusively on the mat. Gandhi sat on his divan, and dictated to one of his secretaries. They wrote voluminously. Mahatmaji performed a number of things simultaneously. He spoke to visitors. He dictated. He wrote. He prayed. He had his sparse dinner of nuts and milk, and presently he even laid himself down on the divan and went off to sleep. It was then that someone turned off the lamp, and people walked out of the hut.

Sriram now felt that he could not continue to sit there. Although no one bothered to ask him what he was doing, he could not stay any more. When he saw the girl was preparing to leave the hut, he felt he had better get up and go: otherwise someone might say something unpleasant to him. The girl lifted Gandhi's spinning wheel and put it away noiselessly, and tiptoed out of the room. She passed without noticing him at first, but the fixed stare with which he followed her movements seemed to affect her. She went past him, but suddenly stopped and whispered: "You will have to go out now," and Sriram sprang up and found himself ouside the hut in one bound.

She said rather grimly: "Don't you know that when Bapuji sleeps, we have to leave him?"

He felt like asking, "Who is Bapuji?" but used his judgment for a second, understood that it must refer to the Mahatma, and not wanting to risk being chased out by the resolute girl, said, "Of course, I knew it. I was only waiting for you to come out."

"Who are you? I don't think I have seen you before."

This was the question he had been waiting to be asked all along, but now when it came he found himself tongue-tied. He felt so confused and muddled that she took pity on him and said, "What is your name?"

He answered, "Sriram."

"What are you doing here?" she asked.

"Don't you remember me?" he said irrelevantly. "I saw you when you came with a money box in the market, the other day—"

"Oh, I see," she said out of politeness. "But I might not

47

remember you since quite a lot of people put money into my box that day. Anyway, I asked you now what you are doing here?"

"Perhaps one of the volunteers," Sriram said.

"Why, 'perhaps?' " she asked.

"Because I'm not yet one," he replied.

"Anybody cannot be a volunteer," she said. "Don't you know that?" she asked.

"Don't I know that? I think I know that and more."

"What more?" she asked.

"That I am not an anybody," he replied and was amazed at his own foolhardiness in talking to the girl in that fashion, she who could put him out of the camp in a moment.

"You are a somebody, I suppose?" the girl asked laughing.

"Well, you will help me to become somebody, I hope," he said, feeling surprised at his own powers of rash and reckless speech. She seemed a match for him, for presently she asked, with a little irritation, "Are we going to stand here and talk the whole night?"

"Yes, unless you show me where we can go."

"I know where I ought to go," she said. "You see that hut there," she pointed to a small hut four doors off Gandhi's, "That's where all the women of this camp are quartered."

"How many of them are there?" Sriram asked just to keep up the conversation.

She answered sharply, "More than you see before you now," and added, "Why are you interested?"

Sriram felt a little piqued, "You seem to be a very ill-tempered and sharp-tongued girl. You can't answer a single question without a challenge."

"Hush! You will wake up Bapuji, standing and talking here," she said.

"Well, if he is going to be awakened by anyone's talk, it

48

will be yours, because no one else is doing the talking," he replied.

"I have a right to ask you what you are doing here and report to our *Chalak* if I don't like you," she said with a sudden tone of authority.

"Why should you not like me?" he asked.

"No one except close associates and people with appointments are allowed to enter Bapuji's presence."

"I will tell them I am your friend and that you took me in," he replied.

"Would you utter a falsehood?" she asked.

"Why not?"

"None except absolute truth-speakers are allowed to come into Mahatma's camp. People who come here must take an oath of absolute truth before going into the Mahatma's presence."

"I will take the vow when I become a member of the camp. Till then I will pass off something that looks like truth," he said.

"When Mahatma hears about this he will be very pained and he will talk to you about it."

Sriram was now genuinely scared and asked pathetically, "What have I done that you should threaten and menace me?"

This softened her, and for the first time he noticed a little tenderness had crept into her tone, "Do you mind moving off and waiting there? We should not be talking like this near Mahatmaji's hut. I will go to my hut and then join you there." She turned and disappeared; she had the lightning-like motion of a dancer, again the sort of pirouetting movement that she had adopted while carrying off other people's coins in a jingling box. She passed down the lane. He moved off slowly. He was tired of standing. He sat on a boulder at the edge of the river, kicking up the sand with his toes, ruminating on his good fortune. He had never hoped for anything like it. It might have been a dream. This time yesterday he could not have thought he would talk on these terms to the money-box girl. He realized he had not yet asked her her name. He remembered that he had felt hungry and thirsty long ago. "I wish they would give us all something to eat in Mahatmaji's camp." He remembered that Mahatma ate only groundnuts and dates. He looked about hoping there would be vendors of these articles. The Taluk Office gong sounded nine. He counted it deliberately, and wondered what his granny would make of his absence now. "She will fret and report to the police, I suppose!" he reflected cynically. He wished that he had asked his teacher to go and tell granny not to expect him home till Gandhiji left the town. On second thought it struck him that it was just as well that he had not spoken to the teacher, who would probably have gone and spread the rumor that his interest in Gandhi was only a show and that he was really going after a girl. What was her name? Amazing how he had not yet asked her it, and the moment she came back he said, "What is your name?"

"Bharati," she answered, "Why?"

"Just to know, that's all. Have I told you my name is Sriram?"

"Yes, you have told me that more than once," she said. "I have heard again and again that you are Sriram."

"You are too sharp-tongued," he replied. "It is a wonder they tolerate you here at all, where peace and kindness must be practiced."

"I am practicing kindness, otherwise I should not be speaking to you at all. If I didn't want to be kind to you I wouldn't have gone in and taken my *Chalak's* permission and come right away here. We must have permission to talk to people at this hour. There is such a thing as discipline in every camp. Don't imagine that because it is Mahatmaji's camp, it is without any discipline. He would be the first to tell you about it if you raised the question with him."

"You have the same style of talk as my grandmother. She is as sharp-tongued as you are," Sriram said pathetically.

She ignored the comparison and asked, "What about your mother?"

"I have never seen her. My grandmother has always been father and mother to me. Why don't you meet her? You will like her, both of you speak so much alike!"

"Yes, yes," said the girl soothingly, "someday I will come and meet her as soon as this is all over. You see how busy I am now." She became tender when she found that she was talking to someone without a mother, and Sriram noticing this felt it was worthwhile being motherless and grandmother-tended. She sat on the same step, with her legs dangling in the river, leaving a gap of a couple of feet between them. The river rumbled into the dark starlit night, the leaves of the huge tree over the ancient steps rustled and sighed. Far off bullock carts and pedestrians were fording the river at Nallappa's Grove. Distant voices came through the night. Mahatmaji's camp was asleep. It was so quiet that Sriram felt like taking the girl in his arms, but he resisted the idea. He feared that if he touched her she might push him into the river. The girl was a termagant. She would surely develop into the same type as his grandmother with that sharp tongue of hers. Her proximity pricked his blood and set it coursing. "There is no one about. What can she do?" he reflected. "Let her try and push me into the river, and she will know with whom she is dealing," and the next moment he blamed himself for his own crude thoughts. "It is not safe with the

Mahatma there. He may already have read my thoughts and be coming here." He was a Mahatma because awake or asleep he was fully aware of what was going on all around him. God alone could say what the Mahatma would do to someone who did not possess absolute purity of thought where girls were concerned. It meant hardship, no doubt, but if one was to live in this camp one had to follow the orders that emanated from the great soul. He struggled against evil thoughts and said, "Bharati!" She looked startled at being called so familiarly and he himself felt startled by the music of her name.

"What a nice name!" he remarked.

"I am glad you like it," she said. "The name was given by Bapuji himself."

"Oh, how grand!" he cried.

She added, "You know my father died during the 1920 Movement. Just when I was born. When he learnt of it Bapuji who had come down South made himself my godfather and named me Bharati, which means I hope you know what."

"Yes, Bharat is India, and Bharati is the daughter of India, I suppose."

"Right," she said, and he was pleased at her commendation. "After my mother died, I was practically adopted by the local Sevak Sangh, and I have not known any other home since," she said.

"Do you mean to say that you are all the time with these people?"

"What is wrong in it?" she asked. "It has been my home."

"Not that. I was only envying you. I too wish I could be with you all and do something instead of wasting my life."

This appealed to her and she asked, "What do you want to do?"

"The same as what you are doing. What are you doing?" he asked.

"I do whatever I am asked to do by the Sevak Sangh: sometimes they ask me to go and teach people spinning and tell them about Mahatmaji's ideas. Sometimes they send me to villages and poor quarters. I meet them and talk to them and do a few things. I attend to Mahatmaji's needs."

"Please let me also do something along with you," he pleaded. "Why don't you take me as your pupil? I want to do something good. I want to talk to poor people."

"What will you tell them?" she asked ruthlessly.

He made some indistinct sounds. "I will tell them whatever you ask me to tell them," he said, and this homage to her superior intelligence pleased her.

"H'm! But why?" she asked.

He summoned all his courage and answered, "Because I like you, and I like to be with you."

She burst into a laugh and said, "That won't be sufficient. . . . They . . ." she indicated a vast army of hostile folk behind her back. "They may chase you away if you speak like that."

He became sullen and unhappy. He rallied and said presently, "Well, I, too, would willingly do something."

"What?" she taunted him again.

He looked at her face helplessly, desperately, and asked, "Are you making fun of me?"

"No, but I wish to understand what you are saying."

She relented a little, presently, and said, "I will take you to Bapu, will you come?"

He was panic-stricken. "No, no. I can't."

"You have been there already."

He could give no reasonable explanation and now he realized the enormity of his rashness. He said, "No, no, I would be at a loss to know how to talk to him, how to reply to him and what to tell him."

"But you sat there before him like someone always known to him!" she said. "Like his best friend." She laughed and enjoyed teasing him.

"Somehow I did it. I won't do it again," he declared. "He may find me out if I go before him again."

Suddenly she became very serious and said, "You will have to face Bapuji if you want to work with us."

Sriram became speechless. His heart palpitated with excitement. He wished he could get up and run away, flee the place once and for all and be done with it, and turn his back on the whole business forever. This was too much. The gods seemed to be out to punish him for his hardihood and presumption. He cried, "Bharati, tell me if I can meet you anywhere else. Otherwise please let me go." He was in a cold sweat. "What should I say when I speak to him? I would blabber like an idiot."

"You are already doing it," she said, unable to restrain her laughter.

He said pathetically, "You seem to enjoy bothering me. I am sorry I ever came here."

"Why are you so cowardly?" she asked.

Sriram said resolutely, "I can't talk to Mahatmaji. I wouldn't know how to conduct myself before him."

"Just be yourself. It will be all right."

"I wouldn't be able to answer his questions properly."

"He is not going to examine you like an inspector of schools. You don't have to talk to him unless you have something to say. You may keep your mouth shut and he won't mind it. You may just be yourself, say anything you feel like saying. He will not mind anything at all, but you will have to speak the truth if you speak at all."

54

"Truth! In everything!" he looked scared.

"Yes, in everything. You may speak as bluntly as you like, and he will not take it amiss, provided it is just truth."

Sriram looked more crushed than ever. In this dark night he seemed to have a terrible problem ahead of him. After brooding over it for a while he said, "Bharati, tell me if I may meet you anywhere else. Otherwise let me go."

She replied with equal resolution, "If you wish to meet me come to Bapuji, the only place where you may see me. Of course, if you don't want to see me anymore, go away."

This placed him in a dilemma. "Where? How?" he asked.

"Come to the door of Bapu's hut and wait for me."

"When? Where?"

"At three a.m. tomorrow. I'll take you to him." Saying this, she jumped to her feet and ran off towards her hut.

Granny had slept fitfully. She had gone up to Kanni's shop five times during the evening to inquire if anyone had seen Sriram, and sent a boy who had come to make a purchase there to look for Sriram everywhere. At last the schoolmaster who lived up the street told her as he passed her house, "Your pet is in Mahatma's camp. I saw him." "Ah! What was he doing there?" asked granny, alarmed, for her the Mahatma was one who preached dangerously, who tried to bring untouchables into the temples, and who involved people in difficulties with the police. She didn't like the idea. She wailed, "Oh, master, why did you allow him to stay on there? You should have brought him away. It is so late and he has not come home. As his old teacher you should have weaned him away from there."

"Don't worry, madam, he is perfectly safe. How many of us could have the privilege of being so near the Mahatma? You must be happy that he is doing so well! Our country needs more young men like him."

Granny replied, "It is teachers like you who have ruined our boys and this country," and turned in, slamming the door.

When Sriram arrived and knocked she was half asleep and in the worst possible mood. She opened the door, let him in, bolted the door again, and went back to her bed saying, "I have kept some rice in that bowl mixed with curd and the other one is without curd. Put out the lamp after you have eaten." Lying in bed, she listened to the sound of Sriram putting away his plate and leaving the kitchen. And then she turned her face to the wall and pretended to be asleep. She hoped that her grandson would understand her mood, come over, and assure her that he would not get into bad ways: but the young man was otherwise engaged. He was in a state of semi-enchantment. Bharati's presence and talk still echoed in his mind, and he recollected the thrill of her touch. He liked to think that when he was not noticing she had touched his arm and patted his shoulder. He thought how he would prefer the rest of his life listening to her banter, but that meant—here was the conflict—he would have to go into the Presence. All else seemed to him insignificant beside this great worry. If it had been any other day he would have pulled his granny out of her sleep and narrated to her all the day's events. If she happened to be in a bad mood he would have pulled her out of it. He knew now that she was not in a proper temper. He could sense it the moment he stepped on the threshold, but he preferred to leave her alone; he felt he had a far greater problem to tackle than appeasing the mood of a mere granny.

He went to bed and slept in all less than an hour. Bharati

wanted him there at three a.m., and he needed an hour to reach the place. He got up before one, washed and bathed and put on special clothes, bent over his granny's bed to whisper, "I have to be going now. Bolt the door."

She essayed to ask, "What! At this hour? What has come over you?" but he was gone on soft footsteps, closing the door behind him.

He stood at the entrance to Mahatmaji's hut, holding his breath. It was very difficult to decide what he should do now. She had asked him to be present at the portals of the Great Presence, but perhaps she had been fooling him. He feared that any sound that he made might arouse the Mahatma and bring the entire camp about his ears. He stood ruefully looking at the camp. Street dogs were barking somewhere. Occasionally the branches of trees over the river rustled and creaked. He stood looking ruefully towards the women's quarters. There a lantern was burning; people seemed to be awake and moving about. He thought, "What if the lantern is burning? They may be sleeping with lights on. Women are cowardly anyway." The stirring he heard might be their rolling in their beds, noisy creatures! Unaccountably he was feeling irritated at the thought of women, the species to which Bharati belonged. He saw a light in Mahatmaji's camp. The door was shut. He heard soft footsteps moving in there. Long ago the Taluk Office gong had struck some small hour. He could hardly believe he had actually sacrificed his sleep and was standing here in the cold wind, at an unearthly hour. Even the scavengers, the earliest to rise in the town, were still asleep. He felt suddenly afraid that he might be attacked by thieves or ghosts. Or if a policeman saw him and took him to be a prowler, how should he explain himself? He couldn't very well say, "Bharati asked me to wait at Mahatmaji's hut at about three a.m." He wanted to turn and go away: he could at least go home and make up to his grandmother instead of hanging around here and wondering what to do. He could tell her: "I went to see the Mahatma, but changed my mind and came away. Why should I get to know him and then into all sorts of difficulties? Don't you think so, granny?" And she was sure to revive and look happy again. He gave one forlorn look at the women's quarters and turned away, his mind completely made up to earn the concrete goodwill of a granny rather than the doubtful and strange favors of bigwigs like the Mahatma and snobs like Bharati. Heaven knew who else would be there. But still the pull of Bharati was strong and he could not get away from the place so easily as he had imagined. He wanted to make just one more attempt to see her and bid her good-bye. Perhaps she was in a situation in which he could help her; people might have tied her up to her cot and gagged her mouth. Anything might happen to a beautiful girl like her. Otherwise there could be no explanation for her absence. Anyway, he felt it would be his duty to go and find out what was wrong and where. He'd have willingly gone near the women's quarters, but he lacked the necessary courage and did the next best thing; once again repeating a rash act he tiptoed towards Mahatmaji's hut. His idea was to peep in unobtrusively, and see if Bharati was there or anywhere else safe and sound and then move off. But in his befuddled state it did not occur to him that possibly he might be seen before he saw anyone. And it happened so. The door of Mahatmaji's hut was half open. Light streamed out through the gap. Sriram went towards it like a charmed moth. If he had paused to reflect he would not have believed himself to be capable of repeating a foolhardy act a second time. But through lack of sleep, and tension of nerves, a general recklessness had come over him, the same innocent charge that had taken him tumbling into the hut the previous evening, took him there again now. He peeped in like a clown. The door was half open; he had overestimated its width from a distance, for he could not peep in without thrusting his head through.

"Oh, there he is!" cried Bharati, with laughter in her voice. "You may open the door if you wish to come in," she said. Sriram felt again that the girl was making fun of him. Even in the great presence, she didn't seem to care. Here at least Sriram had hoped she would speak without the undertone of mischief. He felt so irritated at the thought that he replied with all the pungency he could muster in his tone: "You have—I waited for you there—"

"Come in, come in," said the Mahatma. "Why should you be standing there? You could have come straight in."

"But she asked me to wait outside," said Sriram stepping in gingerly. From the door to where the Mahatma sat the distance was less than ten feet, but he felt he was taking hours to cover it. His legs felt weak and seemed to intertwine; he seemed to be walking like a drunkard, a particularly dangerous impression to create in the Mahatma who was out to persuade even the scavengers to give up drinking. In a flash it occurred to him that he ought to have a sensible answer ready if the Mahatma should suddenly turn round and ask, "Have you been drinking toddy or whisky?" But his trial came to an end, when Gandhi said, "Bharati has just been mentioning you." He spoke while his hands were busy turning a spinning wheel, drawing out a fine thread. A man sitting in a corner, with a pad resting on his knee, was writing. Mahatmaji himself, as always, was doing several things at the same time. While his hands were spinning, his eyes perused a letter held before him by another, and he found it possible, too, to put in a word of welcome to Sriram. Through the back door of the hut many others were coming in and going out. For each one of them Mahatmaji has something to say. He looked up at Sriram and said: "Sit down, young man. Come and sit as near me as you like." There was so much unaffected graciousness in his tone that Sriram lost all fear and hesitation. He moved briskly up. He sat on the floor near Mahatmaji and watched with fascination the smooth turning of the spinning wheel. Bharati went to an inner part of the hut, threw a swift look at Sriram, which he understood to mean, "Remember not to make a fool of yourself." The Mahatma said, "Nowadays I generally get up an hour earlier in order to be able to do this: spinning a certain length is my most important work: even my prayer comes only after that. I'd very much like you to take a vow to wear only cloth made out of your own hands each day."

"Yes, I will do so," promised Sriram.

When the gong in the Taluk Office struck four, the Mahatma invited Sriram to go out with him for a walk. He seized his staff in one hand and with the other supported himself on the shoulder of Bharati, and strode out of the hut—a tall figure in white. He had tucked his watch at his waist into a fold of his white *dhoti*. He pulled it out and said: "Half an hour, I have to walk. Come with me, Sriram. You can talk to me undisturbed." A few others joined them. Sriram felt he was walking through some unreal dream world. The Mahatma was in between him and Bharati, and it was difficult to snatch a look at her as often as he wanted. He had to step back a quarter of an inch, now and then, in order to catch a glimpse of her laughing face. They walked along the river bank. The sky was rosy in the east. Gandhi turned and spoke some business to those behind him. He suddenly addressed himself to Sriram. "Your town is very beautiful. Have you ever noticed it before?" Sriram felt unhappy and gasped for breath. The morning air blew on his face, birds were chirping, the city was quiet: it was all well known, but why did the Mahatma mention it especially now? Should he say "Yes" or "No"? If he said "Yes" he would be lying, which would be detected at once; if he said "No," God knew what the Mahatma would think of him. He looked about. A couple of scavengers of the colony who had joined the group were waiting eagerly to know what he would say; they were evidently enjoying his predicament, and he dared not look in the direction of Bharati. The Mahatma said: "God is everywhere, and if you want to feel his presence you will see him in a place like this with a beautiful river flowing, the sunrise with all its colors, and the air so fresh. Feeling a beautiful hour or a beautiful scene or a beautiful object is itself a form of prayer." Sriram listened in reverential silence, glad to be let off so lightly. When Gandhiji spoke of beauty, it sounded unreal as applied to the sun and the air, but the word acquired a practical significance, when he thought of it in terms of Bharati. Gandhi said: "By the time we meet again next, you must give me a very good account of yourself." He laughed in a kindly manner, and Sriram said, "Yes, Bapuji, I will be a different man." "Why do you say 'different'? You will be all right if you are fully yourself."

"I don't think that is enough, Bapu," said Bharati. "He should change from being himself, if he is to come to any good. I think he is very lazy. He gets up at eight o'clock, and idles away the day."

"How do you know?" Sriram asked indignantly.

"It's only a guess," said the girl. Sriram felt angry with her for her irresponsible talk. Everyone laughed. The Mahatma said: "You must not say such things, Bharati, unless you mean to take charge of him and help him."

During the last fifteen minutes of this walk the Mahatma said nothing; he walked in silence, looking at the ground before him. When the Mahatma was silent the others were even more so. The only movement they performed was putting one foot before another on the sand, keeping pace with him; some were panting hard and trying hard to suppress the sound. The Mahatma's silence was heavy and pervasive, and Sriram was afraid even to gulp or cough, although he very much wanted to clear his throat, cough, sneeze, swing his arms about. The only sound at the moment was the flowing of the river and the twitter of birds. Somewhere a cow was mooing. Even Bharati, the embodiment of frivolity, seemed to have become somber. The Mahatma pulled out his watch, looked at it briefly and said, "We will go back. That is all the walk I can afford today." Sriram wanted to ask, "Why?" but he held his tongue. The Mahatma turned to him as they were walking back, "You have a grandmother, I hear, but no parents."

"Yes. My grandmother is very old."

"Yes, she must be, otherwise how can you call her a grandmother?" People laughed, Sriram, too, joined in this laughter out of politeness. "Does she not miss you very much when you are away from her so long?"

"Yes, very much. She gets very angry with me. I don't know what to do about it," said Sriram, courageously rushing ahead. He felt pleased at having said something of his own accord; his only fear was that Bharati might step in and say something nasty and embarrassing, but he was happy to note that Bharati held her peace. Mahatmaji said: "You must look after your granny, too. She must have devoted herself to bringing you up."

"Yes, but when I am away like this she is very much upset."

"Is it necessary for you to be away from her so much?"

"Yes, Bapu, otherwise how can I do anything in this world?"

"What exactly do you want to do?"

It was now that Sriram became incoherent. He was seized with a rush of ideas and with all the confusion that too many ideas create. He said something, and the Mahatma watched him patiently; the others, too, held their breath and watched, and after a few moments of struggle for self-expression, Sriram was able to form a cogent sentence. It was the unrelenting pressure of his subconscious desires that jerked the sentence out of his lips, and he said, "I like to be where Bharati is." The Mahatma said, "Oh, is that so!" He patted Bharati's back and said, "What a fine friend you have! You must be pleased to have such a devoted friend. How long have you known him?"

Bharati said like a shot, "Since yesterday. I saw him for the first time sitting in your hut and I asked him who he was."

Sriram interposed and added, "But I knew her before, although I spoke to her only yesterday."

The Mahatma passed into his hut, and went on to attend to other things. Many people were waiting for him. Bharati disappeared into the Mahatma's hut the moment they arrived. Sriram fell back and got mixed up with a crowd waiting outside. He felt jealous of Bharati's position. She sought him out later and said, "You are probably unused to it, but in Bapu's presence we speak only the absolute truth and nothing less than that, and nothing more than that either." He took her to task: "What will he think of me now when he knows that I have not known you long enough and yet—"

"Well, what?" she twitted him.

"And yet I wish to be with you, and so on."

63

"Why don't you go in and tell him you have been speaking nonsense and that you were blurting out things without fore-thought or self-control? Why couldn't you have told him that you want to serve the country, that you are a patriot, that you want to shed your blood in order to see that the British leave the country. That is what most people say when they come near the Mahatma. I have seen hundreds of people come to him, and say the same thing."

"And he believes all that?" asked Sriram.

"Perhaps not, but he thinks it is not right to disbelieve anyone."

"But you say we must only speak the truth in his presence."

"If you can, of course, but if you can't the best thing to do is to maintain silence."

"Why are you so angry with me? Is it not a part of your duty not to be angry with others?" asked Sriram pathetically.

"I don't care," said Bharati. "This is enough to irritate even the Mahatma. Now what will he think of me if he realizes I am encouraging a fellow like you to hang about the place, a fellow whom I have not known even for a full day yet!" Sriram became reckless, and said breezily, "What does it matter how long I have known you? Did you think I was going to lie to him if you had not spoken before I spoke?" These bicker-ings were brought to an end by someone calling "Bharati" from another hut. Bharati abandoned him and disappeared from the spot.

Bharati's words gave him an idea. He realized his own omission, and proposed to remedy it next time he walked with the Mahatma. Sriram's anxiety lest he fall asleep when the Mahatma was up kept him awake the whole night. He shared the space on the floor with one of the men in the camp. It was a strange feeling to lie down in a hut, and he felt he was becoming a citizen of an entirely new world. He missed the cosy room of his house in Kabir Street. He missed the two pillows and the soft mattress and the carpet under it; even the noises of Kabir Street added much to the domestic quality of life, and he missed it badly now. He had to adopt an entirely new trend of life. He had to live, of his own choice, in a narrow hut, with thatch above, with a dingy, sooty smell hanging about everything. The floor had been swept with cow dung and covered with a thin layer of sand. He had to snuggle his head on the crook of his arm for a pillow. He had to share this place with another volunteer in the camp, a cadaverous, serious young man wearing *khadi* shorts, a *khadi* vest, and a white cap on his closely-shaved head. He had a fiery look and an unsmiling face. He was from North India, he could only speak broken English, and he was totally ignorant of Tamil words. This man had already stretched himself on the floor with a small bag stuffed with clothes, under his head.

Bharati had told Sriram, "You had better stick on here, around the camp, if you want to be with Mahatmaji. You won't have any comforts here, remember. We are all trained to live like this." Sriram sniffed and said, "Oh, who wants any comforts? I don't care for them myself. You think I am a fellow who cares for luxuries in life?" There was a class of society where luxuries gave one a status, and now here was the opposite. The more one asserted one cared for no luxury, the more one showed an inclination for hardships and discomfort, the greater was one's chance of being admitted into the fold. Sriram had understood it the moment he stepped into the camp. Here the currency was suffering and self-mortification. Everyone seemed to excel his neighbor in managing in uncomfortable situations, and Sriram caught the spirit, though it took him time to grasp the detail and get accustomed to it.

There had been a meeting in the evening and after that the Mahatma retired at his usual hour of seven thirty, and it was a signal for the entire camp to retire. Bharati sought out Sriram and gave him a plateful of rice and buttermilk and an orange, and she also held out to him a small jasmine out of a bouquet which had earlier been presented to the Mahatma by some children's deputation. He received the flower gratefully, smelt it, and asked, "How did you know I like jasmine?"

"It is not so difficult a thing to know," she said, and dismissed the subject immediately.

She said, "I have found a place for you to sleep, with a volunteer named Gorpad."

Gorpad was half asleep when Sriram had entered his hut. Bharati peeped and said, *"Bhai . . ."* and something in Hindi and turned and disappeared from the spot. The other lifted his head slightly and said, "You can come in and sleep."

"Only on the floor?" Sriram asked.

"Of course, of course," said the other.

"Why?" asked Sriram.

"Why? Because Mahatmaji says so."

"Oh," said Sriram, feeling that he was treading on dangerous ground. "I see that otherwise there is no reason why we should sleep on the floor."

"What do you mean by 'otherwise?'" said the other, argumentatively.

Sriram settled himself beside the other, and said, "I didn't mean it."

"Mean what?" said the other. He seemed to be a pugnacious fellow. Sriram felt afraid of him. What did the girl mean by putting him in with this fighter? Could it be that she disliked him, and wanted him to be beaten? If she disliked him, she would not have given him a jasmine flower. It was well-known that jasmine was exchanged only between persons who liked each other, and yet the girl gave him a jasmine with one hand and with the other led him into the company of this terrible man. The other might sit on his chest while he slept and try to choke him.

Gorpad said, "You are new, I suppose?"

"Yes," said Sriram. "I am new to this place. It is through Mahatmaji's kindness I am now here, otherwise I should have gone home and slept."

"Yes," Gorpad said, seeming to understand the situation in a fresh light. "You are welcome here. We are all persons who have to live like soldiers in a camp. We are indeed soldiers in our fight to eject the British from our land. We are all prepared to sacrifice our lives for the task. We sleep here on the bare floor because the major part of our lives we shall have to spend in jail, where we won't be given such a comfortable bed unless we are A- or B-class prisoners. We are not important enough to be classified as A or B, and you had better get used to it all and we are always prepared to be beaten by the police, *lathi*-charged, dragged to the jail, or even shot. My father died ten years ago, facing a policeman's gun."

Sriram said, not to be outdone in the matter of political reminiscences, "I know Bharati's father also died in the same way, when he was beaten by the police."

"That was during the first noncoöperation days in 1920; her father led the first batch of *Satyagrahis* who were going to take down the Union Jack from the Secretariat at Madras. He was beaten with a police *lathi,* and a blow fell on his chest and he dropped dead, but my father was shot. Do you know he was actually shot by a policeman's rifle? I was also in the crowd watching him. He was picketing a shop where

67

they were selling toddy and other alcoholic drinks, and a police company came and asked him to go away, but he refused. A crowd gathered, and there was a lot of mess and in the end the police shot him point-blank." He wiped away tears at the memory of it. "I will not rest till the British are sent out of India." His voice was thick with sorrow, "My brother became a terrorist and shot dead many English officials. Nobody knows his whereabouts. And I should have also joined him and shot many more Englishmen, but our Mahatma will not let me be violent even in thought," he said ruefully.

Sriram, wishing to sound very sympathetic said, "All Englishmen deserve to be shot. They have been very cruel."

"You should not even think on those lines, if you are going to be a true *Satyagrahi*," said the other.

"No, no, I am not really thinking on those lines," Sriram amended immediately. "I was only feeling so sorry. Of course we should not talk of shooting anyone, and where is the gun? We have no guns. My grandmother used to say that there was a gun in our house belonging to my father. Do you know that he died in Mesopotamia? He also was shot point-blank."

"He died in the war, the last war?"

"Yes," said Sriram.

"Then he must have been a soldier in the British army," Gorpad said with a touch of contempt in his voice.

Sriram noted it, but accepted it with resignation. He added as a sort of compensation, "They say he was a great soldier."

"Possibly, possibly," said the other with patronage in his voice. Sriram bore it as a trial. That night he picked up a great deal of political knowledge. Gorpad went on speaking till two a.m. and afterwards both of them left for the river, performed their ablutions there, and by the time the camp was awake Sriram had returned fresh and tidy, so that Bharati said, "You are coming through your first day with us quite well." Through diligently listening to Gorpad he had picked up many political idioms, and felt himself equipped to walk with the Mahatma without embarrassment.

He told the Mahatma, "It is my greatest desire in life to take a vow to oust the British from India."

The Mahatma looked at him with a smile and asked, "How do you propose to do it?"

Sriram could not find a ready answer; it was one of the many occasions when he felt that he had spoken unnecessarily. He caught a glimpse of Bharati on the other side; her mischievous face sparkled with delight at his confusion. He felt piqued by her look. He said haughtily, "With your blessing, sir, I shall make myself good enough for the task. I shall be with you as long as possible, and if you will kindly guide me you can make me a soldier fit to take up the fight to make the British leave our country."

The Mahatma took this resolve with every sign of pleasure. He remained silent for a while as his footsteps pitterpatted on the sands. A somber silence fell on the gathering. "Well, young friend, if God wills it, you will do great things. Trust in him and you will be all right."

To Sriram this seemed a rather tame preparation for a soldierly existence. If it had been possible, he would have strutted before Bharati in khaki and a decorated chest, though the world was having a surfeit of decorations just then. Presently the Mahatma himself spoke, dispelling his notions: "Before you aspire to drive the British from this country, you must drive every vestige of violence from your system. Remember that it is not going to be a fight with sticks and knives or guns but only with love. Until you are sure you have an overpowering love at heart for your enemy, don't think of driving him out. You must gradually forget the term 'Enemy.' You must think of him as a friend who must leave you. You must train yourself to become a hundred per cent *ahimsa* soldier. You must become so sensitive that it is not possible for you to wear sandals made of the hide of slaughtered animals; you should prefer to go barefoot rather than wear the hide of an animal killed for your sake, that is if you are unable to secure the skin of an animal that has died a natural death."

Sriram said, "Yes, I promise," but while saying it his eyes were fixed on Mahatmaji's feet; he struggled to suppress the questions, that were welling up in his mind. The Mahatma read his thought and said, "Yes, these are sandals made of just such leather. In our tannery at Wardha we specialize in it. No one in our Ashram wears anything else." Sriram wanted to ask, "How do you know when an animal is dying, and how do you watch for it?" but ruthlessly put down the question as an unworthy one, which might betray him.

Sriram was told that he could accompany Mahatmaji in his tour of the villages on condition that he went home, and secured granny's approval. Sriram tried to slur the matter over, he said it would not be necessary, he hinted he was an independent man used to such outings from home. The Mahatma's memory was better than that. He said with a smile, "I remember you said that she didn't like to see you mixing with us here."

Sriram thought it over and said, "Yes, master, but how can I forever remain tied to her? It is not possible."

"Are you quite sure that you want to change your style of life?" asked the Mahatma.

"I can think of nothing else," Sriram said. "How can I live as I have lived all these years?" He threw a quick glance at Bharati as she came in with some letters for the Mahatma. Her look prevented him from completing the sentence, which would have run, "and I always wish to be with Bharati and not with my grandmother."

The Mahatma said, "I shall be happy to have you with us as long as you like, but you must first go home and tell your grandmother and receive her blessing. You must tell her frankly what you wish to do, but you must cause her no pain."

Sriram hesitated. The prospect of facing granny was unnerving. The thought of her was like the thought of an unreal troublesome world, one which he hoped he had left behind forever: the real world for him now was the one of Bharati, Gorpad, unslaughtered, naturally-dying animals, the Mahatma, and the spinning wheel. He wanted to be here all the time: it seemed impossible for him to go back to Kabir Street, that *pyol,* and that shop, and those people there who treated him as if he were only eight years of age. He stood before the Mahatma as if to appeal to him not to press him to go and face his grandmother, but the master was unrelenting. "Go and speak to her. I don't think she is so unreasonable as to deny you your ambitions. Tell her that I like to have you with me. If you tour with me the next two weeks, you will observe and learn much that may be useful to you later in life. Tell her she will feel glad that she let you go. Assure her that I will look after you safely." Every word filled him with dread when he remembered the terms in which granny referred to the Mahatma. He dared not even give the slightest indication as to how she would react. He felt a great pity for the Mahatma, so innocent that he could not dream of anyone talking ill of him. He felt angry at the thought of granny, such an ill-informed ignorant and bigoted personality! What business had she to complicate his existence in this way? If he could have had his will he would have ignored his grandmother, but he had to obey the Mahatma now.

He said, "All right, sir. I will go and get my granny's blessing. I'll be back early tomorrow."

Half a dozen times, on the way, he resolved to turn back and tell Mahatma Gandhi that he had seen granny. How could he find out the truth, anyway? But he dismissed the thought as unpractical, though perhaps not so unworthy under the circumstances. Suppose granny created a row, went into a faint or threatened to kill herself, and made enough noise to attract the neighbors who might come and lock him up in his house, refusing to let him out? Should he face this risk in order to tell Gandhiji that he had seen the old obstinate lady as ordered? Would it not be prudent like a sensible man to tell the old gentleman that it had been done? But probably granny would guess about Bharati behind all this and disbelieve anything he might say about Mahatmaji. Or if she spoke insultingly about Mahatmaji, he couldn't trust himself to listen patiently. He might do something for which he might feel sorry afterwards. He visualized himself suppressing his granny's words with force and violence, but he remembered that it would not be right when the Mahatma was concerned. He would be upset to hear about it. The thing to do was to turn the *jutka* back and tell the Mahatma that he had granny's blessings. But then, being a Mahatma, he might read his thoughts and send him back to granny or he might cancel all his program until he was assured that granny had been seen or begin a fast until it was done. What made the Mahatma attach so much importance to granny when he had so many things to mind? When he had the all-important task of driving the British out he ought to leave simple matters like granny to be handled by himself. His thoughts were in a welter of confusion while he was in the *jutka*, but soon the horse turned into Kabir Street. He paid the fare without haggling and sent away the *jutka* quietly.

He didn't want his movements to become noticeable in the neighborhood.

He found his granny in a semi-agreeable frame of mind. His prolonged absence seemed to have made her nervous, and she tried to be nice to him. She probably feared he would flounce out of the house if she attempted to talk to him in the manner of yesterday. She merely said: "What a long time you have been away, my boy!" attempting to keep out all trace of reproach from her tone. He pretended to settle down. He drew up the canvas chair he had bought for her, and sat down under the hall lamp. His granny fussed about as if she had recovered some one long lost. She set before him a plateful of stuff fried in ghee, saying, "They sent this down from the Lawyer's house: The first birthday of his eighth son. They don't seem to miss anything for any child." Sriram put a piece into his mouth, munched it, nodded his approval and said: "Yes, they have made it of pure ghee. Good people." He crunched it noisily. Granny said: "I kept it for you, I knew you would like it. I was wondering how long I should keep it. You know I have no teeth. Who would want stuff like that when you are not here? Don't eat all of it, you will not be able to eat your dinner."

"Oh, dinner! I've had my dinner, granny."

"So soon!"

"Yes, in the Ashram camp, we have to dine before seven usually. It's the rule."

"What sort of a dinner can it be at seven!" she cried in disappointment, "Come and eat again, you ought to be fit for a real dinner now."

"No, granny. It is all regulated very strictly. We can't do anything as we like. We have got to observe the rules in all matters. We get quite good stuff there."

"Have you got to pay for it?" asked granny.

"Of course not," said Sriram. "What do you think? Do you think Mahatmaji is running a hotel?"

"Then why should they feed you?"

"It's because we belong there."

"Do they provide a lot of public feeding?"

Sriram lost his temper at this. He was appalled at granny's denseness. "I said they feed all of us who belong there. Don't you follow?"

"Why should they feed you?"

"It is because we are volunteers."

"Nice volunteers!" cried granny, threatening to return to her yesterday's mood any second. "And what do they give you to eat?"

"*Chappatis,* curd, and buttermilk and vegetables."

"I'm glad. I was afraid they might force you to eat egg and fowl."

Sriram was horrified, "What do you take the Mahatma for! Do you know, he won't even wear sandals made of the hide of slaughtered animals!"

Granny was seized with a fit of laughter. Tears rolled down her cheeks. "Won't wear sandals!" she cried in uncontrollable laughter. "Never heard of such a thing before! How do they manage it? By peeling off the skin of animals before they are slaughtered, is that it?"

"Shut up, granny!" cried Sriram in a great rage. "What an irresponsible gossip you are! I never thought you could be so bad!"

Granny for the first time noticed a fiery earnestness in her grandson, and gathered herself up. She said: "Oh! He is your god, is he?"

"Yes, he is, and I won't hear anyone speak lightly of him."

"What else can I know, a poor ignorant hag like me! Do I read the newspapers? Do I listen to lectures? Am I told

74

what is what by anyone? How should I know anything about that man Gandhi!"

"He is not a man; he is a Mahatma!" cried Sriram. "What do you know about any Mahatma, anyway?" asked granny. Sriram fidgeted and rocked himself in his chair in great anger. He had not come prepared to face a situation of this kind. He had been only prepared to face a granny who might show sullenness at his absence, create difficulties for him when he wanted to go away, and exhibit more sorrow and rage than levity. But she was absolutely reckless, frivolous, and without the slightest sense of responsibility or respect. This was a situation which he had not anticipated, and he had no technique to meet it. It was no use, he realized, showing righteous indignation: that would only tickle the old lady more and more, and when the time came for him to take her permission and go out, she might become too intractable. She might call in the neighbors, and make fun of him. He decided that he must change his tactics. Springing up, he asked: "Granny, have you had your food? How I am keeping you away from it, talking like this!"

"It doesn't matter," she said, almost on the point of giggling. "How many years it is since I had a mouthful of food at night—must be nearly twenty years. You couldn't have seen me in your lifetime eating at night." There was such a ring of pride in her voice that Sriram felt impelled to say: "There is nothing extraordinary in it. Anybody can be without food." He wanted to add, "The Mahatma has fasted for so many days at an end, and so often," but suppressed it. The old lady was in no need of being told anything. She added at once, "No! When Mahatma Gandhi fasts, everybody talks about it."

"And when you fast at nights only, nobody notices it, and that is all the difference between you and Gandhiji?"

She was struck by the sharp manner in which he spoke.

She asked: "Do you want your dinner?"

"Yes, just to please you, that is all. I am not hungry, I told you that. And this stuff is good, made of good ghee. You may tell them so. I've eaten a great quantity of it and I'm not hungry."

Granny came back to her original mood after all these unexpected transitions. She said: "You must eat your dinner, my boy," very earnestly. She bustled about again as if for a distinguished visitor. She pulled a dining leaf out of a bundle in the kitchen rack, spread it on the floor, sprinkled a little water on it, and drew the bronze rice pot nearer, and sat down in order to be able to serve him without getting up again. The little lamp wavered in its holder. He ate in silence, took a drink of water out of the good old brass tumbler that was by his side; he cast a glance at the old bronze vessel out of which rice had been served to him for years. He suddenly felt depressed at the sight of it all. He was oppressed with the thought that he was leaving these old associations, that this was really a farewell party. He was going into an unknown life right from here. God knew what was in store for him. He felt very gloomy at the thought of it all. He knew it would be no good ever talking to his granny about his plans, or the Mahatma or Bharati. All that was completely beyond her comprehension. She could understand only edibles and dinner and fasting at night in order to impress a neighbor with her austerity. No use talking to her about anything. Best to leave in the morning without any fuss. He had obeyed Mahatmaji's mandate to the extent of seeing her and speaking to her. The Mahatma should be satisfied and not expect him to be able to bring about a conversion in the old lady's outlook, enough to earn her blessing.

Granny was very old, probably eighty, ninety, or a hundred. He had never tried to ascertain her age correctly. And she would not understand new things. At dead of night, after assuring himself that granny was fast asleep, he got up, scribbled a note to her by the night lamp, and placed it under the brass pot containing water on the window-sill, which she was bound to lift first thing in the morning. She could carry it to a neighbor and have it read to her if she had any difficulty in finding her glasses. Perhaps she might not like to have it read by the neighbors. She would always cry: "Sriram, my glasses. Where are the wretched glasses gone?" whenever anything came to her hand for reading, and it would be his duty to go to the cupboard, and fetch them. Now he performed the same duty in anticipation. He tiptoed to the *almirah,* took the glasses out of their case silently, and returned to the hall, leaving the spectacle case open, because it had a tendency to close with a loud clap. He placed the glasses beside his letter of farewell, silently opened the door, and stepped into the night.

Part Two

H<small>E WAS</small> an accredited member of the group, and in many villages he was glad to find himself fussed over and treated with respect by the villagers. They looked on him with wonder. He formed a trio with Bharati and Gorpad and whenever the villagers wanted to know anything about the Mahatma, they came and spoke to him reverentially, and that gave him an opportunity to work off all the knowledge he had gathered in his contacts with Gorpad and Bharati. It was a way of learning the job while being on it. Till then he had had no notion of village life. He had been born and bred in the township of Malgudi, and even there his idea of the bounds of the universe were confined to Kabir Street, Market Road, one or two other spots. Whenever he heard the word "villages," his mental picture was always one of green coconut groves, long and numerous steps leading down to the large tank, with elegant village women, coming up bearing pitchers, and the temple spire showing beyond the tank *bund,* low-roofed houses with broad *pyols,* and mat-covered wagons moving about dragged by bulls with tinkling bells around their necks, the cartmen singing all the time. He owed his idea to all the various Tamil films, which he had frequently seen at The Regal. But he saw nothing of the kind here. Reality was something different. Some villages were hardly a cluster of huts. For the first time he was seeing actual villages and on the first day, at a village ten miles from Malgudi, he felt so bewildered that he asked Bharati secretly:

"Where is the village?"

"Which village?"

"Why, any village," he said.

"Doesn't this look like a village to you?" she asked.

"No," he replied. They had found time for a little chat, after the Mahatma had retired for the evening.

"What a pity," she said, "that it's so! But learn, young man, this is really a village. I'm not lying. There are seven hundred thousand other villages, more or less like this in our country."

"How do you know?" he asked, more to prolong the conversation.

"I learnt from wise men," she said.

"How wise?" he asked.

She ignored his frivolity and started talking of their mission. They were out to survey the villages which had recently been affected by famine. It was a mission of mercy; Mahatmaji had set out to study the famine conditions at first hand, and to put courage and hope into the sufferers there. It was a grim, melancholy undertaking. The Mahatma attached so much value to this tour that he had set aside all his other engagements. A distant war being fought in Europe, and probably about to start in the Far East, had its repercussions here. Though not bombed, they still suffered from the war; one did not see A.R.P. signs or even a war poster, but small wayside stations acted as a vital link, a feeding channel, to a vast war reservoir in Western Europe. The wagons at the sidings carried away night and day timber cut in the Mempi forests, the corn grown here, and the able-bodied men who might have been working on their land.

However grim the surroundings might be, Sriram and Bharati seemed to notice nothing. They had a delight in each other's company which mitigated the gloom of the surroundings. Gorpad alone looked oppressed with a sense of tragedy. He spoke less, retired early, mortified himself more and more. He said: "See what the British have done to our country: this famine is their maneuvering to keep us in enslavement. They are plundering the forests and fields to keep their war machinery going, and the actual sufferer is this child," pointing at any village child who might chance to come that way, showing its ribs, naked and pot-bellied. "There is no food left in these villages," he cried passionately. "There is no one to look after them; who cares for them? Who is there to help them out of their difficulties? Everyone is engaged in this war. The profiteer has hoarded all the grain beyond the reach of these growers. The war machine buys it at any price. It's too big a competitor for these poor folk."

"Why does he say all that to me?" Sriram reflected while impatiently waiting to be left alone with Bharati. "I'm not responsible for it." Gorpad was an iron man and could be trusted to leave them alone because he had something else to do and, when his back was turned, their eyes met and they giggled at the memory of all the sad, bad matters they had just heard or noticed.

Sriram's vision of a village was nowhere to be seen. Hungry, parched men and women with skin stretched over their bones; bare earth, dry ponds, and miserable tattered thatched roofing over crumbling mud walls; streets full of pits and loose sand, unattractive dry fields—that was a village. Sriram could hardly believe he was within twenty miles of Malgudi and civilization. Here pigs and dogs lounged in dry gutters. Everything in these parts had the appearance of a dry gutter. Sriram wondered how people ever managed to go on living in such places. He wanted to stop and ask everyone: "How long are you going to be here? Won't you return to Malgudi or somewhere else? Have you got to be here forever?"

The Mahatma defeated the calculation of officials by refusing to give a program of his tour, and by visiting unexpected places. The officials politely asked him to tell them where he wished to go. He merely replied: "Everywhere, if I can." Or, "I wish I knew."

"But we'd like to make proper arrangements."

"For me? Don't trouble yourself. I can sleep in any hut. I can live where others are living. I don't think I shall demand many luxuries. Don't worry. We can look after ourselves. I'm not a guest, here, I'm a host. Why don't you join us, as our guest?" He said this to the District Collector. "We will promise to look after you, giving you all the comforts that you may want."

Quite a band of officials followed him about on his tour. Mahatma Gandhi toured the villages mostly on foot. He halted wherever he liked. He stationed himself at the lowliest hut in the village if it was available, or in a temple corridor, or in the open air. For hours he walked silently, holding his staff and supporting his arm on one or the other of his disciples. Often he stopped on the way to speak to a peasant cutting a tree or digging a field.

Sriram felt it unnecessary to know which village they were passing at a particular time. All were alike: it was the same routine. Gandhiji's personal life went on as if he had been stationary in one place; the others adjusted themselves to it. He met the local village men and women, spoke to them about God, comforted the ailing, advised those who sought his guidance. He spoke to them about spinning, the war, Britain, and religion. He met them in their huts, spoke to them under the village banyan tree (no village was so bare yet that it was without its banyan tree). He trudged his way through ploughed fields, he climbed hard rocky places, through mud and slush, but always with the happiest look, and no place seemed too small for his attention.

Gandhiji's tour was drawing to an end. He was to board a

train at Koppal, a tiny station at the foot of the Mempi Hills. The Mahatma wanted his arrival and departure to be kept a secret and, except a couple of officials deputed to see him off, there were no outsiders on the platform. The Station Master, a small man with a Kaiserlike moustache, who wore a green lace-edged turban and *dhoti*, with the help of his porter had dragged a huge antique chair onto the platform. He had tidied up his children, six of them in a row, and made them stand quietly aside in the shade of a Gold Mohur tree in bloom. He had to act as Mahatmaji's host in between tapping various messages. He had begged Mahatmaji to occupy the chair on the platform. "I can stand as well as anyone else," said the Mahatma, looking around at his followers. Sriram noted the sadness in the other's face, and urged him, "Please take your seat, Bapuji," and the Mahatma sat down, his followers standing around. The little Station Master was excited and agitated and beads of perspiration ran down his eyelids. Beyond the railway line there was a row of hills, standing against purple skies. The Station Master panted for breath, and constantly nudged and instructed his children to behave themselves although they were all the time standing stiffly as if on a drill parade. Mahatmaji said: "Station Masterji, why don't let them run about and play as they like? Why do you constrain them?" "I'm not constraining them, master. It's their habit," he said in the hope of impressing the visitors with the quality and training of his children. The Mahatma said: "Friend, I fear you are trying to put them on good behavior before me. I would love it better if they ran about and played normally, and picked up those flowers dropping on the ground, which they want to do. I'm very keen that children should be free and happy." True to his custom, the Mahatma took out the garlands and fruits given to him on the way, called up the children, and distributed

85

them. Their father fidgeted, his nerves on edge lest someone should suddenly misbehave. The sky was turning red beyond the railway line. A bell sounded inside his little office. He ran to it, and came back with more dew drops clouding his face: "The Seven Down has left Periapur. It'll be here in fifteen minutes. At the stroke of eighteen forty-two." He looked anxious in case the train might defeat his promise. The Mahatma said: "You may attend to your work in your cabin. Don't bother about us."

"May I?" he asked desperately. "I've to write the fare records, sir, and prepare the line to receive the train."

"Certainly, go on," said the Mahatma.

For the first time during all these weeks Sriram felt depressed and unhappy. The thought of having to live a mundane existence without Mahatmaji appalled him. Not even the proximity of Bharati seemed to mitigate his misery. As the sound of the approaching train was heard, he looked so stunned that Mahatmaji said: "Be happy. Bharati will look after you." Sriram looked at Bharati hopefully. Mahatmaji added: "Remember that she is your *guru,* and think of her with reverence and respect and you will be all right and she will be all right." Sriram took time to digest this sentence. The train steamed in. Mahatmaji entered a third-class compartment. Gorpad, a cold-headed stoic whom no parting moved, told Sriram: "Now you know what your duties are, and how to do them. Sister, you will receive our instructions. *Namaste,*" and climbed into Gandhiji's compartment. His party followed him in. The first bell rang, and then the second. The Station Master came out, and said: "The Seven Down generally halts here only two minutes, but today we have detained it for three and a half minutes, sir." He looked despairingly at the crowd of passengers from other carriages gathered before Mahatmaji's window. The engine was hum-ming. The engine driver from one end and the guard from the other had left their stations in order to see the Mahatma, who returned their greetings and asked: "How can the train move, sir, when its heart and soul are here?" The engine driver withdrew with a grin on his face. The Mahatma said generally, "Now, you will all have to go back to your places." The crowd dispersed and the Station Master waved his flag. Gandhiji told Sriram: "Write to me often. I'll also promise you a fairly regular correspondence. In the future you know where lies your work. Become a master-spinner, soon. Don't be despondent." "Yes, master," said Sriram; the parting affected him too much. Bharati merely said in a clear voice: *"Namaste,* Bapu." Bapu smiled and put out his hand and patted her shoulder. "You will of course keep your program and write to me often."

"Yes, of course, Bapu."

"Be prepared for any sacrifice."

"Yes, Bapu," she said earnestly.

"Let nothing worry you."

"Yes, Bapu."

The sky became redder and darker, and the Seven Down moved away, taking the Mahatma to Trichy, and then to Madras, Bombay, Delhi and out into the universe. Night fell on the small station, and the little Station Master proceeded to light his gas lamps and signals.

Though the Mahatma's physical presence was no longer with him, Sriram had a feeling that his movements were being guided. His home now was a deserted shrine on a slope of the Mempi Hill, overlooking the valley. Down below, the road zigzagged and joined the highway which ended a mile off at Koppal Station. He often saw the mail runner trudging up a curve, with a bag on his shoulder, a staff on one arm (the staff had little bells tied to its end, heralding his arrival even a mile away). Sriram expected no mail, but he loved to watch the runner till he stepped on a rock, and took a diverging crosscut, leading him to various estates and villages on the higher reaches of the Mempi Hills.

This place seemed to have been destined for him, built thousands and thousands of years ago by someone who must have anticipated that Sriram would have a use for an abandoned building. The place was a ruin. A few sculptures showed along the wall. The masonry was crumbling here and there. There was an image of some god with four hands in an inner sanctum overgrown with weed. But it was the most comfortable ruin a man could possess. There were stately pillars in a central hall, with bricks showing; there were walls without a ceiling, but from which exotic creepers streamed down; one of the stubborn, undisturbed pieces of sculpture was a Bull-and-Peacock over the large portal, which had very large-knobbed wooden doors that could not be moved at all on their immense hinges. This was no great disadvantage for Sriram since no one came this way, and even if they did, he did not have anything to lock up. If he wished to be out of sight, he had only to slip away beyond a curtain of weeds, into a cellar. He could hear the train arrive and depart far away. He could hear the voices of villagers as they moved up in groups from the villages down below to the estates above. His possessions were a spinning wheel, a blanket on which to sleep, and a couple of vessels, some foodstuff, and a box of matches. He lit the wick of a small lantern whenever he wanted to work at night. He had set duties to perform everyday when he woke up with the cries of birds. "Oh, God, it's much better in Kabir Street," he used to think. "The birds make so much uproar here that they won't allow a man to sleep in peace. In spite of this he got up from bed. He was going through a process of self-tempering, a rather hard task, for he often found, on checking his thoughts, that they were still as undesirable as ever. He had thought that by practicing all the austerities that he had picked up in Gorpad's company, he could become suddenly different. Mahatmaji had blessed his idea of self-development. He had said: "Spin and read Bhagavad Gita, and utter *Ram Nam* continuously, and then you will know what to do in life."

Sriram carried a change of dress and went downhill to a brook and bathed. He felt so invigorated after the cold bath that he sang aloud all alone in his wilderness. He went on repeating: *"Raghupathi Raghava Raja Ram, Pathitha Pavana Seetha Ram"*—Mahatmaji's litany. When he sang it, he had a feeling of being near him and doing something on his orders. He was overcome with such a sense of holiness that he nearly danced in joy when he went back to his retreat. He carried the two pieces of dress he had washed in the brook and put them out to dry on the green fence surrounding the shrine. He was very proud of wearing cloth made with his own hand. Bharati had taught him how to insert the cotton thread, how to turn the wheel, and how to spin. Gandhiji had presented him with a spinning wheel in one of the villages with the explanation: "This is the key to your future." Sriram had felt too respectful to ask what he meant. But he took the wheel with proper reverence and literally put it close to his heart, although it was a heavy cumbrous apparatus. Bharati tried to teach him how to use it during their sojourn in one of the villages. He tried his hand at spinning and committed countless blunders while learning. He never managed to produce more than a couple of inches of yarn at a time, without snapping—it looked more like bits of twisted cotton wool than yarn. Bharati could not restrain her laughter when she saw his handiwork. She remarked: "You will waste all the cotton in India and Egypt before you make for yourself a yard of yarn." After this, she held his fingers down at the correct pressure at the spinning point, but when she took away her hand, Sriram let go his fingers too, and the cotton fell down and became worthless for any purpose.

All through the tour he had worked at it, his lessons starting the moment they came to a halt for the day. Everyday Mahatmaji inquired: "Well, what is the progress?" And before he could answer Bharati generally broke in and said: "Two more inches, Bapuji; in all he has produced six inches today, but the count must be specially measured. It must be a five-count yarn, probably the same count as a lampwick!" The Mahatma said: "Well, there will be a time soon when he will give you a hundred count. Don't be too proud, little daughter."

"I'm not," Bharati said. "I'm merely mentioning the facts."

"How proud she is! Do you know she won her prize in a *khadi* competition some years ago? Her yarn is kept in an exhibition."

"She scores one over me in everything," Sriram reflected. "It's because of the excessive support she gets. She is being spoilt. That is what is wrong with her. She thinks no end of herself."

"I'm sure Bharati will teach you how to excel her," said the Mahatma, and Bharati lived up to this promise. She allowed Sriram no rest, night or day. Whenever there was the slightest respite from travel, she came up with, "Now, what is the program of the great pupil?" And Sriram dragged the wheel out, took the little packets of cotton, and started nervously.

He dreaded making a mistake and provoking the girl's mirth. He hated her for her levity, and for making him feel like a fool so often. But he kept up a desperate effort. He slipped, he made her laugh, he struggled in the grips of unholy thoughts when she stooped over him, held his hand, and taught him the tricks. He concentrated until his mind was benumbed with the half-whispering movement of the spinning wheel. His fingers ached with holding a vibrant ever-growing thread, and his eyes smarted. Finally he did emerge a victor; that was nearly twelve weeks after Mahatmaji had left. Sriram had stationed himself for his novitiate at one of the spinning centers, about fifty miles from Malgudi. Bharati was perfectly at home there and proved herself to be a task-mistress of no mean order; she did not let go her grip on Sriram until he had spun enough yarn free from entanglement for a *dhoti* and a short shirt. It was a result of continuous work over weeks. But it was worth it. She became very excited at the success of his efforts. She tore off the blank edge of a newspaper and wrote on it in minute letters: "This is to say that Sri Sriram is henceforth to be called a master spinner, and he must be respected wherever he goes." She helped him to bundle off the yarn to a central depot at Madras and secure in exchange woven cloth of the same count. Sriram suddenly felt that he was the inhabitant of a magic world where you created all the things you needed with your own hands. His regret was that he still could not make the one hundred count, and that his yarn was somewhat rugged. But Bharati said: "The forty count is the real cloth that can be used: One hundreds are merely for show and prizes, don't worry about it." On the day he got his *khadi* clothes, a simple *dhoti* and a *jibba* (cut and stitched on the spot by the village tailor), he took off the clothes he had been wearing (mill manufactured), heaped them in the middle of the street, poured half a bottle of kerosene over the lot, and applied a match; his old clothes caught fire and burned brightly. A few members of the spinning center stood around the fire and watched. Some of the villagers looked on with interest. Sriram explained to the gathering, fascinated by the leaping flames: "I will never again wear clothes spun by machinery." The *dhoti* and *jibba* were heavy; he felt as if a piece of lead were interwoven with the texture. But he felt it was something to be proud of. He felt he had seen and reached a new plane of existence. He sat down and wrote to the Mahatma, "Burnt my old clothes today. Spun forty count. Bharati satisfied." And Mahatmaji immediately wrote back to him: "Very pleased. Keep it up. God bless you."

Bharati came uphill at dusk. Sriram became fussy. "How can you walk barefoot in all these places?"

"Why not? We are not born with sandals on our feet. I have not yet got the leather from Wardha, and I shall have to manage with this until we get it. But—" she said with a sigh, "there is probably no one there who can attend to our wants. We don't even know how many of them are in prison. The government have stopped giving even that information." They were sitting on the cool mud floor, with a lamp between them. Sriram studied her face, so full of lines nowadays as if the burden of the country were on her back, with Mahatmaji in prison since the August of 1942. Bharati (of course along with Sriram) was a little cog in a vast complicated machinery that was working, in spite of the police hunting down politics everywhere, to eject the British from the land.

Sriram said again: "You should not walk barefoot."

"Why not? India's three hundred and sixty million walk barefoot." Her national statistics bored him.

92

He said sharply: "They may, but it doesn't mean you should also walk barefoot. There may be cobras about; this place is full of such things."

"Bah, as if cobras would not bite if trodden upon with sandaled feet!"

"You are too argumentative."

"I tell you I am not able to get the usual leather from Wardha," she complained, and then added: "I am not afraid of you, and I don't have to explain to you why I am like this or like that. I am not afraid of cobras either, or the lonely road. Otherwise I should not be here."

"Of course, you need not be afraid of me," said Sriram. "Only you expect others to be afraid of you."

"Yes, because I am your *guru*."

Sriram felt, "The whole thing is extremely false. She ought to be my wife and come to my arms." He wondered for a moment, "What is it that prevents me from touching her? What can she do? She is all alone in this place. Even if she shouts nobody will hear her for ten miles around." He reveled in the picture of this terrific possibility. But it was only a dream. She explained her mission: "I am leaving for Madras, tomorrow, and you won't see me for some time."

"When? Where are you going?"

"I have been summoned for instructions. The police are watchful, no doubt, but I can manage to go up and return without any trouble." She started to go. He wondered, "Why has she come to tell me this? What is the matter? Could I interpret it as her love for me?" He wondered. No one would come two miles barefoot just to say there would be nothing to do for the next three days. She must have come with some other motive. Probably she likes me very much, waits for me to take her hand and tell her what I have in mind; and then she would yield to him. Absurd to think that she was just his *"guru,"* *Guru* indeed! Absurd that a comely young

93

woman should be set to educate a man! Educate him in what? He chuckled at the thought. And she said: "You have become suddenly very thoughtful. Why?" He touched her arm: the lonely atmosphere was very encouraging, but she pushed his hand down gently, remarking, "You rest here till I am back with instructions," and she turned and was off down the road, saying, "Don't show yourself too much outside."

He said: "I will escort you halfway."

"It's not necessary," she said and was off. Sriram watched her go downhill. "Someday, someone is going to abduct her; she doesn't seem to feel that she is a woman," he thought and turned in. He stood brooding over the ruins around him. Far away a train halted and proceeded on its journey, its shaded A.R.P. lights crawling along the landscape. He hoped that the girl would reach her village safely, without any mishap.

Three days later she turned up bringing instructions, and from that moment Sriram's activities took a new turn. Bharati came to him bearing a can of paint and a brush. She handed them over to him with the air of an ordnance chief distributing weapons from the armory. She said: "They have assigned to you all the plantations above. It means a lot of walking. You must not miss any of the dozen villages on the way. The villagers will help you everywhere. We shall be at work in Malgudi and the surroundings. Be careful. I will see you again sometime. With Mahatmaji in prison, we have to carry on the work in our own manner. We must spread his message everywhere."

The Mahatma had in his famous resolution of August 1942 said: "Britain must quit India," and the phrase had the potency of a *mantra* or a magic formula. Throughout the length and breadth of the land, people cried, "Quit India." The Home Secretary grew uneasy at the sound of it. It became a prohibited phrase in polite society. After the Mahatma uttered the phrase, he was put in prison; but the phrase took life and flourished, and did ultimately produce enough power to send the British out. There was not a blank wall in the whole country which did not carry the message. Wherever one turned one saw "Quit India."

On the following day Sriram trudged up the mountain path carrying his little tin can, brush, and a rag, in a satchel slung over his shoulder. He stopped at the first village on the way, selected the most suitable wall, which happened to be the outer wall of a new house, on whose *pyol* the village children were learning the alphabet. Their lips had been reciting the letters of the alphabet in a chorus, which incidentally lulled their teacher into a slight doze, but their eyes were following the bullock carts rattling down the road in a caravan, busses flying past and disappearing in a cloud of churned-up dust, and people passing to and fro. The day was bright and the glare on green trees and boughs and hedge creepers was enticing; their eyes wandered, their minds wandered. And so when Sriram came up to write on the wall they slipped out of their class with a feeling of profound relief. The elders of the village, too, suspended their normal occupations and stood around to watch.

Sriram dipped the brush in paint and fashioned carefully, "Quit India" on the wall. He wished that he didn't have to write the letter "Q," which consumed a lot of black paint. It was no use wasting all the available paint on a single letter. He wondered if, for economy's sake, he could manage without drawing its tail. They were launching on a war with a first-rate, war-equipped nation like England, all their armament being this brush and black paint and blank walls. They could not afford to squander their war resources in writing just a single letter. It also seemed to him possible that Britain had imported the letter "Q" into India so that there might be a national drain on black paint. He was so much obsessed with this thought that he began to write a modified "Q" expending the very minimum of paint on its tail, so that it read until one scrutinized it closely, "Ouit India." The villagers asked: "How long ought this to be on our wall, sir?"

"Till it takes effect."

"What does it say, sir?"

"It is 'Quit'—meaning that the British must leave our country."

"What will happen, sir, if they leave? Who will rule the country?"

"We will rule it ourselves."

"Will Mahatmaji become our Emperor, sir?"

"Why not?" he said shaping the letters, with his back turned to them. He taught the school children to cry, "Quit India" in a chorus. They gleefully obeyed him. Their teacher came and expostulated: "What is this you are doing, sir? You are spoiling them!"

"How?"

"By teaching them seditious behavior. The police will be after us soon. Do you want us to end in jail?"

"Yes, why not? When more important persons than you are already there."

The crowd jeered at the teacher. The boys were ever ready to seize an opportunity to jeer at the old man. The old man was more tough than he looked. He put on his spectacles and looked Sriram up and down. The boys cried: "Oh, the master is looking through his spectacles, oh! oh!" They laughed and cried: "Quit India." The teacher pushed his way through and cried: "Add if possible one 'e' before 't'; what we need in this country is not a 'Quit' India program, but a 'Quiet India.' Why don't you write that?"

Sriram finished his job of writing. He had borrowed a

ladder from someone. He turned round and said to the teacher: "Please do something more useful than standing there and talking, master. Please see that this ladder is returned to its owner (I forgot his name now), and you will have done your bit to free our country."

The teacher relented a little. He came forward and said: "It's not that I don't want to see our country freed. I am as much a patriot as you, but honestly do you think we are ready to rule ourselves? We aren't. Don't delude yourself. We are not ready yet for anything. Let this war be over, and you will find me the first to fight for *Swaraj*. Patriotism is not your monopoly." The boys stood around and cried slogans. Sriram said: "Be careful. You will be beheaded when Britain leaves India. We have a list of everybody who has to be beheaded." The teacher lost his temper completely and said: "How dare you say that! I don't want to see Britain go. I am not one of those who think that we'll be happier when Hitler comes, perhaps with the help of people like you. Let me tell you you will be the first to be shot then." Part of the crowd was appreciative of the teacher's point of view, and said: "The master is right, why should we irritate the *sircar*?" Sriram turned on them with rage and said: "You will not only irritate, you must not recognize the government. You don't have to pay taxes to it at all. They are ten thousand miles away from us. Why do you give them your tax?"

"Fellows like this should not be allowed to go about as they like: that's why I've always asked for a police outpost here. If there had been policemen here, would he have dared to come and lecture like this?"

"How far away is the police station?" asked Sriram.

"The Circle Station is beyond ten stones," replied someone.

"See that!" said Sriram. "Your *sircar* have not given you even a police station! Is it because it is unnecessary when

97

there is a person like this master in your midst?" The boys raised a shout of appreciation and cried, "Quit India" in a singsong manner. It was a vociferous, happy gathering. Their shouts and the general riotous behavior frightened a pair of bullocks drawing a load of hay down the road. The bullocks lowered their heads and pulled the cart into a ditch, and it created a general melee, people running hither and thither, and shouting directions to each other. The carter while pulling the animals back to the road, swore at them and at the disturbance. "These politicians, Gandhi folk, they won't leave anyone in peace. Why do you come and trouble us here?"

Sriram said: "Hey, pull up your cart and listen. Don't talk like a baby. You are old enough to know what you are talking about? What's your age?"

The carter pulled up his reins and said over the jingle of the bells around the necks of his animals, "I think I'm twenty!"

"Twenty! More likely you are fifty."

"Maybe, sir, a little this way and that. I used to be twenty."

"How many children have you?"

"Five sons, sir, and a grandson."

"You are fifty, my dear fellow, and you look it. Don't talk irresponsibly. Do you know Mahatma Gandhi is in jail?"

"Yes, master."

"You know why he is there?" The man shook his head. "So that you may be a free man in this country. You are not a free man in this country now."

Sriram's orbit of operations lay in the mountain villages scattered here and there, connected by more or less self-formed roads, which wound their way through thick wooded vegetation and forests. Their connection with the outside world was through a postal runner, who passed through some of the better villages once or twice a week, bringing in the mails dumped at the railway station at Koppal. There were a few police outposts scattered over the whole area, with a petty officer and a handful of men in each, who kept in touch with their headquarters through the telephone lines passing overhead and often vanishing into the vegetation on the mountain slope. One would hardly associate this remote green wilderness with politics, but it was as good a front line in the fight with Britain as any other.

He went into a part of the jungle where elephants were hauling timber. Huge logs were being cut and herds of elephants picked them up on their trunks and rolled them and piled them on trucks waiting in the heart of the jungle. Sriram penetrated here with his own message. He watched them at work and remarked: "You are cutting down green unripe timber. You know where it is going?" The mahouts on the elephants paused in their tasks, and looked down at him with amusement. Sriram explained, "They are going into the making of ships and rifles and bridges and what not, all of which are to be used for the destruction of this world. They are going into a war which we are forced to fight because Britain chose to drag us into it. We don't have to strip our forests for this task. It's going far away, to far off countries, and the money you are getting is a puffed up, illusory currency, which will lose its value soon. Don't supply these materials for the war; it will take centuries for us to grow all this timber again. Refuse to do this job; it's in your hands. Don't strengthen the hand that is oppressing you."

The timber contractor, who was observing him, came up and pleaded, "Don't trouble us please, after all we are businessmen. If tomorrow, you place an order with us for a fair quantity at a good price—" "This is not the time for acquiring wealth. This is the time to join in the fight for independence." The contractor merely said, "Please leave us alone. We don't wish to get into all this bother." He whispered, "Please don't disturb our labor, please." "I'm not out to create labor trouble. You must not send that timber out of this country for this hellish purpose. All wars are against Mahatmaji's creed of *Ahimsa*. Do you accept it or not?"

"Ah, Mahatmaji. I gave five thousand rupees to The Harijan Fund. I have a portrait of him in my house. The first face I see is his, as soon as I get up from bed."

"Do you know what he means by nonviolence?"

"Yes, yes, I never missed a day's lecture when he came to Malgudi."

"You must also have attended an equal number of Loyalist Meetings, I suppose."

The contractor bowed his head shyly. He muttered: "After all, when the Collector comes and says, 'Do this or that,' we have to obey him. We cannot afford to displease government officials."

"How much have you given to the War Fund?"

"Only five thousand. I'm very impartial; when the Governor himself comes and appeals how can we refuse? After all we are businessmen."

The man had inveigled Sriram into entering his tent under the tree. It prevented the mahouts from wasting their time listening to their talk. The forest resounded with the sound of logs rolling down and mahouts goading the elephants, chaffing among themselves, and laughing. The air had a slight smell of eucalyptus and green leaf, and also of the tobacco that the mahouts had been smoking. The contractor seated him on a chair, took out an aluminum kettle smoking on a stove and poured two cups of tea. Sriram felt depressed at the sight of him. He was a lank man with a clean-shaven head, wearing a knitted *banian* and a *dhoti,* and at his waist he had tucked in a leather purse and some rolls of paper. The man looked prosperous, with a thin gold chain around his neck, and a wristwatch on his left hand, but he looked haggard with overwork. Sriram said: "You are no doubt making a lot of money, but it is worth nothing unless you develop some spirit of—of—" He fumbled for words. He wanted to say "National Service," or "Patriotism," but he was tired of these expressions, they smacked of platform speeches. He said: "If you have a photo of Mahatma Gandhi, pray that he may inspire you with reasonable thinking, that's all I can say." He got up abruptly. The man said: "Drink your tea and go." Sriram said, "I don't want it." He walked out of the tent, slipped through a gap in the hedge, and was off.

He lost count of time. He went on doing things in a sort of machinelike manner. He entered forests and villages and conveyed what he felt to be Mahatmaji's message. Wherever he went he wrote, "Quit India." And it was followed by loyalists' amending it with: "Don't" or "I" before "Quit." In one place a man asked Sriram: "What is the use of you writing 'Quit India' in all these places? Do you want us to quit?"

"It does not mean that."

"Then write it where it can be seen by those to whom it is meant."

"They are everywhere, sometimes seen and sometimes unseen. It is better to have it written everywhere."

"Waste of time and paint," said the man.

"I'm merely carrying out an order, and I cannot afford to stop and listen to too much wisdom."

There was a plantation four thousand feet above sea level, whither Sriram carried on his pot of paint and his brush. It meant nearly half a day's job for him. He arrived at the estate late one afternoon. He saw a picturesque gate post with the sign, "Mathieson Estates," over it. There wasn't a single human being to be seen for miles around. Sriram wondered for a moment: "Is it worth writing any message here?" He looked about and hesitated, but dismissed the doubt as unworthy. He briskly dusted a portion of the gatepost and wrote in a beautiful round handwriting: "Quit India," and turned to go. An estate laborer who was passing, stopped to look at the message and asked: "Are you writing a board?" Sriram explained at length the import of the message. The man listened for a while and said: "Go away. That *Dorai* is a bad fellow. Always with a gun. He may shoot you." Sriram hesitated for a moment whether it would be worthwhile to get shot or go away peacefully. He suddenly felt he need not have come up so far if it were only to go back safely. He hadn't climbed four thousand feet above sea level for nothing. The laborer with the pickaxe went away after uttering his warning. Sriram went forward, towards an ancient bungalow that he saw ahead. "Hope he doesn't have bulldogs," Sriram reflected. He pictured the scene ahead in a somewhat gory way. He had only to approach the steps and the *Dorai* would level his double-barreled shotgun and click and Sriram would go up in smoke and blood. Probably that would fill Bharati with remorse. She would tell herself: "I wish I had shown my love more definitely when he was alive." Anyway why was he doing this? The High Command had not instructed him to go and bare his chest before a gunman.

A seven-foot figure with a red face and sandy hair accosted

him by the porch. He was smoking a pipe, and had one hand comfortably tucked in his trouser pocket. For a second Sriram felt a little reluctant to go forward. "Hullo! Who may you be?" Sriram felt dwarfed by his side. He went up and said in a shrill voice: "I have brought a message."

"Oh, good. From where?"

"From Mahatmaji."

The man took out his pipe and said: "Oh! What?"

"From Mahatma Gandhi."

"Well? What is it?"

"That you must quit India." The other looked abashed for a second. But he recovered his composure in a moment. He said: "Why do you say that?"

"I'm not saying. I'm merely giving you the message."

"Oh! Oh! Come in and have a drink, won't you?"

"No. I never drink."

"Oh, yes, yes. I didn't mean spirits, but you can have anything you want, sherbet, or coffee or tea."

"Oh, I need nothing."

"You look tired, come in, let us have a chat anyway. Boy!" he shouted and his bearer appeared. "Two glasses of orange juice," he ordered. "Look sharp."

"Yes, sir," said the "boy," turning and going away. The servant wore a white uniform with a lot of buttons. Sriram reflected, "This man wants even a particular kind of dress for Indians who act as his servants," and felt an inexplicable rage at it. The other watched his face for a while, "Come along, let us go to the veranda." He conducted him up the steps to the veranda, which had been furnished with wicker chairs, covered with beautiful chintz cloth: there were also a few decorative plants in large pots here and there. Sriram contrasted it with his own surroundings, a ruined building built thousands of years ago, full of snakes and scorpions and with only a mat to sleep on. He could not help asking, "How do you manage to do all this? May I know?"

"Do what?" asked Mathieson.

"Manage so much decoration and luxury so far away?" said Sriram and pointed at all the things around.

Mathieson laughed gently and said, "I wouldn't call this luxury, my friend."

"And all this while millions of people here are going without food or shelter!" he said in a general way, the statistics he had picked up from Bharati deserting him for the moment.

"It is our prayer," said Mathieson, "that all of them may have not only enough to eat soon but also beautiful houses to live in, something, I hope, better than this, which is only a makeshift."

Sriram put down this explanation to racial arrogance. "It is his prosperity and the feeling of owning this country that makes him talk like this," reflected Sriram and wanted to shout at the top of his voice, "Quit, quit, we shall look after ourselves, we don't care for wicker furniture and gaudy coverings for them, we don't care even for food, what we care for—" He was not clear how to end his sentence. He merely said aloud, "What we most care for is to do what Mahatmaji tells us to do."

"And what has he advised you to do?"

"We will spin the *charka,* wear *khadi,* live without luxury, and we shall have India ruled by Indians."

"But you have rejected the opportunity to try it. Don't you think it is a pity you should have turned down Cripps's offer?"

Sriram did not reply for a while. It seemed to him a technical point with which he was not concerned. Such intricate academic technicalities refused to enter his head, and so he merely said, "Mahatmaji does not think so," and there was an end to the discussion. He had a jumble of phrases, Dominion Status, Reservation for Muslims, and this and that; although he had gathered all these from the newspapers they seemed to him beside the point, the only thing that mattered being that Mahatmaji did not think the proposals had anything to do with the independence of India. "It is just an eyewash," he said remembering a newspaper comment. "We don't want all that. We have no use for such proposals. We don't want charity." This last thought so worked him up that presently when the butler came bearing a tray with two glasses of orange juice he wanted to knock the tray down dramatically and say, "I don't want it," but it was a beautiful liquid, yellow and fresh, in a long and almost invisible tumbler, and the climb and exertion had parched his throat. He hesitated. Mathieson handed him a glass and raising his own, said, "Here's to your health and luck." Sriram could merely mumble, "Thanks," and drained off his drink. The passage of the juice down his throat was so pleasant that he felt he could not interrupt it under any circumstance. He shut his eyes in ecstasy. For a moment he forgot politics, Quit, Bharati, strife, and even Mahatmaji. Just for a second the bliss lasted. He put down his glass and sighed. The other had taken an invisible infinitesimal layer off the top level in his glass and was saying, "Care to have another?"

"No," said Sriram and started to leave. The other walked with him halfway down the drive. Sriram said, "Don't rub off the message I have painted on your doorway."

"Oh, no, I shan't. It is a souvenir and I shall keep it proudly."

"But won't you be leaving this country, quitting, I mean?" asked Sriram.

"I don't think so. Do you wish to quit this country?"

"Why should I? I was born here," said Sriram indignantly.

"I was unfortunately not born here, but I have been here very much longer than you. How old are you?"

"Twenty-seven, or thirty. What does it matter?"

"Well, I was your age when I came here and I am sixty-two today. You see, it is just possible I am as much attached to this country as you are."

"But I am an Indian," Sriram persisted.

"So am I," said the other, "and perhaps I am of some use to the people of this country seeing that I employ five thousand field laborers and about two hundred factory hands and office workers."

"You are doing it for your own profit. You think we can only be your servants and nothing else," said Sriram, not being able to think out anything better, and then he asked, "Aren't you afraid? You are all alone. If the Indians decide to throw you out it may not be safe for you."

Mathieson remained thoughtful for a moment and said, "Well, I suppose I shall take my chance, that is all, but of one thing I feel pretty sure! I am not afraid of anything."

"It is because Mahatmaji is your best friend. He wants this struggle to be conducted on perfectly nonviolent lines."

"Of course that is also a point," he said. "Well, it was nice meeting you," he said extending his hand. "Good-bye."

Sriram went down the pathway, overhung with coffee shrubs, hedge plants, bamboo clusters, and pepper vine winding over everything else with very dark green grass covering the ditches on the sides. He felt so tired that he wondered why he did not lay himself down on the velvet turf and sleep, but he had other things to do. He had unremitting duties to perform.

It was the village named Solur three miles away that was

his next destination. The place consisted of about fifty houses on a hill slope. Valleys and meadows stretched away before it. It was seven o'clock when Sriram reached it. The village was astir with activity. Men, women and children were enthusiastically gathered under the banyan tree of the village, in bright chattering groups. A gaslight had been hung from the tree, and one or two people were arranging a couple of iron chairs brought in from one of the richer households in the village. The two iron chairs were meant for some distinguished men who were expected. Sriram went to the only shop in the village, purchased a couple of plantains, and washed them down with a bottle of soda water. He felt refreshed. He asked the shopman, "What time does the meeting begin?"

"Very soon. They are bringing someone to entertain us. It is going to be a nice function. Can't you stay on for it?"

"Yes, I will."

"Where are you coming from?"

"From far away," said Sriram.

"Where are you going?" the other asked.

"Far away again," said Sriram attempting to be as evasive as possible. The other laughed, treating it as a nice joke. The man supported himself by clutching with one hand a rope dangling from the ceiling. It was a boxlike little shop made entirely of old packing cases, with a seat cushioned with gunny sacks for the proprietor to sit on. Bottles containing aerated water in rainbow colors adorned his top shelf, bunches of green bananas hung down by nails in front of his shop almost hitting one in the face, and he had several little boxes and shallow tins filled with parched rice and fried *gram* and peppermints and sugar candy and so forth. He enjoyed Sriram's joke so much that he asked, "I have some nice biscuits. Won't you try them?"

"Are they English biscuits?" Sriram asked.

"The best English biscuits."

"How can you be sure?"

"I got them through a friend in the army. They are supplied only to the army now. Purely English biscuits which you cannot get for miles around. In these days, no one else can get them."

"Have you no sense of shame?" Sriram asked.

"Why, why, what is the matter?" the other said, taken aback, and then said, "Hey, give me the money for what you took and get out of here. You are a fellow in *khadi*, are you? Oh! Oh! I didn't notice. And so you think you can do what you like, talk as you like, and behave like a rowdy."

"You may say anything about me, but don't talk ill of this dress. It is—it is—too sacred to be spoken about in that manner."

The shopman felt cowed by his manner and said, "All right, sir, please leave us alone and go your way. I don't want your lecturing here. Your bill is two annas and six pies . . . two bananas one anna each, and soda six pies. . . ."

"Here it is," Sriram said, taking out of his tiny purse two small coins and a six-pie coin and passing them on to him.

"You see," the other said softening, "this is not the season for bananas and so they are not as cheap as they might be."

"I am not questioning your price, but I want you to understand that you should not be selling foreign stuff. You should not sell English biscuits."

"All right, sir, hereafter I will be careful, after I dispose of the present stock."

"If you have any pride as an Indian you will throw the entire stock in the gutter and won't let even a crow peck at it. Do you understand?"

"Yes, sir," said the shopman, not liking the little circle of watchful people who were gathering. At the end of the street the lecture platform was being set up and groups of people stood around watching. The villagers were very happy. Some lively business was going on there, as well as starting here. The shopman saw an old enemy of his who liked to see him in trouble, standing on the edge of the crowd with a grin on his face. As if to satisfy him the gods had brought this man in *khadi* here, a born troublemaker. He appealed to Sriram, "Now, sir, please go away a little. I must close the shop."

"You may close the shop if you like, but I want you to destroy those biscuits," said Sriram firmly.

"What biscuits?" asked the shopman alarmed. "Please leave me alone, sir."

"You have those English biscuits, you said."

"I have no English biscuits, where should I get them? Even in the black market they are not available."

"If they are not English biscuits, so much the better. My esteem for you goes up, but may I have a look at one of them?"

"I have no biscuits at all," pleaded the shopman. The crowd guffawed. Somebody shouted to someone else, "Hey, here is Ranga in the soup, come on."

"You have got them in that box," Sriram said, pointing to one of the tin boxes.

The shopman immediately lifted its lid and displayed its contents, white flour, luckily for him.

"But did you not say that you had biscuits a moment ago?"

"Who? I? I was merely joking. I am a poor shopkeeper. How could I afford to pay black market rates for biscuits and keep them for sale?"

"He has got them inside, sir. Let him show us the inside of his shop," said one of the wags.

"Shut up and go your way," shouted the shopman. The situation was getting more complicated every moment.

"I am very sorry to note that you are a liar, in addition

to being a seller of foreign black market stuff. I am prepared to lay my life at your threshold, if it will only make you truthful and patriotic. I will not leave this place until I see you empty all your stock in that drain, and give me an undertaking that you will never utter a falsehood again in your life. I am going to stay here till I drop dead at your door."

"You are picking an unnecessary fight with me," wailed the man.

"I am only fighting the evil in you; it is a nonviolent fight."

A woman came to buy half an anna worth of salt. Sriram interposed and said, "Please don't buy anything here." When the woman tried to get past him he threw himself before her on the muddy ground: "You can walk over me if you like, but I will not allow you to buy anything in his shop."

The shopman looked miserable. What an evil day! What an evil face did he open his eyes on when he awoke that morning! He pleaded, "Sir, I will do anything you say, please don't create trouble for me."

Sriram said: "You are completely mistaking me, my friend. It's not my intention to create trouble for you. I only wish to help you."

The woman who came to buy salt said: "The sauce on the oven will evaporate if I wait for your argument to conclude," and she pleaded, looking at the figure lying prone on the ground: "May I buy my salt at the other shop over there, sir?"

Sriram with his head down could not help laughing. He said: "Why should you not buy your salt wherever you like?"

She didn't understand his point of view and explained: "I buy salt once a month, sir. After all, we are poor people. We cannot afford luxuries in life. Salt used to cost—"

Sriram still lay on his belly and raised his head and said:

"It's for people like you that Mahatma Gandhi has been fighting. Do you know that he will not rest till the Salt Tax is repealed?"

"Why, sir?" she asked innocently.

"For every pinch of salt you consume, you have to pay a tax to the English government. That's why you have to pay so much for salt."

Someone interposed to explain: "And when the tax goes, you will get so much salt for an anna." He indicated a large quantity with his hands. The woman was properly impressed and said, opening wide her eyes: "It used to be so cheap formerly," and added, throwing a hostile glance at the shop-man standing on his toes, supporting himself by the dangling rope, with tears in his eyes, "Our shopmen are putting up the prices of everything nowadays. They have become very avaricious," a sentiment with which most of the people were in agreement. A general murmur of approval went round the gathering. The shopman standing on his toe said, "What can we do? We sell the salt at the price the government has fixed."

"You might support those of us who are fighting the government on these questions," said Sriram, "if you cannot do anything else. Do you remember Mahatma's March to Dandi Beach in 1930? He walked three hundred miles across the country, in order to boil the salt water on the beach of Dandi and help anyone to boil salt water and make his own salt."

The shopman was a very picture of misery. He said in an undertone, "I'll do anything you want me to do. Please get up and go away. Your clothes are getting so dirty lying in the dirt."

"Don't bother about my clothes. I can look after them. I can wash them."

"But this mud is clayey, sir, it is not easily removed," said the shopman.

Someone in the crowd cried, "What do you care? He will probably give it to a good *dhobi.*"

"If you can't find a *dhobi,* you can give it to our *dhobi* Shama. He will remove any stain. Even Europeans in those estates above call him for washing their clothes, sir."

Someone else nudged him and murmured, "Don't mention Europeans now; he doesn't like them."

It seemed to Sriram that the people here liked to see him lying there on the ground, and were doing everything to keep him down. When this struck him, he raised himself on his hands and sat up. There was a smear of mud on his nose and forehead and sand on his hair. A little boy, wearing a short vest and a pair of trousers twice his size, came running, clutching tightly a six-pie coin in his hand. He shouted: "Give me good snuff for my grandfather, three pies, and coconut *bharji* for three." He dashed past Sriram to the shop and held out his coin. The shopman snatched the coin from his hand in the twinkling of an eye. Sriram touched the feet of the young boy and importuned him: "Don't buy anything in this shop."

"Why not?"

Sriram started to explain, "You see, our country—" Some two or three people in the crowd pulled the young boy by the scruff, saying, "Why do you ask questions? Why don't you just do what you are asked to do?" They tried to pull away the boy, but he clung to a short wooden railing and cried: "He has taken my money. My money, my money."

People shouted angrily at the shopman, "Give the boy his money."

The shopman cried: "How can I? This is a Friday, and would it not be inauspicious to give back a coin? I'll be ruined for the rest of my life. I am prepared to give him what he wants for the coin, even a little more if he wants; but no, I can't give back the cash. Have pity on me, friends. I am a man with seven children."

The little boy cried: "My grandfather will beat me if I don't take him the snuff. His box is empty. He is waiting for me."

"Go and buy in that other shop," someone said.

The boy answered, "He'll throw it away if it is from any other shop."

The shopman added with untimely pride, "He has been my customer for the last ten years. He can't get this snuff from any other place. I challenge anyone."

The boy clung to the railing and cried, "I must have the snuff packet, otherwise—"

Someone from the crowd pounced upon him muttering imprecations and tore him away from the railing. The boy set up a howl. The crowd guffawed. The shopman wrung his hands in despair. Sriram sat on the dust like a statue, solemnly gazing on the ground before him. Someone pacified the boy, murmuring in his ears, "Come and take your snuff after that fellow leaves."

"When will he go?" whispered the boy.

"He will go away soon. He is not a man of this place," whispered back another man.

"But my grandfather's snuff box must be filled at once."

"I'll come and speak to your grandfather, don't worry."

Sriram sat without moving, listening to everything, but he said nothing.

The crowd at the shop gradually melted away as the gathering at the other end started forming. A second lantern was being taken up the tree. The crowd looked up and said, "Ramu is climbing the tree with the lantern." They pointed at a youth wearing a striped *banian* over his bare body and khaki shorts. His mother watching from below cried, "Hey, Ramu, don't go up the tree. Won't someone pull that boy down? He's always climbing trees."

"Why do you bother, what if boys do climb trees?" asked someone. A quarrel started, the mother retorting, "You wouldn't talk like this if you had a son always endangering himself."

The boy shouted from the tree top, "If you are going to quarrel, I will jump down and make you all scream." The crowd enjoyed the situation. For a moment the shopman, losing sight of his own troubles, gazed at the treetop, and remarked, "That's a terrible boy, always worrying his mother with his desperate antics. She knows no peace with him about."

"Well, he looks old enough to look after himself," said Sriram.

"Yes, but he has been spoilt by his mother, he is always climbing trees, or swimming or teasing people, a rowdy," said the shopman.

"You people trouble him too much. He will not bother anyone if he is left alone, I think," said Sriram. "Everyone is advising and worrying him."

Now came a shout from the treetop: "I have fixed the lantern. Who else could have done it?" The lantern swung in the air and threw moving shadows on the rocky hill slope behind. The crowd jeered and laughed at him. "If anyone jeers at me, I'll cut the rope and throw the lamp on you all," he challenged.

"Devil of a boy," shouted his mother.

It was a pointless banter, it seemed to Sriram. He felt angry at the thought of all these aimless, lighthearted folk in this place. The shopman added, "There is no peace in this village—those two are always bothering everyone in some way or other."

"You are no better," said Sriram angrily. The country was engaged in a struggle for survival. In a flash there passed before his mind Gandhi, his spinning wheel, the hours he spent in walking, thinking and mortifying himself in various ways, his imprisonment; all this seemed suddenly pointless, seeing the kind of people for whom it was intended. He suddenly felt unhappy. All his own activity seemed to him meaningless. He might as well return to the cosy isolation of Kabir Street—that would at least make one old soul happy. What did it matter whether the shopman sold British biscuits or Scandinavian ones or Chinese crackers or French butter? It was only a matter of commerce between a conscienceless tradesman and a thick-skinned public. All this sitting in the mud and bothering and fighting was uncalled-for. He felt suddenly weary. He asked the shopman, "Can you give me a piece of paper and a pen and an envelope? I will pay for it."

"No, sir," said the shopman. "There is no demand for paper and such things at this shop. People who come here are all simple folk, who want something to eat or drink."

"And who ask for only English biscuits, I suppose?" said Sriram cynically.

"Forget it, sir. I'll never do it again," assured the shopman, "if you will only get up from that spot and forget me." Sriram felt pleased at this compliment and at the great importance his personality had acquired. It was very gratifying. He said, "You are not lying, I hope, about the paper and envelope?" he asked, "Possibly you have only the costliest English paper and ink?"

"No, sir, I swear by the goddess in that temple. I have no stock, and I swear by all that is holy I will hereafter avoid all English goods. I will fling into the gutter any biscuit that

I may ever see anywhere. I will kick anyone who asks for an English biscuit. At least in this village there will be no more English biscuits. Meanwhile, may I go to the schoolmaster and fetch you a sheet of paper and a pen? He is the only one who ever writes anything in the place." The shopman said, "Please move up a little. I can't leave the shop open, there are too many thieves about."

Sriram said, "I'll look after your shop while you are away," and added in a sinister manner, "You know how well, I can keep off people." He seemed to enjoy it as a joke. The shopman thought it best to join in and laughed nervously, preparing to close the doors of his shop. His nerves were taut lest Sriram should suddenly change his mind. He added, in order to safeguard himself against this possibility, "You must write your letters, sir, without fail, however busy you may be. I'll be back in a moment." He felt happy when he gave a tug to his brass lock and jumped down. He felt like a free man. This was his first taste of absolute freedom in all his life. "I will be back, sir, I will be back, sir," he cried, running away jingling his bunch of keys. It was an amusing sight to watch that portly man run. Sriram enjoyed the sight for a while, leaned back on the door of the shop decorated with enamel plates advertising soaps and hair oil, and composed in his mind the letter he should write when the paper arrived. His eyes were watching the swaying lanterns dangling from the tree branch over the shrine, and the people assembled for the meeting under it. His mind was busy with the letter: "Revered Mahatmaji, I don't know why we should bother about these folk. They don't seem to deserve anything we may do for them. They sell and eat foreign biscuits. They are all frivolous-minded, always bothering too much about a young scamp who has climbed a tree. I don't know if he has come down; I don't care if he falls down; it'll be a good riddance for all concerned. They will thank us for leaving them alone, rather than for telling them how to win *Swaraj*. They simply don't care. At this very moment I find them engrossed in preparing for a Loyalists' Meeting. What I want to know, my revered Mahatmaji, is—" He wondered what it was that he wanted to tell the Mahatmaji. What was really the problem? He lost sight of the problem. He felt suddenly that he was too tired and unhappy. He was hungry and homesick. He wanted to go back to his Kabir Street home, preferably with Bharati, and forget all this. The banana and soda water were hardly adequate for the strain he was undergoing. He wished he could ask the man for more if he came back and opened the shop door. He was seized with such ineptitude that he watched without stirring the proceedings of the meeting ahead of him. His conscience pricked him all the time. Something told him: "You are here to counteract this meeting, but you are doing nothing about it." He merely told himself, "I can't do anything. I want to suspend everything till I have guidance from my leader. There is no use rushing along without a point." He saw without emotion a set of people arrive in a jeep. A gramaphone ground away, with amplifiers, producing some film songs to which the public marked time. And then someone came up with a harmonium, and accompanied it in a loud voice. Sriram shut his ears at the sound of the harmonium: "Damned instrument," he muttered to himself. His nerves were ajangle with its raucous cry. "I hope when Mahatma Gandhi becomes the Emperor of India, he will make it a penal offense to make or play this instrument. This is also a British gift, I suppose," he told himself. After this music someone presented a scene from the Ramayana, with music and narration. The public enjoyed the show. Right in the midst of it all, the two officers occupying the iron chairs suddenly got up and delivered a speech in very bad Tamil. They explained the importance of the War, how Britain was winning, how it was India's duty to help, and how India should protect herself from enemies within and without. There were policemen in plain clothes, made less plain by their broad belts and khaki shirts, civil officers in tweed and bush coats, with sleek hair; somebody was distributing toffee out of a tin to all the children in the assembly. Sriram said to himself, "I'm here to stop it, but—but—let me first write to the Mahatma and get his advice—" He looked about. He had an excuse to wait. He had to wait for the promised letter paper. But he spotted the shopman in the crowd. "Oh liar!" Sriram commented: "He is probably going to pretend that he is a child, ask for toffee and sell it at black market rates tomorrow at his shop."

As if in answer to his unwritten letter he received a communication from Mahatmaji. It was enclosed in a note to Bharati and said: "Your work should be a matter of inner faith. It cannot depend upon what you see or understand. Your conscience should be your guide in every action. Consult it and you won't go wrong. Don't guide yourself by what you see. You should do your duty because your inner voice drives you to do it. Well, look after Bharati, as well as she looks after you, that's all. God bless you both in your endeavors."

The message had given Bharati an occasion to come up and see him. It was one of his off-days—a day of soldier's leave, as he thought. He had sat at the portal of his ruined temple resigning himself to doing nothing for the day, going through an old issue of a paper he had picked up. It was full of dead news—of the Maginot Line and the like. But that was enough for him. The mail carrier had stepped off the boulder down below long ago on his return journey, and had gone back to the plains. The evening train had crawled in and out of the landscape long ago. The sun stood poised over the Western horizon.

Sriram brought out his rush mat, spread it out and threw himself on it, and was presently absorbed not only in reading all the stale news in the paper, but also all those jokes, tidbits, and syndicated cartoons, which filled the bottom of its columns. He had picked up the paper on the highway, when returning from his expedition at Solur village. It had blown across the highway and hugged a tree trunk. He unwound the sheet from the tree trunk, flashed his torch on it and saw it was an upcountry paper which was well-known for its reactionary views and carping references to Gandhiji, but still it contained some interesting Sunday reading. He felt irritated for a second at the thought that someone should have been scattering such an imperialistic paper in these parts, but he carefully folded it and put it into his bag. He had been the victim of certain moments of extreme boredom, when he felt that the huge teak trees and bamboo clumps and the estate trees covering slope upon slope would destroy his mind. They got on his nerves and made him want to shout aloud in protest. He once tried talking aloud to himself in order to get over the tedium. He asked himself, "Hallo, what are you doing here?" and told himself, "I am fighting for my country."

"What sort of fight is it? You look like a vagabond, with no uniform, no weapon, and no enemy in sight. What sort of fight is this? Are you joking?" and he laughed aloud, "oh, oh, oh!" He spoke at the top of his voice till the hills echoed with his voice, and one or two birds sitting on a tree nearby took off in fright. This exuberance had greatly relieved his mind. Now he hoped to be provided against boredom with this sheet of newspaper. Here at least was something to read instead of watching endlessly those treetops and valleys. It was his lot to be here. He could not kick against it.

He stretched himself on his mat. He had had a block of stone rolled over to serve as a back-support for his couch. He had found it a couple of days before, lying about in the grass and weeds, and had moved it up with difficulty. It had been a job of nearly an hour. There were smoothed out lettering and ornamental carvings on the stone. He had speculated what they might signify, but they were circular letters which looked familiar but eluded study; a message carved probably thousands of years ago by some king or emperor or tyrant one found pictured in history books. History books were full of ruffianly-looking characters, according to Sriram. He had often wondered what earthly purpose was served in reading and allowing oneself to be questioned about side-whiskered *goondas*? Reclining against this tablet he thought that if he had at least passed his examinations normally, he needn't have got into his present life. He might have settled as a good-natured clerk in an office, as his friend Prasanna had done. It was only yesterday he had been a champion street-footballer, but already he was in harness, slaving at the Treasury desk several hours a day.

Sriram reclined comfortably against the ancient tablet, and read a joke in which a "He" and a "She" indulged in a four-line dialogue. "When am I going to get my tie pressed?" To which She gave the smart reply: "Exactly an hour after I get that gown." Sriram read it over again and again, and felt irritated. What was the joke? Where lay its humor? He looked it over and examined it minutely, but failed to spot any sense in it. It was accompanied by a grotesque-looking couple, fat about the waist. Sriram thought: "We can't know what humor Englishmen will enjoy!" He put away the paper and its corners rustled in the wind. Now it was as if he heard the anklet-sound of his beloved, and there she was down below.

Bharati was coming up the road half a mile away. She had never been more welcome. He got up and ran to her with a wild cry of joy. He saw her as an angel come to relieve him of his tedium. She carried a bag in her hand, as usual, and she strode on with such assurance and happiness. She was taken aback when, turning a bend, she was accosted by Sriram. "Hallo!" he cried at the top of his voice: "Here is my *Devata* come!" She slowed down her pace and said: "What has come over you? What will anyone seeing us think!" "Who is there to see and think?" he asked haughtily. "As if a big crowd were milling about!" he said, putting into it all the venom that he felt at his lonely existence. She detected his tone of bitterness but preferred to overlook it, "What do you want? A big fair around you all the time?," she asked lightheartedly, walking on.

He asked, "Where are you going?"

"I'm going to meet you."

"Here I am!" he said.

"I won't take official notice of your presence here, but if you want me to state my business, I will say it and go back. I have come to you with excellent business."

"What is it?" he cried anxiously, following her.

She went on, saying, "Come and hear it at your own place."

At his place, he ceremoniously showed her the mat, and begged her to recline with ease against the tablet. She obeyed him. She stretched her legs, leaned back on the tablet, and while her figure was rousing wild emotions in Sriram, she picked up the letter from her little bag and gave it to him. "Here is a letter from Bapu for you. How do you like it?"

He read it and remained thoughtful. Owls were hooting, the sky had darkened; crickets were making a noise in the dark bushes. He sat beside her on the mat. He could see her heart palpitating her left breast under her white *khaddar* sari. She seemed to be unaware of the feelings she was rousing in him. She said, "Do you know what it means? Bapu wants you to stay on and do your work here. He feels your work here is worthwhile and that you will have to go on with it."

"How do you know he means that and not something else?"

"I know it because I can read what he writes and understand it."

"I can also read what he writes," said Sriram with pointless haughtiness.

"Did you write anything to him?" she asked.

He didn't like the cross-examination. "I might or I might not," he said with anger in his voice.

"Why should you be angry? I'll write to Bapu next time that you are a very angry man."

In answer he suddenly threw himself on her, muttering, "You will only write to him that we are married." It was an assault conducted without any premeditation, and it nearly overwhelmed her.

He gave her no opportunity to struggle or free herself. He held her in an iron embrace in his madness. He lost sight of her features. The hour was dark. He felt her breath against his face when she said, "No, this can't be, Sriram."

Sriram muttered, "Yes, this can be. No one can stop me and you from marrying now. This is how gods marry." Her braid laid its pleasant weight on his forearm. Her cheeks smelt of sandalwood soap. He kissed the pit of her throat. He revelled in the scent of sandalwood that her body exuded.

"You are sweet-smelling," he said. "I will be your slave. I will do anything you ask me to do for you. I will buy you all the things in the world." He behaved like an idiot. She wriggled in his grasp for a moment and at the same time seemed to respond to his caresses. He rested his head on her bosom and remained silent. He felt that any speech at this moment would be a sacrilege. It was a night of absolute darkness. The trees rustled, crickets and night insects carried on their unremitting drone. He wanted to say something about the stars and moonlight, but he felt tongue-tied. The only thing that seemed to be of any consequence now was her warm breathing body close to his.

He murmured: "I always knew it. You are my wife."

She gently released herself from his hold and said, "Not yet. I must wait for Bapu's sanction."

"How will you get it?"

"I shall write to him tomorrow."

"If he doesn't sanction it?"

"You will marry someone else."

"Don't you like me? Tell me—Tell me—" he said in a fevered manner.

She felt the trembling of his body, and said: "I shouldn't be coming here or meeting you if I didn't."

"Wouldn't Mahatmaji have known?"

"No. His mind is too pure to think anything wrong—"

"What is wrong with what?"

"This is very wrong—we—we should not have—I—I—" she sobbed. "I don't know what Bapu will think of me now. I— must—write to him what has happened."

He had never seen her so girlish and weak. He felt a momentary satisfaction that he had quashed her pride, quelled her turbulence. He said aggressively: "Bapuji will say nothing. He will understand. He knows human feelings, and so don't worry. There is nothing wrong in loving. You and I are married."

"When?"

"On the very first day I saw you."

"That's not enough. I can't marry without Bapu's sanction."

He became positive and dynamic. He swore. "We shall marry this very moment." He dragged her by the hand into the inner sanctum. He ran hither and thither feverishly doing various things. He lit the lamp and placed it before the image, whose nose was broken, and arms broken, but whose eyes still shed grace. He ran out and came back with a few leaves and flowers, placed them at the foot of the pedestal. He took out a thread from his spinning wheel saying, "You cannot have a *thali* more sacred than this, nor a priest more holy than this god." When he attempted to place the thread around her neck, she gently drew herself away from him.

A sudden firmness came in her voice, as she said: "Know this, Sriram. If I had not trusted you I'd not have come here again and again." He did not understand why she was saying it. He felt rather bewildered. Why was she talking like this? Perhaps she suddenly remembered that she ought to marry Gorpad or someone else. Yes, now it flashed across his mind there used to be some significant exchange of looks between her and Gorpad. What a fellow to marry, rough as emery paper! A stab of jealousy shook him for a moment and he said, "Will you swear before this god that you will marry only me."

"Yes, if I marry at all, and mark this, if Bapu agrees to it."

"Bapu! Bapu!" It filled him with despair. He wailed: "He is too big to bother about us. Don't trouble him with our affairs."

She said, "I won't marry if he doesn't sanction it. I can't do it."

"If he asks you to marry someone else," he asked pathetically, checking at the last second the word "Gorpad?"

"Bapu has better things to do than finding a husband for me," she said clearly, unequivocally.

He blinked for a moment. The excitement made his throat parched. He wanted to ask something again. But even in that confused state, he was aware that he was saying the same thing over and over. He blinked pathetically. The broken-armed god looked on. Sriram had never bargained for such an inconclusive love-making. It had begun with such spirit that he had felt he would be shot into Elysium next moment, but here he was, standing before a god immobilized and listening to an obscure speech. The girl would probably take him for a fool to leave so much space between them. He tried to remedy it by approaching her again, attempting to storm her as he did a moment ago. The first time he had the advantage of a sudden impulse. But now it didn't work. She just beat down his outstretched arm: "No. You will not touch me again." She said it with such authority that he felt foolish.

"I didn't intend to, if you don't want it. I know you hate me," he said childishly.

She simply said, "Why should I hate you?"

"Because I am bothering you."

"How?" she asked.

"By, by—asking you to marry me. It's wrong, perhaps wrong."

"It wouldn't be if Bapu agreed to it."

He resigned himself. "All right," he said. "As you please—"

"We shall marry," she said, "the very minute Bapu agrees."
She was very considerate.

He felt it was time for him to ask again: "Do you—like me?"

"Yes, when you don't misbehave."

Days of listlessness and suspense followed. Sriram lost sight of her for a considerable period. He thought he had lost her forever. It made him so paralyzed that all day he did nothing but lounge in front of his cottage going over in mind again and again all that had happened that night. He had suspended his usual round of lecturing, agitation, and demonstrations; he didn't seem to think he owed any duty to the country. He ate and stayed in his den all day; he had read the joke about a "He" and a "She" two hundred times already. He saw the train arrive and depart. He saw the postman step on the boulder and go away to the estates. He lounged against the corner tablet and brooded endlessly.

After all, one day she turned up. She came at noon. It seemed significant that she should avoid dusk. The moment he sighted her on the bend, he gave a shout of joy and wanted to ask, "Are you coming now, because it is a safe hour?" But he checked himself. He ran up to meet her at the usual bend of the road. He asked: "What news?" She didn't speak till they were back in their place. She sat down, leaned back on the tablet, took a letter out of her bag. Sriram snatched it hungrily and glanced through it:

"Blessed one, not yet . . . I am going to ask all workers if they are underground to come out. I want you to give yourself up at the nearest police station. Take your disciple, too, along. God bless you both."

Sriram felt stunned. He read the letter over and over, trying to make out its significance. He tried to interpret it. "'Not yet,'" he says. What does he mean?"

"He just means that and nothing more," she replied. "It is never hard to understand what Bapuji says."

Sriram felt amazed at the hardihood and calmness of the girl. She didn't seem to possess any feeling. She spoke of it with such indifference. He was appalled at her calmness. She was probably feeling relieved that Bapuji had vetoed their plans. It suited her very well—Gorpad. And of course, in his sick imagination he felt that probably Mahatmaji was also in favor of Gorpad, he'd naturally prefer to marry her to a grim and dry-as-dust worker like Gorpad. But why couldn't she be plain with him? "Why can't you be plain?" he asked her all of a sudden.

"What do you mean?"

He felt tongue-tied, and asked: "Why should Bapu not want us to marry?"

"He doesn't say so."

He sighed: "I thought he would send us his blessing, but he has only turned down our program." In his disappointment, he felt sore with the whole world, not excluding Bapu. He suddenly asked her: "Don't you feel disappointed that we are not married?"

"I have other things to think of," she said.

"Oh!" Sriram said significantly. "What may they be?"

"I am going to jail . . ." The full significance of the whole thing dawned upon him now. He cried, "Bharati, you just can't do that, what do you mean?"

She replied, "You will have to come, too . . ." She opened the letter and glanced through it again. "Bapu has also given instructions as to how I should occupy my time in jail. 'This is an opportunity for you to learn some new language. I wish you could read Tulasi Das Ramayana without any assistance;

127

you speak Hindi well, but your literary equipment will also have to be equally good. You may ask the jail superintendent to give you facilities if you are going to be classed as B to take your *charka* along. I would like to hear that you are spinning your quota in jail. Don't for a moment ever feel that you are wasting your time. Wherever you may be with a copy of Ramayana and Gita, and a spinning wheel, there you are rightly occupied. Anyway look after your health. Very mild exercise may be necessary. You may get it by walking around the compound if you are permitted . . . If you would rather not be in B class but would like to be an ordinary class prisoner like others, you will have to ask for it. All that I am saying for you applies to your disciple, too.'"

Sriram pleaded, "Don't. Please tell Bapu . . ."

Bharati looked at him with wonder, "After all these months of association and work, how can you speak like this? How can we do anything other than what Bapuji asks us to do?"

Sriram had no cogent answer to give. He hung down his head. For the present he seemed to have forgotten that he was a soldier in the struggle for freedom. She said resolutely, "I ought to be there already. I am reporting to the police station at . . ."

"How long will they keep you in jail?" he asked pathetically.

"How can I say?" she replied. She asked, "Are you also coming?"

He said, "Not now. I want to think it over. But I will readily come if they will keep me in the same prison, preferably in the same cell."

"It won't be possible. The government won't keep us together," she said.

This enraged Sriram. The whole universe seemed to be

organized to defeat his purpose, even the government which differed from the Mahatma on most matters seemed to be in accord with him where it concerned him and Bharati. The worst of it was that Bharati herself seemed to rejoice in the arrangement. He became wild at the thought and said, "Why is everyone opposed to my loving you?"

She took pity on him and said tenderly, "Poor fool. You have lost your wits completely."

"How dare you say that?" he shouted.

"There is no point in your shouting," she said. "Don't let us quarrel. I will be gone in a moment . . . I want to report myself before it strikes four. If they want to send me to The Central or some other jail they must have time to catch the evening train."

"What shall I do without you?" he wailed.

"That is why Bapu has asked you to report, too."

He shook his head. "I have a lot of things to do outside . . . Bapu has given everyone freedom to carry on the *Satyagraha* in his own manner. He doesn't really mean me," he said dolefully. In answer Bharati seized the letter and held it open under his nose. " 'This applies to your disciple also,' he says."

"But that doesn't mean me. It may mean anyone," said Sriram.

"I thought he always understood whom he meant by 'disciple,'" she said grimly. "Anyway the choice is yours. You may do what you think best. I am doing what seems to me the right thing to do."

"How do you know it is the right thing to do?"

"I need not answer that question," she said irritated. "If I had known that you would treat Bapuji's words so lightly—"

Sriram felt crushed by her tone. "Oh, Bharati, don't add to my troubles by mistaking me so completely. I revere the Mahatma, you know I do. Why do you suspect me? Have I not followed every word of what he has been saying . . . Otherwise I should not have been here. I should not have left the comfort of my house. All that I want is some more time to think it over. I am . . ." he brought out his master-piece on an inspiration. "I am only thinking of my grand-mother. I want to see her before I am finally jailed. That is why I asked you how long we should be in prison. She is very old, you know. I will surrender myself after I have seen her once. I must manage to see her."

This idea seemed to soften the girl. She thought it over, leaning back on the tablet. She seemed to appreciate his tender feelings for his grandmother. "That is all right, Sriram. I am sorry I mistook you."

He wanted to touch her arm, but he felt afraid to do so. She would surely say, "Keep off, not until," and that would irritate him again and make him speak nonsense.

She got up. He asked, "Must you go?"

"Yes, it is late for me."

He followed her sheepishly, "When we meet again after the jail, and wherever we may meet . . . will you not forget me?"

"I will not forget you," she said, catching her breath ever so lightly.

He loved her as she drew herself up, more than at any other time in his life, but he also felt afraid of her more than at any other time. He simply said, "If you will not be angry with me, Bharati, I wish to ask one thing."

"Yes?" she said, stopping and looking at him.

He noticed beads of perspiration on her upper lip and wanted to wipe them off with his fingers. He was seized with desolation at the thought that he would not see her any more coming round the bend of the road. He wanted to seize her in his arms and take a stormy leave of her, but he had to content himself with asking, "Will you marry me after we are out of all this, will you promise, if Bapuji permits?"

"Yes, I promise . . ." she said and hurried off before he could talk to her or follow her. He stood where he was and saw her raising her hands to her eyes once or twice in order to wipe off the tears gathering there.

Part Three

A PERSON called Jagadish dropped in one day very casually and introduced himself as a national worker. He said he was a photographer in Malgudi by profession, and claimed he had a formula for paralyzing Britain in India. His studio in Malgudi with its dark interior served as a meeting ground for a group who were bent upon achieving immediate independence for the country. Jagadish came because he was in need of an out-of-town lair for his activities, and he was looking for a place where he could install a small radio set which could also transmit code messages.

He came trudging uphill while Sriram was reclining against his stone tablet. He came with a haversack on his back and wore a *khadi* dress. Sriram had been reading his old newspaper. Bharati's exit from his life had created a vacuum which he found it hard to fill. He felt somewhat confused as to what he should do with himself now. Jagadish set down his haversack, sat beside Sriram and asked, "You are Sriram?"

"Yes."

"I am Jagadish. I used to know Bharati also. We are all doing more or less the same work." This was enough to stir Sriram out of his lethargy. He sat up and welcomed the other profusely with a great deal of warmth and asked, "Where, where is she?"

"In detention . . . We don't know where, but one of our boys met her just before she surrendered herself to the police."

Sriram asked, "Where is this man?"

"He, too, has surrendered himself to the police. Before that he came and saw me."

"Are you also going to court imprisonment?"

"No, I have other things to do. That is why I have come here."

Sriram was happy to find a kindred soul and at once poured into his ears, his own feelings. "I told Bharati not to be a fool . . ."

"Don't say that. In this matter we all judge and act individually. Those who cannot follow Mahatmaji's orders are free to act as they think best."

"How right you are!" Sriram cried, feeling he had blundered into the right set.

The other said, "This is a war in which we are engaged, we are passing through abnormal times, and we do what we think best."

He began to unpack his haversack. Sriram, always hungry and rather tired of the monotonous food he was eating, hoped childishly that something nice to eat would come out of it. He hoped it would be chocolate or fruit or biscuits. Oh, how long it was since he had eaten anything like *idli,* those white sensitive things, made by his granny on most Sundays. Why Sunday and not on any other day? he had often asked. Now Jagadish took from his bag a small box, unwrapped the paper around it and brought out a tiny radio set. "You will have to keep this," he said. "It can transmit as well as receive. I had it in my studio all these days . . . but the police have become very watchful nowadays." He installed it behind the god's image, and camouflaged it with some bamboo leaves.

From then on the god with the eyeless sockets saw a great deal of Jagadish. He was of short stature with a brown wrap around his shoulders. He had a shaggy crop of minute, springy curls, which spread out parallel to the earth, projecting several inches beyond his ears. He parted his shaggy crop in the middle and applied a vast quantity of oil over his curls so that the top of his skull was always resplendent, and often Sriram saw the midday sun shining back from his head in a thousand colors. He was a very dark man with a large bulbous nose, but there was a fire in him that consumed everything before it, and Sriram felt afraid to oppose him. It seemed incredible that an elegant slender creature like Bharati should ever have spoken to this bearlike personality. A stab of jealousy passed through him now. Could it be that she had ever toyed with the notion of marrying him? God knew what he did with himself when he was out of sight. How did he make a living out of photography? Sometimes he didn't appear for days, and when he turned up he explained, "the wedding season you know. More fools getting married, and they drop in to get themselves photographed. I can't afford to waive all the business." Or he explained, "the jasmine season, and this is a heavy time for a photographer. What a lot of young girls come with jasmine buds knitted in their braids—the problem for the photographer is to photograph a girl's face and the back of her jasmine-covered head simultaneously, which is what they demand. Poor things, they sit up all night when they have the jasmine on their hair, for fear of crushing it on the pillows. They arrive at the rate of two a minute. When they are in the darkness of the studio, I try to find out their politics and give them our cyclostyled circulars and the latest news. The studio is a help for us in this job. When anyone comes there he is more responsive than he is anywhere else. People generally come to a studio with a cheerful mind ready to oblige the photographer by being agreeable and responsive, and by listening to all he has to say, the same as being with a barber. They have a feeling that they are obliged to the photographer in some vague way and readily listen to his talk, and I make use of this for our national cause. That's why I keep the studio going, although it's so difficult, without a proper supply of materials. When our country gets independence, if I have anything to do with things, you will see what I shall do to the beggars who are black-marketing films now!" He ground his teeth at the thought of them.

He was soon converting the temple into a fortress. He explained: "The advantage of this place, do you know what it is? Except a few antiquarians, no one knows of its exist-ence. And it is not visible from outside. I've observed it from various points. It cannot be seen from the road down below. I wonder why anyone built a temple here at all. I believe it must have been used as a place for conspirators a thousand years ago," and he laughed grimly. Sriram laughed. He began to like him.

"Don't think this is always going to be safe," said the other. "Sooner or later they will find it."

"There is an underground chamber," began Sriram.

"Yes, where I know aged cobras live, if you prefer them to the police. But we have to manage somehow between the cobras and the police."

"Yes, yes, with so much to do—"

Jagadish handed him a small axe and told him to cut the bamboo foliage, large branches of it, and drag them up. Sriram went at it till the skin on his palm smarted and peeled off. Jagadish induced Sriram to climb the rampart of the old temple and stick the foliage here and there according to his directions. He was shouting energetically. Standing in the sun all day, his face shone like mahogany with sweat. He said, "I can screen this whole mountain if it comes to that." Sriram felt tired and indignant. He wondered, "Why should I let this fellow order me about, when he does nothing but stand around and instruct?" Probably it would have been more pleasant to have gone to jail. But Jagadish never gave him much opportunity to dwell on such thoughts. He said: "We are waging a war, remember. Mahatmaji in his own way and we in our own. All our aims are the same."

"But I thought we were all working out the Mahatma's orders."

"We are, we are," he said vaguely. "I used to be a devoted follower too. I'm still one, but he is no longer there to guide us. What can we do? He permits us all to carry on our work to the best of our abilities."

"But strictly nonviolently," said Sriram.

"Of course, this camouflaging is not violence. It doesn't hurt anybody. It's done only that we may be left alone to work out our plans without interference. I don't want even that postman to see too much of this place. After all, he is a member of the Imperial Government."

His next assignment was more complicated. He found he had become a blind slave of Jagadish, and a word of encouragement from him pleased him to the depths of his soul. He felt proud of his position. He thought that perhaps the other associates hardly ever got a good word from him. All day long, he sat up with the radio behind the god, with a writing pad on his lap, and a pencil between his fingers, taking down the news and messages coming from Rangoon, Singapore and Germany, which purported to give the hour-to-hour progress of the war in Europe and the Far East. Sriram worked far into the night. His pencil wore out every three days. He had never worked so hard in his life. The only reward he got was Jagadish's "Very good! Excellent job. More of our troops have joined the Indian National Army. They will soon be marching into India." He sat by the lamp and went over the reports with concentration as Sriram sat chasing out the gnats and beetles that were trooping in towards the light. Jagadish made several markings on the messages, and carried them off to be cyclostyled and distributed from his studio at Malgudi.

The radio said: "This is Tokyo calling. Here is Subhas Chandra Bose, your own leader at the mike, addressing you on a special occasion." A few seconds later the message said, "This is Subhas Chandra Bose speaking." Sriram sat up respectfully. "What good fortune that I should hear his voice!" At the sound of it, Sriram felt reverence for this man who had abandoned his home, comfort, and security, and was going from country to country, seeking some means of liberating his Motherland. With what skill he had managed to slip away from his home in Calcutta in spite of police vigilance, disguising himself as a *sadhu!* Sriram felt he was peculiarly fortunate to be hearing the hero's voice. Subhas Chandra Bose's voice said, "Men of the Indian Army, be patriots. Help us free our dear Motherland. Many of your friends are here, having joined the Indian National Army which is poised for attack on your borders. We are ready. We shall soon be across, and then you can join the fight on our side. Till then don't aim your guns at us, but only at the heart of our enemy." And then followed a ten-point program of National Service that the men of the Indian Army should undertake. Sriram wrote at breakneck speed. He felt as if the commanding presence of Subhas Chandra Bose itself was at his elbow and dictating. He filled up several sheets of the pad in respectful silence. He was overawed by the look of the radio now as its lamps burned red. Outside crickets chirped, a train rattled away somewhere, and the bamboo clumps rustled. The radio went on and on. Its red eyes glowed, and threw a red glare on the ankle of the god on the pedestal. Sriram lost count of time. He had never written so much in his life. That the broadcast came through in English was a great trial, for his spelling was none too good.

Subhas Chandra Bose was saying: "And now, standing-by for a most important message, be attentive." Sriram wanted to catch it without fail, without any possibility of a mistake, but just at that moment a contrary noise began to emanate from the radio. It was as if a bee had started buzzing in time with the Great Message. Sriram felt distressed. If the thing went on undisturbed for a few seconds more, the message would be over. He strained his ears, but the other noise was becoming too loud. He ground his teeth. His left hand strayed towards the knob of the radio, and turned it. It only seemed to irritate the radio further. He lifted his eyes from the paper and glared at the radio. He saw on the dial on the outside of the glass sheet, illuminated by a small light inside, a very small cockroach; its pale body quivered with the battery of noise from the radio. Sriram felt a revulsion at the sight of its white belly pressed against the glass dial. He could see, but not reach it. He felt sick and angry. He cried, "You cursed creature, how dare you come and interfere with this most important message! Get away." He tapped the glass with his finger. He felt indignant, "Am I here to wear out my pencil, taking down your stupid loathsome noises!" His tapping was so furious that whether it affected the insect or not, he tapped the light away, and all noise from the machine ceased. The radio was dead. Sriram laid aside his pad and pencil and shook the radio, but nothing happened. He turned the knobs, shook his fist at it, and cursed and cried, but nothing happened. He asked pathetically, "Couldn't you have waited for five minutes more? Why should this have happened just when the most serious part of the message was coming through? What would Jagadish say about him now? Sriram looked at the radio and realized his utter helplessness. He had seen youngsters who could take any mechanism to pieces and assemble them again. He wasn't fit to turn even a screw. His own limitations came back to him with a good deal of force, and he said, "I am a fool, I have been brought up as a fool by that granny of mine. It is a wonder that a girl like Bharati cares for me at all!"

This note of self-reproach was fully endorsed when Jagadish turned up at two a.m. After putting the radio out of commission, Sriram sat for a while wondering what to do, blew out the lamp, kicked open his mat and lay down on it. When Jagadish arrived, and struck a match to look for the lamp, Sriram woke up and cried excitedly, "Who are you?" A sleepy vision of the very dark man illumined by a match flare was unnerving. "Hush, it is myself. Get up." Sriram sat up, rubbing his eyes. The lamp was lit. Jagadish gave him a slight shake in order to wake him fully; he sat beside him and asked, "What is special today?" Sriram triumphantly held out his pad to him. He snatched it, crying excitedly, "Ah, a message from Subhas Babu! How lucky you are to have heard him. Good boy! Good boy! You shall be a big man when our country becomes free and independent." He ran his eyes down it muttering, "These are men who are gods on earth; whose deeds must be recited in odes to posterity. I'll have a *lavani* composed of Subhas Babu's life, his sacrifice, patriotism, courage, and make it compulsory to sing it every day in every school in this country." He went on reading aloud, "My countrymen, heroes of our Indian Army—" in a singsong manner, interlarding it with appreciative comments of his own, such as "Very good," "Precisely," "It is a great mind speaking!" "Listen and learn, all ye good folk," and so on and so forth. Till he

came down to: "Now be attentive. In the first place all of
you who—" He turned the paper over in his hand and asked,
"Where is the continuation?"

"There is no continuation. The message stopped there.
Someone has been tampering with the broadcast."

"What do you mean? Let us see." He dashed to where the
radio was and turned its knob. There was no sign of life.
He shook it and cried, "What has happened to this blessed
radio?"

"How can I say? Am I a radio engineer?"

"Don't get into an argument with me about it. It'll not
take us anywhere. Subhas Babu must have said some very
vital things, and you have chosen to choke the radio."

"No. You are wrong. It choked itself. Probably a cockroach
I saw there must have done it."

Jagadish clenched his great fist and remained silent. Sriram
feared he would hit him. If he did, he wouldn't go down
without a fight. He looked at a corner where he kept a
bamboo staff for cobras and scorpions. He wondered for a
moment whether he should make an immediate dash to it?
Would the other give him the necessary time?

After many moments of grim silence the man said, "Well,
let us not bother about it any more. As soldiers, we must
learn not to brood over what is definitely past, and mind
you, what is definitely past." He said, "Give me that pencil."
Sriram passed the pencil to him. Jagadish adjusted the lamp,
read the message carefully, and after spending one minute
thinking, filled in the rest of the sheet briskly. "You must,
you must and you must." He wrote with inspiration. It took
him nearly an hour to complete the writing of the message;
he looked over it and shook his head with satisfaction. He
gave the pad to Sriram and commanded, "Now read it, young

man. This is exactly how he would have gone on if the cock-roach had not stood there acting like a censor." After this triumph a sudden sorrow assailed him. He was reminded of the radio. "The last battery set—you could have spoken back to Subhas Babu, if you had only been careful. It was a two-way radio—I suppose I'd better take it back with me and repair it. As a soldier I will not cry over split milk."

"Is it 'split' milk?" Sriram asked nervously.

"Of course it is," asserted Jagadish. "When milk goes bad, it splits into water and solid, you know. It's no use crying over split milk," he repeated.

Next afternoon, a little while after the train blew its whistle, Jagadish arrived with a bundle of papers hidden under his shirt. For the purpose of carrying that quantity of paper he wore an inner shirt with an enormous pocket and over it another large cloaklike shirt, and looked so big with all this literature hidden about his person that Sriram sometimes wondered if the impressiveness of his personality might not be due to excessive padding.

Jagadish unwound the robes about him and took out a bundle of papers, and once again Sriram childishly as ever expected him to produce some nice eatable. "Come on, sit down," said Jagadish. Jagadish first went to look up and down and assure himself that no one was watching. He dra-matically attempted to close the large door which creaked on its mighty hinges, but could be moved only half an inch forward. Sriram watched him without a word. After these preparations, he pulled Sriram to a seat beside him on the mat. He pressed a sheet of cyclostyled messages into his hand,

and said, "Read it." Sriram read aloud, "Men of the Indian Army, etc., etc.," all that he had monitored on the previous day, but it continued for several paragraphs more. "First, don't coöperate with our enemy Government. Lay down your arms and lay down your lives, if necessary. You will be the heroes of the day when the Indian National Army marches into Delhi and flies its flag on the Red Fort, the very place where our men are now imprisoned." And it went on and on, giving precise directions to the army as to what it should do, for the liberation of the country. Sriram now felt a profound admiration for the man. "How did you manage to get the rest of the message?" he asked innocently.

"Don't bother, how," replied Jagadish. "Where there is a will there is a way. All out of this," he said proudly touching his forehead. "I could easily guess how the rest of the message would have run. It is just a matter of thought-reading, more or less," he declared proudly. "It is an extremely important message for our army at this moment. It is very vital to us. And it is to your honor that you got it first, although (never mind, let us not think of what is past) you couldn't get the full message; nothing is lost, and so don't bother about it. Furthermore it should be your honor to see that the message reaches those for whom it is intended."

Sriram was somewhat confounded. He asked, "What should I do?"

"Listen to me carefully. I will give you fifty copies of this and you will take them to the army camp at Belliali. The poor fellows there cannot have any notion of what is happening in the world since they are not allowed to listen in to truth, but only to the cock-and-bull stories that the British War Department issues. Our boys must know the truth. They must know where Subhas Babu is, where the Indian National Army is stationed, and what is to be done. It is our duty to propagate truth wherever it may be. Has not Mahatmaji told us so?"

"Yes, yes," agreed Sriram to whom this argument appealed. "What will you do with the rest of the copies? Why don't you let me carry some more?"

"No, I can spare only fifty. I have made one hundred and fifty copies in all. These are days of paper shortage, remember. I am going to send fifty copies to Lakshi camp, and take fifty myself to the third one at . . . You will have to go up tonight and complete the task allotted to you."

"Agreed," said Sriram.

Before parting Jagadish said, "We shall probably all three of us get shot in this enterprise. But don't bother. Our lives are not very important. Our work is more important."

"I don't care whether I live or die," said Sriram, remembering the frustrations he had experienced with Bharati. What was the use of dragging on one's existence with this girl always inaccessible? Probably this national fight would never be over, and if over, might probably involve her in further activities. She was bound to be pursuing something else all her life. . . . This thought caused him so much weariness that he declared with all sincerity his readiness to die. He added, "If I fail to return, will you tell Bharati what I think of her?"

"What do you think of her?" asked the other with amusement.

"That if she had married me I should probably not have died or something like that."

"Well, I will tell her that. If I am shot, you can take charge of my studio. It is yours for the asking."

Sriram felt too moved to speak. "You are kind," he murmured. "How good you are!"

The other just twirled the end of his fancy scarf. "But I

am afraid you will find it hard to run it, with the position of chemicals being what it is! Anyway, I wish you luck."

The pamphlets were written on a convenient size which could easily be carried concealed on one's person. Sriram placed them neatly in a small bundle in a long strip of a towel, brought together its corners and tied them, put the towel around his waist and knotted it; over it he put on his *khadi* vest, and over it his *jibba*. The messages pressed his stomach uncomfortably, but he bore it with fortitude. He went down hill at nightfall. Jagadish had given him precise directions.

Sriram walked down the road and waited under a tree for a bus. There were one or two villagers sitting under the tree, waiting too. It was dark, and beyond the horizon there was the glow of Malgudi town. He sighed like an outcast. "What a wretched hour it was when I set out to face life! Granny!" he addressed her mentally, "I want to be back but I can't be, don't worry. All troubles must end. I wish they would release Mahatmaji. As long as he is in prison we will fight this devilish government. How dare they lay their hands on him? If they hadn't done that, Bharati would be out and happy, and Mahatmaji would have given his consent to her marriage."

"Eh? What do you say, sir?" asked one of the villagers, peering at him curiously.

Sriram became cautious and asked, "Who is there?" He looked closer, and asked, "What are you waiting for?"

"The bus is late today," they said by way of conversation, and Sriram agreed, "It should have been here long ago, isn't that so?"

"How is the war going, sir?" asked one of them, the usual question that any villager would put to any man who looked informed.

Sriram suddenly became very cautious. He asked, "Why?"

The other said, "Because if it is over soon, we shall all be free from troubles."

"I don't know," Sriram drawled. In the darkness he could not make out the features of the man to whom he was talking. It might be a police spy or a constable himself.

"How is the war going, sir?" persisted the man.

"Well, the papers say this and that, and that is all I know," replied Sriram.

"But someone says that it is all false! My brother knows a lot of people and he said that the English are being defeated everywhere. He said that the Germans are already in Madras. If they come, will they release our Mahatmaji from prison?"

Sriram wished to divert the question and asked, "Have you seen Mahatma Gandhi?"

"Yes, sir, he passed through our village," began the man and the headlights of the bus became visible far off. The man picked up his bundle, ran to the middle of the road crying, "Unless we stop the bus, he won't stop." By the time the bus arrived he had stood right in the middle of the road gesticulating wildly.

"You will be run over!" cried Sriram.

The driver jammed his brakes and cursed: "What are you doing? Do you want to kill yourself? Why don't you join the army and die if you want to die?" he asked and laughter came from the bus.

The villager cried, "I wish to go to—"

"Clear off and don't stand there talking. There's no place even for an ant in this chariot."

"Let him in," cried the conductor, to whom this meant extra income. Such passengers were unaccounted for at the end of the day.

"I will sit on the floor," pleaded the villager.

"Five annas," cried the conductor.

"Three annas," cried the passenger. "Last week you took me for three annas."

"Last week is not this week," cried the conductor.

Sriram who had watched the proceedings with detachment till now suddenly came forward, "Take him in for three annas, if you did so last week."

"Yes, sir," said the conductor, awed by Sriram's manner.

"And drop me at . . . How much?"

"Three annas, sir."

"I will stand on the footboard if there is no space inside," said Sriram.

The conductor became officious. He said, "You may come in, sir. I'll make room."

All the passengers craned their necks out of the bus; the engine was hissing like a serpent. "No, I will stand on the footboard," said Sriram and clutched the handrail when the bus moved. "He probably thinks I am a bus inspector off duty," reflected Sriram, clutching the cold handrail and the night breeze blew on his face. Within the bus someone was snoring, someone was explaining the war and its progress on all fronts, someone was talking about God and Fate, a child was crying, a woman was yawning; the driver and conductor exchanged some private jokes and giggled: they are probably enjoying the thought of their ill-gotten money and the sharing of it, thought Sriram. The bus ached and groaned under its load. Sriram feared that its bottom might fall out. Unfortunately, he was not a bus inspector. All the same he assumed a voice of authority and asked, "Conductor, what is your limit of loading?" and the conductor replied with humility, "The Government have set aside the rule, sir. We may take in as many as we can hold. This is war time, sir, otherwise, how many poor folk would get stranded on the highway?" Many murmurs of approval came from the passengers. "What with these air raids and troubles, it would be most dangerous to get stranded on the road," someone ventured. The bus rocked past sleeping villages. The lights were shaded according to the wartime rule, and the head-lights threw a faint patch of light ahead. Someone was hum-ming a tune; all these human sounds were welcome to Sriram's ears, which had grown atrophied through his lonely existence. He revelled in the music of human voices. The bus slowed down and he jumped off at a village called San-gram. The time was about eleven at night and the entire village was asleep. He waited on the road till the bus was out of sight, and then patted his person to see if his material was intact: a wire-cutter in his inner pocket, and the precious message at his waist. When he stopped, a lump pained him at the belly. "If only to be relieved of this pain, I must scatter the message," he reflected. He twined down a road on his left. He walked on the extreme side of the road since one or two military lorries were passing, and he did not want to be noticed. He came up against a vast jungle of barbed wire entanglements, enclosing a group of bamboo and mud huts, with a private road winding through. The main entrance was on the other side. This was a military depot and training center, and from here all day the rattle of convoys agitated the silence.

Presently he found himself cutting a portion of the barbed wire fence. The snap resounded through the place: he feared somebody might machine-gun him. He heard the footsteps of the patrol sentry, and lay low. He thought, "Well, this is my last moment. Suppose I am sent to hell?" He remembered all the details of hell that his grandmother had given him in childhood, and shuddered. "There is no sense in getting shot by an unknown sentry," he reflected. "One unknown man shooting another unknown man, a ridiculous thing to happen!" On the strength of this, he put away the cutter. He took out a little glue, sat down and applied it neatly to the back of a few sheets, pasted the notices on the pillars supporting the wire and facing the inner barracks. The barb scratched the skin of his forearm. "Blood is drawn, and this is the utmost I'm prepared to shed on Jagadish's orders." After this, he rolled up his sheets into one mass, and flung it into the enclosure. He saw under the starlit heaven the notices fluttering down. "The boys may pick up and read the messages at their leisure tomorrow morning," he reflected, and turned back.

Jagadish said, "Why that lack-luster and far away look in your eyes, young man? You do a lot of service to the great cause. But without your heart really in it. May I know why?" Sriram had nothing definite to reply. "I should have said, 'Look pleasant, please,' or 'Smile, please,' as becomes a photographer. You must put your heart into your job, my dear young man, otherwise you will not help our country. We are passing through crucial times as our statesmen say, and we have to do something. I have a suspicion that you let your thoughts play too much around a certain person. Am I right?"

"Yes."

"Well, that's a futile occupation, since it's the government who think it would be in your best interests to keep you two apart. You don't even know where they are keeping her."

"That's true," said Sriram dolefully.

"But I know where she is," said Jagadish. "I've my own agents. She is not actually in any regular prison, all jails being full now. She is in a hurriedly made up one— You know the Old Slaughter House? She is in it, along with a number of other women prisoners."

"How do you know?"

"I know a guard who works there. He likes me because he is an old customer, whose old photograph in my stock helped him in some family litigation. He will help you to meet your friend, if you are inclined that way." Sriram's heart palpitated. This was as if the dead had come to life, or at least were promising to come to life. "A nice fellow, he will help you, at the risk of his own life, to meet and talk to Bharati for about half an hour."

"When? When?" Sriram asked anxiously.

"As soon as you have done your job smartly. Some business about chrome ore, and I need your assistance."

"You mean I shall be rewarded for my services."

"Yes, that's what I mean. One good turn deserves another."

"Who is going to be benefited by my good turn?" Sriram asked.

"Well, the country. A train load of chrome ore is leaving at a certain railway station for England. It should not reach the port. If it reaches the port, it will return to us in the form of triggers and what not and plague us. . . . I can't think of anyone but you to assist me in this job."

It was inevitable that soon the police should publish Sriram's photograph and announce a reward for anyone giving information of his whereabouts.

Sriram had a racking fear that Jagadish might be playing

a practical joke. "If he is playing a joke, heaven help him," he told himself. "I will crush his skull with a big stone," and he revelled in visions of extraordinary violence. He pulled his mind back sharply when he realized how Bharati would react. The thought of Bharati softened him. He told himself he would not hesitate to fall at the feet of any villain if Bharati desired him to do so. Anything to please her and earn her approval. His whole being acquired a meaning only when he was doing something in relation to Bharati. He wondered how he should conduct himself when she came out and the photographer, too, was there. He hoped that his jealousy would not drive him to do wild things. Anyway he hoped that the photographer would mind his business and leave him alone in order to pursue his life as he liked; he hoped the fight with the British Government would end soon. He hoped Britain would leave India so that he might return to Kabir Street and live in peace with Bharati and granny! Ah, that was the trouble. What would granny do about it? She would probably nag Bharati night and day and compare her with her brother's granddaughter in looks and competence in household duties, but he hoped Bharati would turn round and challenge her to say whether that village niece of hers would have faced a charging police force or spoken to Mahatmaji. As he reclined on his couch at the entrance to his cave and looked at the top of the blue gum trees his mind roamed unchecked.

In a moment Jagadish had come up and was standing by his side. He said, "Very unsafe, young man. If it had been a policeman instead of myself, you would still have been sitting there, daydreaming, and he'd have put a nice collar round your neck and led you along to the jail."

Sriram, rather irritated, asked, "What's wrong with daydreaming?"

153

"There is much that is not right. You must be more watchful. Our cave is probably not visible from outside, but someone may think of exploring these parts. You are probably not seen but don't imagine that can last forever. You should always watch, even through the camouflage. Be careful."

"All right," Sriram said, cowed by the other's manner, very much like a tiger in the circus ring which subsides on the spot indicated by the ringmaster, with a rolling growl. Jagadish took his seat beside him with the remark, "And if you imagine that it's better the police come after you, so that they may detain you at the Old Slaughter House, you are mistaken. They will do nothing of the kind: it's reserved for women prisoners." At the mention of the Old Slaughter House, Sriram softened. The associations of the Old Slaughter House might not be quite pleasant for everyone, but for Sriram it produced the happiest associations and a very profound sense of peace. "Old Slaughter House? Old Slaughter House?" Sriram said, adopting a playful attitude for the first time these many days. "Old Slaughter, the sound is familiar! What has that to do with us?" "Its virtue is that it is an Old Slaughter House, and not a new one," said Jagadish. "Many a goat trembles when it passes that building, but it makes you smile and joke. All the slaughter of the place is forgotten. . . . Yet it's still a place that attacks the heart, doesn't it?" he said. Sriram felt completely happy. He would have gone on talking of the Slaughter House for the rest of his days: it was an opiate which made him forget politics, history, police, and his own loneliness. "If you wish to visit the place, you will have to make certain alterations to your good self," Jagadish said. He explained, "First you must look unlike the photo the police have published. If someone wants to make money by informing, you should not help him to do so. I fear the police have published your photo far and wide, and any street urchin may denounce you. It shows the evil of leaving one's photos about. I have an advantage in this respect—there is no photo of me and they have only described me: having been so busy photographing others, that is the chief advantage. You have been scattering your portraits about like a film star."

"Yes, yes," Sriram had to agree dolefully. He recollected the cheap four-for-one-rupee quick photos that he had indulged in some time after he came into his wealth. Often Sriram had seen his picture displayed on the advertisement boards of the photographers; and the walls of his house were full of his own pictures. He remembered his grandmother saying: "In our days people hung portraits of gods and ancestors; you have nothing but your own! I wonder why you do it?"

"Does it mean the police have taken the photos from our house at Kabir Street?" Sriram asked, assailed by a sudden thought.

"Definitely. That's the first thing they will have done."

"I wonder what granny would have said."

"She will repeat it all when she sees you next. Don't worry," he replied. He studied Sriram closely and said: "You will have to change your appearance. You will have to undertake some drastic changes. First and foremost grow a nice small moustache. A little one that droops at the ends will make you look slightly like a Mongol, but let that not weigh on your mind, they are looking for you, not for a Mongol. And then, do you think you could shave off your crop in order to complete the picture?"

Sriram's heart quailed at the suggestion, remembering all the heartaches he had undergone in order to get rid of his old tuft and grow his present crop. His granny would not hear of it at first. She was certain that it would spoil his appearance, but one day he had just slipped away to the temple tank on whose steps barbers sat and shaved their customers. He induced an old barber to cut off his tuft and run the machine over his ears, and on his lap he emptied all the pocket money he had purloined from his own sealed money box. He had widened the slit of the money box and shaken out the coins, when his granny was in the kitchen. To disguise rattling he had muffled it with a piece of cloth and carried the operation on till it shed eight annas in small coppers. His granny kept shouting from the kitchen, "What is that noise?" "Which noise?" shouted back Sriram, and had gone on with his job. He had had no clear idea how much a barber would demand for a crop-cut. He put it down at six annas, and two annas extra for any unlooked-for expense. But the barber at the tank had demanded a rupee to cut off the thick curly tuft Sriram had possessed. By haggling Sriram brought it down to six annas; and the barber went on muttering disappointed remarks to the tune of snapping scissors. Sriram saw himself in a small mirror produced out of the barber's tin box, and was delighted. He felt he had rid himself of a couple of pounds of tuft: it lay on the stone steps of the tank: and Sriram remembered how he shivered at the sight of the appendage, for no known reason. They were long and curly tresses, and he said: "Sell it and you will get ten rupees for it." The barber lost his temper at the suggestion: "You take me for a hawker of hair. Mind how you speak, young gentleman. I should have cut your throat if it hadn't been yourself but someone else. Look, I don't want anything, but give me the *dhoti* you are wearing: that's the usual custom under these circumstances."

Sriram was aghast: "And how shall I reach home?"

"Bathe in this tank and run before anyone notices. Anyway haven't you got your piece cloth under your *dhoti*? That'll do for a young man of your age." So saying he almost tugged the ends of Sriram's *dhoti*, and Sriram had to dodge him. "Oh!" cried the barber in great surprise. He made queer faces to indicate his feelings. "Do you mean to say that you go about with—" He described vividly the underclothes of respectable and honest citizens, and commented on the habits of the modern generations. The topic was so below-the-waist that Sriram blushed and finally wrenching himself free ran off. All this flashed across his mind now. He took his hand to the top of his head and ran his fingers over it and said to Jagadish: "I can't sacrifice this crop. I like it."

Sriram spent a sleepless night wondering how he could change his appearance. He even thought that he might disguise himself as a *purdah* lady and not show his face at all. Jagadish laughed all his propositions away. He seemed intent on disfiguring him in his own manner, bent upon shaving him like an egg and making him as ridiculous as possible. Perhaps he wanted to make him the laughing stock of the world and ruin his chance once for all with Bharati. She would refuse to take a second look at his face for the rest of his life. He wondered why he should not refuse to do anything that Jagadish suggested. Even the Slaughter House might be a huge practical joke or turn out to be a real slaughtering place after all! But his fears had no value. Whatever he might feel or fear, the fact was always there that Jagadish was inescapable, and one had to do what he ordered.

Jagadish granted a period of three weeks for a respectable moustache to develop on Sriram's upper lip. He bought him a small bottle of coconut oil for massage to help a quick growth. "How many things I have to do before I can see Bharati!" Sriram reflected. Jagadish checked the growth on the other's upper lip day after day. He nodded his head discouragingly each time. "Very slow, very slow, too slow," he said as if Sriram himself were responsible. Sriram clicked his tongue apologetically. The period of three weeks was by no means wasted. In association with Jagadish and under his expert guidance, Sriram did a variety of jobs which he hoped would help the country in its struggle for freedom: he set fire to the records in half a dozen law courts, in different villages; he derailed a couple of trains, paralyzed the work in various schools; exploded a crude bomb which tore off the main door of an agricultural research station, tarred out "V" for Victory and wrote over the emblem "Quit India." He became so seasoned in this activity that a certain recklessness was developing in him. He had no fear of the police: they seemed to him a remote, theoretical body, unconnected with his affairs. He knew he could always slip through. They were looking for him everywhere, except where they could find him. Jagadish kept repeating: "Britain will leave India with a *salaam,* if we crush the backbone of her administration." He was always talking in terms of backbone. Sometimes he said: "Britain's backbone is, you know where?"

"On her back, I suppose?" said Sriram facetiously.

"Do you know where that back is?"

"Behind her front, I suppose," said Sriram, still facetiously. He was beginning to enjoy these bouts, which were a relief in his lonely, drab life, isolated from all human association. Jagadish forgave him his tricks. He explained: "The prospect of the Slaughter House makes you sharp-witted, doesn't it?" He explained with a good deal of tolerance, "Britain's backbone must be smashed, and it lies in the courts and schools and offices and railway lines; from these she draws the strength for her survival." It was an intricate logic which Sriram could not easily grasp. He asked pathetically, "Why do we not smash her front also?"

"Because it's far away, and we can't reach so far."

Jagadish dragged him about and made him his instrument and agent. Sriram was actually beginning to enjoy the excitement and novelty and above all the game of hide-and-seek with the police. It gave him a feeling of romantic importance. He felt that he was a character out of an epic, and on his activities depended the future history. But now and then some kind of misgiving assailed his mind, when sitting concealed in a ditch in Jagadish's company, he saw the flames rising from a railway station or a government building and lighting up the night. Once he whispered, "Do you think Britain will be affected by this fire?"

Jagadish declared unequivocally, "Churchill will already have known of it. It will make him groan. It will make him sit up. It must go on and on every hour of the day, all over the country, until Britain tells us, 'We are bundling ourselves out tomorrow, do what you like with your country.'"

Sriram asked next, "I wonder what Mahatmaji will say about all this!"

"I don't know," replied Jagadish. "It is not his line. But when the results turn out satisfactorily, I am sure he'll say, 'You did well, my boy.'"

Sriram felt doubtful. He shook his head. "I'm not sure. Only Bharati knows exactly what Mahatmaji will say or think. . . ." And then his thoughts went off to the Slaughter House.

Jagadish seemed to weaken slightly at this point: "We have not willfully caused anybody's death. I'm always careful to see that no life is lost, but if in spite of our precautions, some people are accidentally caught in a mess and killed, we can't help it."

"A lot of people are also shot down by the police when they disperse the mobs that gather to help us," said Sriram.

"But that is none of our concern," said Jagadish, and

added, "In a war lives are bound to be lost. However, the job of the moment is more important than any amount of theoretical speculation. Mahatmaji taught me this philosophy when I was with him at Wardha. Anyway, don't bother too much about these questions. He has asked us to work for the movement according to our individual capacities."

On a certain day Jagadish examined Sriram's face and declared, "The most satisfactory moustache that I ever saw in my life!" With a razor and scissors he helped Sriram to give its end a downward turn. He produced also some old silver-rimmed spectacles, and mounted them on his nose. He provided him too with an ill-fitting, closely-buttoned coat, and a white turban for covering his head. He ordered him to tie up his *dhoti* bifurcated, like all respectable men. After all this, Sriram looked into a mirror, the very tiny one which he used for his shaving, it did not reveal a full picture, but it showed enough for him to remark: "I look like a wholesale rice merchant." Jagadish nodded appreciatively and said with considerable delight in his tone, "True, true . . . If I could only put a dark caste mark on your forehead, that'd indeed complete the picture."

Sriram as he sallied forth at about seven, after sunset, felt so different that he wondered why he should expect Bharati to admit him at all. He chuckled at the thought, "Bharati may wonder why a rice merchant has taken a fancy to call on her, all of a sudden." The spectacles gave him a dull ache on the bridge of his nose, and kept constantly slipping down, and pestering him with a dull, misty vision. "This is what comes of not surrendering oneself to the police when Bharati advises one to do so," he reflected. At the little station, he climbed into the train going towards Malgudi. There were a few sleepy passengers in his compartment. He ignored the whole lot. "It's no business of a self-respecting rice merchant to speak to these folk," he reflected and sat looking at his fellow-passengers with indifference. Jagadish had proved himself to be a genius: the moustache was a tremendous asset, it was as if Sriram had worn a mask over his face, the transformation was so complete.

From Malgudi station it was an hour's walk southward through Market Road to the Slaughter House. As he passed along the familiar roads, Sriram felt sentimental and unhappy. It seemed as if he had left this world ages ago. Beyond those rows of silent and darkened shops was the house of his grandmother.

Jagadish had given precise instructions. The rice merchant crouched behind the eastern wall of the old Slaughter House. Bharati would come to the lavatory at the corner, stand up on a large stone, rolled into position for the purpose, look down and talk to him. Sriram was wondering if Bharati would notice his moustache in the darkness; he wondered if he could reach up and touch her hand. He patiently waited. The Taluk Office gong sounded two in the morning. He felt sleepy. He remembered Bharati asking him to meet her at three a.m., when the Mahatma came to Malgudi. "She seems fond of spoiling other peoples' sleep," he reflected. He sat there on the ground. The Taluk Office gong struck the next hour. "How long am I to stay here?" he reflected. "Has someone been playing a prank?" Angry thoughts were rising in his heart. "Hey," cried a voice. He looked up hopefully. Over the wall a head appeared, but it was not Bharati's. It was one of the wardresses. "Where is . . . ?" Sriram began stretching himself up on his toes. "Hush, listen. She won't come."

"Is she not coming?"

"No. Catch this." She dropped a letter. "Read it," said the head, "and be off."

The rice merchant moved away clutching the piece of paper in his hand, his head buzzing with a thousand speculations.

Under the first street lamp, he spread out the note. It was a piece torn out of a memo pad. On it was the hurried pencil scribbling: "I cannot bring myself to see you today. It seems degrading to have a meeting under these conditions. Bapu has always said that it is dishonorable to assume subterfuges. In a jail we must observe the rules, or change them by *Satyagraha* openly, if possible. Forgive me. We shall meet again. But before that, please go and see your granny. A detenue who came in here told me that she was very ill. It is your duty to risk your life to see her. Go before it is too late."

Not many people were able to recognize him when he ascended the steps of 14 Kabir Street. He saw Kanni, the shopman, coming out of the house. He was softly closing the door behind him. He didn't recognize Sriram, who for a moment forgot that he could not be recognized, and cried, "Kanni!" almost involuntarily. His voice betrayed him. Kanni halted, and suddenly cried, "Oh! it's our young master! O, Ram, what is it you have been doing to yourself, deserting your house and the old lady who was your father, mother, and cousin and everything? Have you no heart? Thank God, you have come at least, anyway. But you are too late." "Why? Why?" screamed Sriram. "What has happened?" "She is dead. She died at ten o'clock last night." Sriram ran past him into the house. There, in the old familiar place, under the good old hall lamp, lay the old lady. A white sheet was drawn over her. A couple of women from the neighboring houses were sitting beside her, keeping vigil.

Sriram was sorrow-stricken. The familiar household; the old almanac still there under the roof tile: the copper vessel in which she kept drinking water still on the window sill. The easy chair which he had bought for her with his first money was still where he had put it. He had a glimpse of a past life. He went up to the corner of the house which used to be his and examined his books, pens, clothes; he opened the lid and looked into his old tin trunk. All the articles with which he had grown up were there, kept safe and intact. The vigil-keepers followed his movements with dull sleep-filled eyes. Sriram wept. But he could not wipe away his tears; he realized that his spectacles were a nuisance: he suddenly plucked them off and flung them down, feeling: "I'm answerable to Jagadish for it. I'm betraying myself." Kanni stood in the doorway, respectfully watching. "How imperious she looks! Even now!" he cried. "A great Soul." "I can't believe she is dead. She looks asleep! How do you know that she is dead?" Sriram asked. Kanni merely laughed grimly. "You had better telegraph to all your relatives. I'm sure many would want to have a last look at her face." Sriram sat down on the floor, beside the old lady, quietly sobbing. The women looked at him for a moment, and silently lapsed into mournful silence. They turned to Kanni and asked, "Is he the only relative to arrive or should we wait for some more?" Kanni preferred to ignore their question. The night was absolutely still and silent. Even the street dogs were asleep. Except the low voices conversing under the dim light, the entire world was asleep, following the example of granny herself. Sriram suddenly rose to his feet, went to Kanni, put his arm round his shoulder, and whispered, "Kanni, I am very hungry. Can't

163

you open your shop and give me something to eat? There is nothing in the kitchen."

"How can there be anything? She was ill so long: those ladies were bringing her milk and gruel."

"I'm very hungry, Kanni," Sriram said again pathetically.

Kanni jingled his keys, and said, "Come with me." They crossed the street. Kanni unlocked the door of his shop and lit a lamp. Sriram climbed the platform and went in, then bolted the door again from inside. The shop was hot and stuffy. Bananas hung down in bunches, buns and biscuits filled various glass containers; all, of course, were presided over by the European queen with apple cheeks. Sriram complained that it was stuffy. Kanni explained, "I don't want anyone to suspect your presence, though handing you over and collecting the reward might prove a better proposition than running a business in these difficult days!" Sriram had not realized how hungry he was. He demanded and ate everything that he saw. Kanni took out a paper and calculated: "That would be two rupees and four annas. I will put it down into your account."

Now that he was no longer hungry, Sriram said: "Tell me about my granny. What was wrong with her?"

Kanni paused for awhile before answering. "Ever since the police came asking for you in this house, she lost . . . if I may say so, her original spirit. She was always feeling that you had betrayed her. You may know all about Mahatma and so on, but all she knew was what people told her, that you had run after a girl. The old lady was much hurt. She hardly ever came out after that, and when the police came to take away your photograph, she was upset very much. She felt that she could not hold up her head in public again. She was always saying that you had betrayed her. The police came and questioned me, too, about you. I said, 'You are merely wasting my shop time. I am not to be bothered about every scapegrace in the town because I have the ill-luck to have a shop opposite his house,' and that satisfied them. I wish you had not gone away without telling her. It worried her too much. She kept saying, 'What can a little cobra do even if you have brought it up on cow's milk. It can only do what its breeding tells it to do.' "

Sriram was visibly annoyed at this comparison. "She was a very bitter-tongued person; that's why I preferred to go away without telling her at all. What chance did one have of talking to such an unreasonable character." He forgot for a moment that he was talking about someone dead.

"People came and told her hair-raising tales about you. She was alarmed by your activities. What was the matter with you? I never thought the young master I had known so long ago could ever grow up into a *zigomar*."

Sriram felt hurt by this comparison with an old classical bandit. He said with a lot of self-pity, "I wouldn't have come if I wasn't eager to see my granny."

"That's true," said Kanni "The Market Road doctor has attended often; even this evening he was there with his tube and needle and stayed till she passed away."

"Was she talking all the time?" asked Sriram.

"She wasn't, but she might have been. Why think of all that now?" Kanni said. "Let us think of what we should do next."

"Yes, what is to be done?"

"The funeral. Get through it quickly. Are you going to wait for relatives?"

These were tough and complex domestic questions to which he was unaccustomed. He brooded over them. The word 'relative' brought to his mind only his grand uncle whose dark descendant he was expected to marry; and plenty of others, a batch of miscellaneous folk who dropped in for a meal or two occasionally from their village, and always spoke of lands and litigations. Granny used to find their talk fascinating and forgot to notice Sriram's arrivals and departures, while he generally sneaked out to a nearby cycleshop and learnt to balance himself on the pedal of a bicycle taken on hire. Sriram had a sudden vision of being responsible for gathering that entire crowd again: they might stand around the corpse and lament over their lands and litigations. He was aghast at the thought. He said: "I don't care for anyone."

"Yes, I know. I, too, think you should not keep the body too long. Better hurry through the funeral. But at least let the lady have the satisfaction of having her pyre lit by her grandson. That may assuage her spirit."

"I don't know what to do about such things," Sriram wailed.

"I will help you," said Kanni.

"One thing. I can't go with the funeral procession," said Sriram. "I will manage to come at the end if you will manage the other things."

"Even the police may not interfere now. After all, they are also human," said Kanni.

Sriram went back into his house, took another look at his granny. The two vigil-keepers were asleep. They sat hunched up and slept with their heads on the floor, curled beside the body, "They look more dead than granny," thought Sriram. A cock crowed somewhere. Sriram went out, softly closing the door behind him. Meanwhile Kanni had locked the shop, and was returned. "She is in your charge," said Sriram. "Will you be there at eight? Do everything nicely. Don't bother about expense."

"Yes, I know. I can always get my debts. I have kept your account in full detail. You should have no misgiving even about an anna. I have even put into the account what I have been paying the doctor from time to time. Are you sure her relatives will not be angry with us later?"

"What do you care whether they are angry or pleased? What have we to do with them? A set of useless rustics," said Sriram with a certain amount of unnecessary bitterness in his voice.

At about eight Sriram was on the cremation ground beyond the Sarayu river. A couple of pyres which had been lit on the previous day were still smoldering. Bamboo and discarded pieces of shroud were scattered here and there. A funeral procession was crossing Nallappa's Grove. The bier was decorated with flowers and some men wearing white shirts and rings on their fingers were shouldering the corpse. "Must be devoted relatives," he thought. "They are bearing the burden. But poor granny has no one to carry her." Once again he felt angry at the thought of those village relatives. The heat was intense although it was not even eight in the morning. "This is a very hot place," he reflected. Bullock carts were crossing the river; villagers on their way into the town with baskets on their heads chattered incessantly. He noticed people coming to the river for a wash. His mind made a dull note of all that his eyes saw. His main job now was to await the arrival of granny. Why were they taking all this time? Probably priests were holding up the body so that they might get a higher fee for funeral citations. Or could the police have held up the procession? For a moment a fantastic fear seized his mind lest the police should have suspected foul play and held up the body for a post-mortem. The pampered body carried by the devoted relatives was now brought in through the gate and laid down on the ground. They were going through a lot of ceremonial activities . . . Granny's pyre was also being built up with dried cow-dung cakes, on a small platform: all the arrangements were supervised by Kanni's shop-assistant, who was haggling with fuel suppliers, and ordering the graveyard assistants about. They obeyed him cheerfully, which made Sriram wonder why they obeyed him at all. "It is in some people's blood to be respected by all kinds of people," Sriram reflected, watching with a certain amount of envy all the fuss that the rich were making with the body in their hands.

Led by Kanni, who bore in his hand a pot of fire, a couple of neighbors, the manager of the Fund Office, and two priests, granny arrived on a bier made of bamboo, carried by four grim subhuman professional carriers. Sriram rushed to the small wooden doorway to meet the procession. Kanni was the first to step through. He held the pot of fire to Sriram, saying, "Really, it is your duty to carry it." Sriram took charge.

Granny's face was uncovered and faced the sun. Sriram felt a pang of fresh sorrow at the sight. The bier was laid on the ground. "Sriram, bathe in the river and come back soon with wet clothes on you. She is at least entitled to so much consideration." The words came from the old family priest. Sriram realized that he was still in the garb of a wholesale rice merchant, and felt ridiculous. The old priest had officiated at festivals and domestic ceremonies ever since Sriram could remember, including the grand ceremony of his first birthday. The old man was several years granny's senior, but remarkably wiry and alert, with his greenish eyes and hook nose, and greed for ceremonial fees. He asked Sriram, "Have you two rupees in coins?" While Sriram fumbled for an answer, the ever-watchful Kanni descended on him wrathfully. "Why do you ask that? Haven't we agreed on a lump sum for everything?" The priest who was squatting beside the body turned and said,"Whoever said the lump sum included this? This can never go into that. This is a separate account. Our elders have decreed that the Dear Departed should have two silver coins on his or her chest from the hand of the nearest and dearest. It is said to smooth out the passage of the soul into further regions. I am only repeating what the *shastras* say; our ancestors knew what was best for us. I am merely a mouthpiece."

"And what happens to the coins?" asked the Fund Office Manager. The priest pretended to ignore the question, but Kanni said, "It goes the way of other coins, that is into a priest's money box." "Yes, it does. Do you expect the soul to carry the silver with it? You must view it all in the proper light; you must take only its philosophical meaning. We carry nothing from this earth," said the priest and quoted a Sanskrit verse. He suddenly looked across at the other part of the ground where the rich men were conducting their ceremonies, "See there. They are devoted and very correct. They are not omitting a single rite."

"We are not omitting anything either," said Kanni angrily. His tone cowed the priest who mumbled, "Don't think I am after money: I only do things in order to satisfy a great soul known to me for several decades now." He looked up at Sriram and said, "Now go and bathe quickly. Nothing can begin until after that." He paused and added, "You will find a barber there. You will have to shave off your moustache and the top of your head. Otherwise it would be very irregular. The *shastras* say . . ."

"I will not shave my moustache nor my head," said Sriram emphatically.

"All right," said the priest. "It is my duty to suggest what the *shastras* say, and it is left to you to follow it or modify it in any manner. Of course modern life makes it difficult to follow all the rules, and people have to adjust themselves. There are even people who like to perform their funerals with European hats on in these days. What can one do about them? 'It is wisdom to accept what has come to pass,' say the *shastras* and we bow our heads to that injunction."

Sriram presently returned from his bath in the river dripping wet with his hair sticking on his head and his clothes stuck to his body. They had now laid the corpse on the pyre. The pyre beyond was already aflame and the party was leaving the ground. "They are very businesslike," said the priest. He seemed to admire everything they did. Sriram felt piqued, and Kanni said, "Don't go on talking unnecessarily."

All the rites before the lighting of the pyre started. The old lady lay stretched out on the cow-dung fuel. The priest placed a small vessel into Sriram's hand and asked him to pour the milk in it over the lips of the dead. Sriram poured the milk, chanted some *mantras,* and finally dropped the fire over granny's heart, which was actually below a layer of fuel. The fire smouldered and crackled. "Now it is all over with her," Sriram said.

The Fund Office Manager suddenly cried, "See there, see there." He was excited. They looked where he pointed. The big toe on the left foot of the lady was seen to move. "Pull out the fire, pull out the fire . . ." Someone thrust his hand in and snatched off the burning piece. The old lady's sari was already burning at one end. Sriram flung a pail of water on it and put it out. Now with the fire out, they stood around and watched. The toe was wagging. "She is not dead. Take her out," cried Sriram.

"I've never heard of such a thing. You can't do that," the priest cried. People seemed to have suddenly lost all common sense.

"You want us to burn granny alive, do you? Get out of our way, priest," cried Sriram. He kicked away the pile of fuel, lifted the body and placed it down again on the ground. "I knew something was wrong. I knew granny wouldn't die," said Sriram. He sprinkled water on her face, and forced some milk down her throat, and fanned her face. The priest stood aside with a doleful expression. Kanni seemed too stunned to speak. The shop-assistant was running in circles, announcing the glad tidings and collecting a crowd. The Fund Office Manager cried, "Let us not waste time. I will fetch the doctor." He started running towards the city. Kanni cried, "Oh, what doctors, these days! They don't even know whether a person is alive or dead! If we had failed to notice in time, oh, what doctors!"

Under their nursing, the movement in the toe gradually spread. All the toes showed signs of revival, and then her leg, and then her arms. The old lady seemed to be coming back to life, inch by inch. Her eyes were still shut. Sriram murmured, "Granny, granny, open your eyes. I am here." At this moment all politics were forgotten, all disputes and wars, Britain, even Bharati. "Get up, granny, you are all right." Now her heart began to throb, her breathing returned, ever so faintly. Sriram let out a cry of tremendous relief. He called the shop assistant. "My granny will not die, she is not dead. God bless her." He dragged Kanni by his hand and said, "Kanni, granny is alive." He nursed his granny with one hand and put the other around Kanni's shoulder and sobbed. His face was wet with tears. Kanni patted his back and said, "Don't, don't, be brave. You must not break down. She may open her eyes and she must see a happy face."

The rattle of an old car was heard far off. Everyone cried, "Doctor's car." Presently a little car with a flapping hood was struggling over the sand and pebbles at the Nallappa's Grove crossing, and on through the rough sandy track leading to the southern door of the crematorium. The doctor was a puny man wearing an enormous white overall, with a straggling crop of hair resembling Einstein's; a small man above whom everyone seemed to tower. He jumped out of his car, followed by the Fund Office Manager. "Is this true, is this true?" cried the doctor running forward. He stopped suddenly and said, "Someone go and fetch that bag from the car." Presently he knelt above the old lady, took her wrist in his hand, pulled out his watch, held his fingers under her nostrils, and smiled at Kanni. "Yes, she is not dead."

·"Oh, doctor, can't you even say whether a person is dead or alive?" asked Kanni.

"Why go into all that now? Let us be happy that she is back from the other world." The doctor brooded. In his experience this was the first situation of the kind. Previously he had known only one-way traffic. He rubbed his chin thoughtfully. "How is she, doctor?" asked Kanni. "Her pulse is good. She will need some rest and recuperation." He took several things out of his bag. He sterilized a syringe needle, took out a phial, and injected the needle into granny's forearm. She twitched at the touch of the needle and groaned slightly. The doctor looked at her with approbation. "Well, freaks like this just happen. We can't say why or how. Last night she was practically dead. I don't know. This is enough to make one believe in soul, *karma*, all that." He stood looking at her and biting his lips. "I read about a similar thing in a medical journal years ago but never thought it would come within my view." Granny was reviving little by little. Her breathing was becoming normal. The doctor said, "It is not right to keep her here when she becomes fully conscious. She must be moved. Why not take her back home? Take her in my car."

The priest interrupted, "How can you suggest such a thing? No one who has been carried here can ever step into the town bounds again. Don't you know that it will . . . it will . . ."

"What will happen?"

"Happen! The whole town will be wiped out by fire or plague. It is very inauspicious. Do anything you like, but she can't come back into the town."

This point of view gathered a lot of support. The news spread into the town. People began to throng into the cremation ground. Everyone who came said, "This is a big problem. What are you going to do with her?"

In deference to this view she had to be carried to one of the small abandoned buildings on the river bank, which had once been used as a toll-gate station, and since the river was between her and the town, she was out of bounds. She was kept at the Toll Office, and nursed by the doctor. Her world hummed around her, Kanni, the Fund Office Manager, Sriram, the old hook-nosed priest, and the two mournful women who had kept vigil. They nursed and fed the old lady as she lay on a bed in the old building. The doctor's little car drove up half a dozen times a day and Kanni practically abandoned his shop in order to conduct the operations. A vast concourse began to arrive in order to witness the miracle. Some close relatives of granny who had not seen her for years came and cried, "Oh, sister, how good to see you! No one sent word to us that you were dead."

"Word was not sent because there was nothing to send."

"But when a close relation is dead, is it not . . . ?"

"But she was not dead, so why send word?"

"How did you know that she was not dead?" asked the relatives, and the conversation flowed on in rather bewildering channels. Sriram feared all along that this crowding and publicity would ultimately lead to trouble. He tried to keep himself aloof from the crowd. When too many people arrived he went away to the back of the building, while Kanni and the others managed the visitors. He overheard people ask, "Where is that grandson of hers?"

173

"Oh, that never-do-well adventurer is probably in Burma," said Kanni.

But none of this helped. A police inspector in plain clothes and two constables arrived on the third afternoon as Sriram, having fed his granny and eaten a meal brought in a vessel by the Fund Office Manager, was enjoying a siesta in the shade of a tree behind the toll-gate building. Granny and her attendants were peacefully sleeping. The inspector looked down at Sriram and said, "Get up."

"Why?" asked Sriram, rising. "What do you want?"

"You are under arrest," said the Inspector. "We have been looking for you for a long time now."

"Who gets the reward?" asked Sriram with heavy cynicism. The inspector did not reply.

He said, "We know the special occasion which has brought you here, and we don't want to make any fuss, provided you make none. That is why we have stationed our jeep over there. I have some more men in it. You may come with us as soon as you are ready. Don't be too long."

Sriram said, "Yes, give me a little time."

"I am armed and will shoot if you try to escape," the inspector said.

Sriram went to take a look at granny. He found her sitting up and conversing with the two people near her. The moment she saw Sriram she cried, "Oh, boy, when did you come back? They told me that you were here, but with a moustache. Whatever made you grow one, my boy? Take it off, don't come before me with that, whatever else you may do."

"Yes, granny," he said obediently. He was so happy to find her old spirit had revived. One need have no doubt that it was she who was speaking. There was the genuine ring in her tone. Her personality seemed to have returned from the other world, unscathed by the contacts there. He sat down

174

on the edge of her bed, took her arm into his hands, and stroked it. She looked at him closely and said, "You are down and out, no doubt about it." She shook her head dolefully. "Whatever induced you to get mixed up with all those people? I can't say. I tried to bring you up as a respectable citizen. If you didn't go up for your B.A., it wasn't my fault. No one can blame me for it. But is it all true, all the things people say about you?"

Sriram thought and replied slowly, "Don't believe a word of anything you hear. People talk falsehoods, remember."

Granny's face puckered in a happy smile. "Vile-tongued folk!" she cried. "May all those that talk ill, think ill, slander you, or mislead you, or tempt you out of your way. . . ."

At this point Sriram had a slight misgiving that the old lady might mean Bharati. He tried to divert her attention. "Don't exert yourself, granny, lie down."

"Why should I? There is nothing wrong with me. You believe that doctor! Let him come before me. I will tell him what I think of him. He would have burnt me alive if he had had his way!" She laughed grimly. Presently she recollected the interrupted curse she had intended to hurl on someone. "Whoever has been responsible for taking you out, whether it be man, woman or whatever, may they perish and suffer in the worst hell!" After uttering her imprecation she felt both relieved and happy.

Sriram thought of the police waiting outside, and said, "Don't exert yourself, granny, you must not talk too much."

"Why not? And who says that?" she asked. "I will speak as much as a I like and no one shall stop me." At this point one of the policemen peeped in at the doorway and granny asked, "Who are you?" so authoritatively that he withdrew his head immediately.

"Who is he?" asked granny.

"Someone to see me," said Sriram. He went on stroking her arm so soothingly that she presently felt drowsy. He gave her a few ounces of milk. She said, "I am glad to see you. Good boy, don't let people tempt you out of your way. Be with me. Don't leave me again." Sriram helped her to stretch herself on her bed again. She was soon asleep. He walked over to the police officer and said, "Let us go." Kanni followed him to the jeep. Sriram said, "Kanni, look after granny till I am back. I don't know how long they will keep me. Try to see me and tell me how she is. I think the Collector will let you see us in jail. I don't know what you are going to do about her." He stood with bowed head for a moment, and then as though the problem were beyond any solution, he stepped into the jeep.

Kanni said, "Don't be anxious. She is like a mother to us. We shall take care of her."

Part Four

H^E WAS in detention at the Central Jail. He occupied a cell with a few others. He slept on the hard cement floor. They woke him up at five in the morning. This irked him most. He sometimes wished that they wouldn't pull him out of his retreat in a soft dream into the harsh reality of the prison world. And then the hurried getting up and washing at the dribbling water tap, and the public toilet; this sickened him at first. He prayed that they might let him wait at least till the others had gone. But that could not be; the warder stood over him and the others and hustled them. Sriram once attempted to approach the Most High of this world, in regard to this, when he came to inspect the prison. The Superintendent of the Prison lagged behind the Most High respectfully, with all the other officials trooping behind. Sriram had been in a file awaiting inspection at the central yard, which was surrounded by the horrible slate-colored barracks; the great man was marching by, throwing a haughty glance at the file. The prisoners had been advised to stand stock-still, and not to utter a word or move a muscle, when the man passed; they were not to speak unless spoken to. But when Sriram saw the great god approach his part of the file, he could not resist the impulse to step forward and begin: "I have a complaint and a request to make, sir." At once several people seized him and pulled him out of the way; and the great man passed on, pretending not to have noticed anything. After he was gone, Sriram was summoned to the Superintendent's Office. The guards held his biceps and kept him standing at attention before the superintendent's table. The superintendent looked up and said: "You have violated the jail discipline and you are liable to receive punishment."

"What punishment?" Sriram asked. The man, who had trailed like a meek puppy behind the visitor an hour ago, stamped his foot under the table and shouted, "I will not have you talk to me in that manner, understand?" Sriram felt cowed. He feared the other might go mad and kick him: he was the overlord here and was entitled to kill people, if he chose. People might talk of monarchy being abolished, but here was absolute monarchy. This was his world, ruled by his authority, and no one could do anything about it, so Sriram said meekly, "Yes, sir"; the very first time in his life he had adopted a tone of meekness. The other was pleased with his submission and asked, "Why did you step out of the line? What did you want to say?"

Sriram felt it would be better to speak plainly, "I wanted to ask if something might not be done to provide us some privacy for our toilet."

The Superintendent sniggered, "So you thought you might get things done over my head? Eh?"

"Not that, sir, but it hadn't occurred to me earlier, that's all," Sriram said.

The other said, "You saved yourself by not talking more, understand? If you had spoken to him, you would have been put in chains. Remember, we don't want indiscipline in this prison, understand?"

"Yes, sir," Sriram said, completely crushed by his manner.

The other softened a little at this and said, "Ask me for anything you may want."

"Yes, sir." Sriram found that this was the best way of talking to the man; the only idiom that didn't upset him.

The Superintendent asked, "What did you say you wanted to tell the I.G.?"

"I wanted to ask about the privy arrangements," he said feeling tired of all the repetition and publicity.

"Oh, is that so?" the other asked, and added, "Here is the reply to your representation."

"What, sir?"

"You will not be getting any arrangement other than what you have already got, understand?"

"Yes, sir," said Sriram, uttering the soothing word, "but may I know why?" The guards pinched his biceps, alarmed at his impudence. But the Superintendent did not seem to mind. He merely replied, "If it had been any other time you would have been shot without a word, remember. You are not our guest, but our prisoner. You are not a classified prisoner, but one in custody under the Defense of India Rules, remember."

"But there has been no trial. How long am I to be here?"

"There is no need for a trial in cases such as yours. The whole world knows why you are here."

"I was only trying to do my duty," Sriram said. The Superintendent kicked the table and said, "I'll not have you fellows talking politics here." The word "politics" seemed to sting him.

"Yes, sir," Sriram said, and this again soothed the man's temper. He said as a concession, "You are neither Gandhi's man nor an ordinary criminal, but more dangerous than either." Sriram could express no opinion in the matter himself. The word "Gandhi" brought to his mind the memory of Bharati and he heartily wished that he had surrendered himself to the police with her. They would probably have treated him as an honorable political prisoner. "Where is Bharati?" "Is she by any chance in this jail?" "If so won't you let me see her?" "Is she keeping well?" Questions by the score buzzed in his head, as he stood staring at the wall.

The Superintendent said, "I'm glad you are paying close attention to my words. But let me say at once, it won't pay you to be troublesome, within these walls. What are you thinking?" he demanded suddenly.

"I was only wondering how long I shall be kept here. It's already several months. I have lost count of the months."

"It is unnecessary for you to keep count of anything, it's not going to be of any use to you. Your stay here will be as long as His Majesty wishes you to be here, that is all. We're instructed to keep you not very differently from your other friends here, under sentence of various terms of rigorous imprisonment. That's all, dismiss." The guards clicked their heels, saluted, and turned Sriram round. As he was going the Superintendent threw after him the remark, "You will ask me for anything you want."

"Yes, sir."

"That's all, dismiss." And the guards marched him off.

The days, weeks, and months, that followed were similar, one day following another without much distinction. Sriram began to feel at home: he looked forward to the little excitements that came to him in the course of his existence. When he was taken to break stones in the quarry behind the jail, he welcomed it as a change: the rocks that he hewed were hot under his seat, the sun scorched his body, the iron hammer with which he broke the stones peeled his skin, but still he liked the job because it took him, though under surveillance, outside the jail. He was with a gang of men, miscellaneous criminals, who were there for anything from murder down to confirmed pocketpicking. Most of them were planning what they would do at the end of their term. Some of

182

them were planning to return again and again, and spend the rest of their lives here. Sriram felt uneasy in this rough company, who laughed at the softhanded, softheaded man. They simply could not make out why he should have courted all this trouble from the police because someone wanted him to do something, and not because such exploits as derailing a train brought him a share of profit. This was a fresh outlook that had not occurred to Sriram in his self-centered political existence. He had a feeling that he was running up against a new species of human being, speaking like monsters, but yet displaying sudden human qualities; they were solicitous that he should not undernourish himself; they pitied him for his inability to relish the food: a tough ball of boiled millet with very watery buttermilk. (The buttermilk was a recent addition because somebody had agitated for it in the press and in the assemblies, and the buttermilk content was just enough to satisfy the technical needs of all agitators in general). While he ate he thought of all the good things that his granny had made for him and remembered how even during his very last visit to her, at their house, she had offered him something that a neighbor had sent. He felt agony at the memory of the crunchy, ghee-flavored rice; he could almost hear the music of his bite, while he held up his aluminum platter to receive his quota. The very manner in which he munched made his fellow prisoners comment. "You still think of *Badam Halwa?*" asked the Culpable Homicide not amounting to murder. They were sitting side by side during the break for food at midday. "If ever I leave this place, I am going to spend a hundred rupees on *Badam Halwa* at the corner shop. You know, Krishna Vilas's. The shop is small but it is a wonderful place, he serves on clean banana leaves and not on plates. You know his *idlies* are almost as if made of the lightest . . ." Sriram was at a loss for a comparison.

183

and his companion helped him with similies of jasmine, rose petals, soft butter, and so forth. Sriram added passionately, "And you know he gives free *chutney* to go with it, you can't see the like of it anywhere else on the globe. You must have known the corner hotel?"

"No," his companion shook his head. "I am from Bellary, I am not familiar with the town."

"I know that hotel," the guard added, joining in their conversation, "it's a good place, but I go there rarely. I haven't much chance of getting out of this place."

"You are like us?" said one of the prisoners and all of them laughed happily at the joke.

Mealtimes were the best. Sriram's neighbor, a veteran forger, whispered to him, "Don't tell anyone. I am getting some good things to eat and drink next Thursday. I will give you some when I get them."

"What is it?" asked Sriram unable to control his curiosity.

"Some *vadai,* and the nicest chicken *pulav.*"

Sriram retched at the mention of the chicken. He made a wry face: "Chicken! Chicken! Oh! I can't stand the thought of it!" he said, his face twisting with disgust. "I don't eat those things!" he cried. "I have not even eaten cakes because they contain eggs."

The forger was amused. He rolled with laughter till the guard, who had been friendly hitherto objected: "Stop that, where do you think you are!" The Central tower threw a welcome shade. The afternoon was languid, though warm. The Superintendent would be snoring in his quarters, enjoying his afternoon siesta: there was really no one to object to anything; and this was the only hour when the prison ceased to be a prison for a while and gained a human and habitable atmosphere; the warders themselves acquired a friendly mellowness, and all conversation flowed on the

184

human level. This was the hour at which it was impossible to continue the rigors of the jail atmosphere: it was almost like the midday recess at Albert Mission School of Sriram's younger days. The forger pleaded with the warder: "Don't bother us for a while, please. A man needs some rest after all the labor of the day. Please leave us alone for a while." And then he turned his attention to Sriram: "I know they will use the purest ghee and nutmeg leaf and cinnamon bark for the *pulav*. If you scoop a handful of it, ghee will drip down your fingers; it's so rich. Don't say that you won't have it. You must accept it. It will do you good. Once you taste it, you will keep demanding it every day. That's the worst of it. It'll be impossible to get it into the place every day, though once in a way we can do anything. Our friend here and his friends will not mind what we do. He knows he will get his share." A gong struck the hour. The warder jumped to his feet and said: "Get up and march," and he led them back to their quarrying at the back of the jail.

At night, Sriram had companions in his cell. Before lying down on their cement beds, wrapped in their blankets, they sat up talking. The sentry at the corridor cried, "Hush! Don't talk." One fellow, the one who had committed housebreaking and murder, took it into his head to sing a hymn and insisted upon all the others joining him. *"Rama, Rama, Sita Rama,"* he sang musically, and urged all the others to follow the chorus. He said, "This is the only thing which is real," in a very philosophical manner. "You must know what is real and what is unreal. You must know the nature of the world in which we live. You must repeat the name of the Lord ceaselessly." And he began a singsong devotional recitation of the Lord's name. Others followed. If they stopped, he shouted in the dark, "What Satan's offspring is in this room with me? I will cast him out." Sriram could not help asking, "If you were so religious, why couldn't you have remained outside and led your followers?"

"It's because the police would not let me be, that's all," he said.

"Of course, but for the police, we would all be happier men," someone said. After this they all started their chant again. The sentry came and peeped at them. They guffawed. He muttered something and went away. The leader said in the dark, "I am not afraid of anyone, I am not afraid of any jailer."

"It's because you are so experienced," said another admiringly.

"I would have been swinging in that shed long ago, but the judge understood that I didn't kill because I wanted to. I only wanted to break the bones of that ill-fated fool."

"Which ill-fated fool?" asked Sriram, unable to check his curiosity. Here was a collection of men who formed a new species. He might have to spend the rest of his life as a member of this family.

The other answered: "I only wanted him to give me the keys, as so many others had done, but he suddenly ran to the window, shouted for the police, and when I tried to run away, he jumped on me and held me down. What could I do? I had to do something. I thought I might crack his legs and— but he pushed me, that didn't work. These people force us to do unhappy, unpleasant things." He ruminated for a while and sighed, "No use thinking of it, but the magistrate understood, and when I leave the jail, I shall take him some fruits, oranges, plantains, things like that. Let us not waste our time." And he began his chant with the others joining in. Sriram wanted to speak to them about politics, Mahatmaji and nonviolence, and the British rule. He began to speak but he was cut short by the man saying, "Who cares who rules? We don't belong to that world. I've seen all these Gandhi followers in prison, and they think they are honored guests! If you had been careful you could have enjoyed that too. They'd have put you in a bungalow with a cook and pocket money and they would have given you books to read and sherbet to drink."

Sriram's blood boiled at his words. "How dare you speak like that of those who are suffering for the country's cause? You are mistaken. You are completely mistaken." He wanted to get up and hit him, but he remembered that Bharati would have labelled him a traitor to the nonviolence creed of Mahatmaji. Perhaps she would have said, "I don't want to look at your face again. Get out of here." And so he merely mumbled, "Don't talk in that utterly ignorant manner of our patriots."

The other growled, "Who are you to talk to me in that tone?" There was a pause. The forger at his side nudged and said, "Say you regret it. Don't rouse him. He is very strong." Sriram heard heavy steps approaching him from the other end of the cell. The man stood over Sriram and growled: "I insist upon saying that your political prisoners are no true prisoners, do you understand? I've been in ten jails so far. I have seen a lot of them. They feel they are in their father-in-law's house, visiting for *Deepavali*. I know what I'm talking about. I won't have you correcting me, do you hear?"

"I don't agree with you," said Sriram. "They are great patriots. They put themselves through much suffering."

"I will knock your teeth out, if you contradict me, am I clear?"

"I will say what I please," said Sriram defiantly. "Even the British Government could not make me do what I didn't like to do!"

The other sneered: "H'm, this is what comes of reading and writing. You don't know obedience of any sort, let me tell you. People should never go to a school. They talk too much."

"If I had been out, I'd have made you prostrate yourself before Mahatmaji, and confess your crimes," said Sriram with passion.

At the mention of the Mahatma, the other brought his palms together and said, "Don't drag his name in here; that great saint."

"He is also in prison, I suppose you know that," said Sriram.

"He may be, what is that to you? Do you think you are also Mahatmaji because you are here?"

"Go back to your bed, man," commanded Sriram. "You don't know what you are talking about."

"You call yourself Mahatma's disciple, and you have derived no good from it. What business have you to come in our midst?"

Sriram said in disgust, "Go back to your bed, man, I won't talk to you."

The gangster swung his arm to hit Sriram. Sriram felt the rush of air in the dark, and ducked his head, and the other went back to his bed; Sriram felt happy and relieved only after he heard him stretch himself out and utter a long noisy yawn, which he prolonged into a song, till the sentry cried through the bars, "Hush! Silence. No more talk."

During the day the various duties he had to perform and the variety of derelict humanity he watched in the prison kept his mind away from too much gloom. But when the last

of the prisoners in his cell fell asleep and snored, his loneliness came down on him and he became a prey to introspec-
tion. He was seized with a desire to meet and talk to Bharati.
Where was she? Dead? Married to someone else? Or hanged
in the prison? There was no way of knowing. He was amazed
at the isolation that had been devised—inhabiting the same
planet, people were completely cut off from one another.
States and their police minions seemed capable of devising
any torture for human beings. Bharati had probably married
Gorpad and gone to North India. It was months and years
since they had met. He had lost count of time. The only
reckoning they had was morning, midday and night punctuated by meal hours, drudgery, and occasional excitements
such as that caused by the bully in his cell. He wondered if
Bharati would ask, "Who are you?" if he appeared before
her. He was seized with the obsession that day by day he was
deteriorating so much that he wouldn't be fit to be seen by
her. He was losing his identity. He had lost his patriotic aim.
He wondered what he had done to warrant anyone calling
him a political sufferer. But for Jagadish he would not have
done things that he wouldn't wish to enumerate before any
decent person now. If it had not been for Jagadish he would
probably have gone on living in his ruined temple until the
police forgot him. And then he might have been worthy of
associating with Bharati. The thought of her produced in
him a certain uneasiness: he heartily wished that she had
not been such an uncompromising zealot. Everything that
she thought or said or expected was set on grooves and
was hard to practice. To all practical purposes he was a
back number now, nothing better than the associate of
forgers and homicides: their world was his world. Why should
he be thought of differently? The longer he stayed here the
more likely he was to drift away from Bharati. It was im-

perative that he should get away. How? He revolved in mind all the things he had read in story books—of files and hacksaws being smuggled into prisons and people working their way out. The more he thought of it, the more unhappy he became. The sheer helplessness of the whole business weighed him down. He became silent and glum. All night he was racked with dreams of being caught while escaping, taken out and shot, the shooting party being directed by Bharati. He woke up in cold sweat and was greatly relieved to find that after all he was still in the solid and homely prison. Why was Bharati causing him worry even in his dreams? Why couldn't she make herself agreeable and amenable like any other normal sweetheart?

The Fund Office Manager sought special permission to meet him.

The call came to him when he was at work in the weaving shed. A warder came to say, "You are allowed to see a visitor today, between three and four in the afternoon."

Sriram felt excited. "What visitor?" he cried. "Man or woman?" He had a wild hope that his visitor might be Bharati. Could it be? What would he say to her? How was he going to talk to her? How could he tell her all that he wanted to within the time? Perhaps she would spurn him when she saw him. Better not see her. Could he send word back that he would not see anyone? All this passed through his mind in a flash. He asked: "What sort of a person?"

But the warder said, "See for yourself. The interview is in the Chief's room. If you don't waste too much time asking questions, you can have a few minutes with the visitor."

Sriram followed the other meekly, dropping his job.

His neighbors muttered: "Your mother-in-law is probably come to see you, with sweets!"

At the entrance to the Chief's office, the warder halted for just a second to look him up and down, flick off a cake of dirt on his jacket, and pull up his dress in general: he murmured: "Remember how you should behave before the Chief. If you make any trouble, he will have you whipped."

Sriram answered, "I don't like whipping," to which the other retorted, "Don't talk back. It is enough if you do what you are told." It was only after Sriram had mumbled an unqualified affirmative that he would behave properly that the warder pushed him in. He saw the Fund Office Manager waiting for him. He looked intimidated by his surroundings; he sat on a stool, his legs dangling, afraid to cross them. The Chief looked up briefly and said, "Prisoner, you have special permission to meet a visitor today." Sriram felt abashed to stand there in that uniform and face the Fund Office Manager. He stared at the Manager, who stared back at him. The Chief was busy looking through the papers on his table. "You may speak," he ordered. "I can't allow this interview to be prolonged beyond four p.m. If you have anything to say to each other, go ahead, and don't waste time." Sriram felt like a fool. He had a feeling that the Manager would break the ice and begin a conversation. But the man seemed bereft of speech. The Chief tried to ease the situation again by interrupting his study of the papers to order, "Guards, wait outside." Two men, who had mounted guard over Sriram, saluted, clicked their heels, and went out. This brought a slight improvement, but still the interview did not proceed beyond the stage of mutual staring. The Fund Office man seemed to be stunned by the sight of the Sriram he saw before him now. He seemed to doubt whether this lank, sallow, close-cropped man in striped knickers and jacket could be the one he had come to see. Sriram noted his surprise and hesitation and said to himself: "When even the Manager is so reluctant to admit my identity, what will Bharati do? Perhaps she will say, 'Get out, you *budmash*. Who do you think you are?'" The chief looked at his watch and fretted. He said: "You may talk about anything except politics and other banned subjects." Sriram suddenly found his voice to ask, "How is everybody, Manager?"

"Very well, very well," the man said swinging his short legs, still afraid to cross them.

"Tell me about granny," said Sriram.

"That is why I have come here," said the Manager. "We had a communication from her today."

"Communication! Where from?"

"Don't you know? She is in Benares now?"

"When did she go there?"

"Oh, you don't know all the story? When she revived at the cremation ground, some orthodox people said that she could not come back into the town because it was inauspicious and might blight the city. She respected their wishes and stayed in the toll-gate house for some days, and then said she would go to Benares. We helped her to take the train at Talapur."

"Benares! What is she doing at Benares?"

"She is with a number of others, who spend their last years there, old persons who are waiting to die. They cheerfully await their death, and look forward to the final fire and the final ablution in the sacred Ganges."

"Did she ask for me?"

"Oh, she was so—" the Manager began and at this point the Chief said, without looking up from his papers, "Not allowed. Talk of something else."

"But it is not politics," began Sriram.

"Don't argue. Talk of something else," ordered the Chief.

Sriram helplessly glared at him and said to the Manager: "And then what happened?"

"She is quite well in Benares. There is a whole street of them, old people who have retired there to the banks of the great Ganges, awaiting their end. Some have been there for years. That's as it is enjoined upon old people in the *shastras*. No one could wait for a happier end."

The man from the Fund Office seemed to be so impressed with this that he became very eloquent, and Sriram could not help asking, "You, too, want to retire there?"

"Yes, in good time. If God wills it. Everyone can't be as fortunate as your granny!" He paused to reflect, gently swinging his short legs. He had respectfully left his sandals outside the office and Sriram noted how dirty his feet were, and blackened with dust and wear. When he came back to the sordid world again the Manager said, "She has given instructions regarding the disposal of the rent of her house. She wants the amount to be sent to her."

"Is someone living in the house?"

"Of course, of course. Didn't you know?"

Sriram seemed to be hopelessly out of date, he seemed to know nothing of what had happened anywhere. "It was her instruction that a tenant should be found for the house, and accordingly we found one to pay a rent of forty rupees only, which they are crediting to the old lady's account in the bank."

It was an appalling thought for Sriram, that someone else should be living in the old house, shutting and opening its doors. "Who are they?"

"Some yarn merchant."

"Yarn merchant! I never thought we would have to surrender our old house to a yarn merchant!" he said with disgust.

"It's no surrender. They will vacate at a month's notice."

This information somehow filled Sriram with uneasiness. "Where am I to live?" he thought. "Where am I to accommodate Bharati, when we marry?" Although he had lived away from the old house for so many years, he still had a feeling that everything was all right so long as grandmother lived there and so long as he could think of it as a home. He was filled with nostalgia. Its brass-bonded, slender pillars, the *pyol* over the gutter, and the coconut-tree tops beyond the row of buildings.

"This is the point," said the manager. "She wanted me to tell you about it, and if you didn't want this money—it's been accumulating, as I have already told you, into a considerable amount—she said it might be sent to her. She seems to have exhausted all the cash she had taken with her. This can be done, I suppose?"

"Of course, why not?"

"I am merely carrying out her instructions. She wants me to consult your wishes in the matter."

"Do anything she asks you to do. If she needs more money, don't hesitate to take it out of my funds. Poor granny! I wish I had more time to give to her affairs. She has done so much for me. How is she? Does she feel very lonely?"

"Far from it. A friend came from Benares today. She is keeping very well; bathes thrice in the Ganges, and prays in the temple, cooks her food, has good company. A sublime life; it's this friend who has brought the letter."

Sriram thought of his house again and felt unhappy. "They are probably driving nails in all the walls and what has happened to all my books and other things?" He gave a list of articles he possessed.

And the Manager said soothingly, "Don't worry about all that. They are all safely kept. In that end room, which we have reserved for our own use."

"What other news? How is the war?"

"Don't talk of that," said the Chief.

"How is everything else?"

The man got up to say something, but Sriram interrupted with: "I don't even know what year or month it is."

"Nothing on those lines," said the Chief. "No politics, no war."

Sriram in the solitude of midnight in his cell developed the notion of escape. He revolved in his mind all the technique of escape that he had read or heard about. Smuggled files and rope formed, of course, the staple points in the whole business. Scaling the walls and crawling through ventilators were an inevitable feature. He dwelt on reminiscences of Monte Cristo's escapades; it was all very interesting and kept his mind busy planning. His admiration for the old prisoners became genuine; his sympathies were really widening. He realized how impossible it was to do anything within the walls of a prison, except what the jailer permitted. (The warders seemed to take a personal pleasure in carrying out their duties, they were incorruptible and could not in any manner be influenced.) And yet how did people smuggle in hacksaws and things like that? While his hands were busy digging the earth or turning a wheel, his mind revelled in dreams of filed bars and nimble ascents up dangling ropes, escapes which story film writers presented so slickly. This dream became so troublesome that he could not contain himself any longer. Lying on his cement bed at night he was busy weaving a rope that would go up to the ventilator in the ceiling, through which the night sky was visible, the only glimpse of a shining free world. His only consoling thought, perversely enough, was that perhaps Bharati herself was languishing similarly within the bounds of the Old Slaughter House. It was not that he wanted to see her suffer, but the idea of her suffering established a community of interest. If he succeeded in escaping from the jail, he would smuggle the tip to Bharati wherever she might be so that she might climb out of her prison, and meet him outside its formidable walls, and hug him as her hero. Or she might insist upon going back to her cell, refusing to walk out of it unless they opened the gates for her in a right royal manner. She might spurn him for his labor. She was incalculable in her behavior. She would want the sanction of Bapuji, perhaps. Bapuji would probably applaud the proposal, if it could be proved that Sriram's technique would enable all prisoners to climb out of jails, they would at once understand its national implications: how the British could be driven to despair if they were made to realize that their prisons could hold no one. It might drive them mad and make them swear, "Well, we will quit. We can't hold India any longer." It was wishful thinking on a very big scale, but that could not be helped. It was the only excitement that he could ever conjure up. In his desperation he consulted the bully in his cell when an opportunity occurred. One evening he was unusually friendly, and Sriram slipped over to his cement bed and sat there. He whispered: "Why don't we all escape from this hell?"

The other laid a clammy sympathetic hand on Sriram and said, "It's usual to get that feeling. But nowadays I don't get it. I just do my *Bhajan* and feel all right. You must also join us in our *Bhajan*."

"Well, we will speak about that later. But now let us discuss how we should escape."

"How?" asked the other.

"You must help us. You are experienced. Have you never escaped from a prison?"

"Yes, twice, that's why I'm doing my seven years now."

"You should not have allowed yourself to be caught."

"Well, these things just happen, we can't help it," said the other philosophically.

Sriram was interested in the method and asked, "How did you escape?"

"Easy," said the other, looking up at the ventilator. "We were just six in a cell. We spun out the blanket strands, raised ourselves on each other's shoulders, tied up the rope, and climbed out; it didn't take much time. We were crossing *cholam* fields in about an hour. No one would have found us again, but a fellow who had come out with us broke the lock of a house on the way and he was caught."

"Shall we do something like that and get out of here?"

The other thought it over and said, "Why should I? What have I to do outside?"

"But I wish to get out. I can't stand this place anymore," said Sriram.

"If you didn't like this place, you should not have done things to bring you here, that's all," said the other. "Even if you manage to get out, they will bring you back in no time, it's not worth all the trouble. You can't hide your face."

"I will grow a beard."

"They will pluck out your beard just to see how you look. This is how you bring dishonor on even holy *sadhus,* who have beards."

"I promise I will keep out of the way of the police."

The other shook his head. "What is the use of going out

197

if you can't move about freely?" He seemed to take pleasure in teasing him, and to disapprove of people who didn't appreciate their life in jail. Finally, Sriram took out his trump card and said, "I want to escape because a girl I want to marry is out there."

"Where?" asked the man ruthlessly. Sriram was afraid to give the reply, but he blurted it out before he could hold it back. "She is in jail, too."

"Oh! Oh!" the other cried, amused. "Do you mean to say you are going to slip into her jail and ask the jailer to officiate at your nuptials?" he asked coarsely. Sriram felt angry and regretted that he had ever mentioned his angel to this coarse man. God knew what terrible things he would say now. He remained silent, afraid to open his mouth. And the other said: "If she is the kind to go to jail, listen to my advice, leave her alone. You can't bring up your children in jail. There must be someone to look after the house. It's not at all right that both a man and his wife should be the jail-going sort."

"How is it with you?" Sriram asked.

"I have three wives, here and there, and they run the homes in my absence: if they didn't, I wouldn't hesitate to put sense into them. That's the way. You are not going to be here all your life. When you are let out, go and marry a good girl, I tell you. This jailbird will be no good for you."

"She is not a criminal; she has gone to prison on Mahatmaji's command."

"Oh! Oh! Oh!" the other sneered. "Why do you drag in that great man's name here?"

Sriram grew annoyed. Somehow the mention of Bharati seemed to rouse in the other the worst ideas. Sriram abruptly rose to his feet and went to his bed muttering, "Go on and sleep. Let us not talk anymore."

"You are afraid I shall tell the Chief, aren't you?" the other sneered. "If you don't join me with gusto in our *Bhajans*, I will report you to the Chief."

"I'm not afraid," said Sriram defiantly.

"Well, we will see. Don't be surprised if they lock you up in a solitary cell. You will have only the walls to talk to," said the other. He took a fiendish pleasure in promising hell for Sriram.

Sriram paused for a moment and said, "I have not wronged you. Why do you hate me?"

The other said sulkily, "I have no sympathy for those who don't believe in God. I don't like fellows who speak ill of God."

"I have not said a word against God," Sriram said, wondering at the turn the subject was taking. "What have I said?"

"I won't repeat it," the other replied. "If you don't respect God, you will be whipped in jail, remember. That's my experience. You should listen to a man with experience, that's all."

"I am in need of no advice from anyone," said Sriram haughtily.

The forger turned in his sleep and swore, "Are you going to sleep or keep on talking all night? A wretched place! It's become worse than the market place. No peace for a man who wants to sleep. I will call the guard if you fellows don't shut up at once."

In answer the bully let out a loud, challenging song in a stentorian voice, enough to wake the whole town. There was a sound of running feet outside. Sriram sneaked back to his bed. The guard asked through the bars: "What's going on here?"

"People are chattering and chattering. This has become

worse than the market place," said the bully from his bed.

A friendly warder brought them the news of the outside world: "Mahatma Gandhi is becoming the Emperor of India," he said one day. "I heard it just today from a person who knows these things. Some men have come by plane from England with such a proposal."

"Don't be silly. How can they want the Mahatma to become the King of India, when they have put him in prison for fear that he may become one?"

"Didn't you know? It seems he is out of prison."

"I don't believe it."

"I swear he is. They released him long ago because he was ill and his wife died. A woman who comes here to cut grass told me so."

"It is not safe to have any transaction with grass-cutting women. They will get you into trouble," said a veteran prisoner.

"How do you know?"

"It is because I have suffered. They are sirens. They will seduce you before you know where you are. And then you will have trouble everywhere. They don't like such goings-on in a jail."

"But this is an old woman who cannot seduce anyone. She is a grandmother, so don't fear."

"Then it is all right. Go on."

"Her son is in the army. Her grandson sells newspapers in the market and he tells her what goes on in the world." Every one of the prisoners and their guards as well, eagerly crowded round him to ask, "What is happening? What is happening? Tell us." "It seems that some men have come from England and they want to make Mahatma a King." They clapped their hands in glee. "Oh, how good to hear this!"

"Why does it make you so happy?"

"Because, if Mahatmaji becomes the king of our country, he will not allow anyone to be kept in prison. He doesn't like it. It's because he is a very good man. It seems the British don't like him because he says such things."

"They like him now, all right."

The indulgent warder looked on as the prisoners discussed these matters among themselves, while going through their various duties. The warder didn't, however, like the idea of a prisonless state. He said: "How can there be no prisons? There will always be prisons whoever may become the king." This was a ticklish technical point. The best thing was to consult the political expert in their midst. They turned to Sriram for guidance.

Sriram was breaking the stones unmindful of what they were saying. He was listening to their discussions but he chose not to display any enthusiasm. He said, "I don't know anything about anything."

They plied him with questions: "Is it a fact or is it not a fact?"

"How should I know? I am in your midst."

"Will they release us all from prison?"

"All? I don't think so; they are likely to release only political prisoners."

The warder seemed to feel relieved to hear it. "Ah, you say so. Political prisoners are different. There are some in the other block. I have heard that some of them are leaving every day. That is a different thing altogether. But you are all not political prisoners."

They all said, "What if we aren't? We are also human beings. Why should we not be treated well, too? Whatever you may say, Mahatma Gandhi will help us. Do you mean to say that Mahatmaji will not care for us? He is a kind man."

Their curiosity could not be contained. Night and day they worried about it, until one day a newspaper was smuggled in through the good offices of the friendly warder, and put into Sriram's hand for perusal and explanation. While his audience sat around him, and the guard watched over them, at the quarry outside the jail, Sriram read out to them the *Daily News* from the first line to the last. It was as if he had been given a sudden vision of a broad and active world. He read of the impending political changes, of the proposed division of India into Hindustan and Pakistan, of Mahatmaji's firm refusal to countenance the proposal, of the Cabinet Mission, and the endless amount of talking that was going on at Delhi, of death, disaster, and convulsive changes. The greatest triumph for Sriram was that the British were definitely quitting India. He said proudly, "I myself wrote on all the walls 'Quit India,' and you see it has taken effect."

People looked at him with wonder. He became a hero in their midst. "Will they give you some reward for all your work now?"

He read, and this was heartening, of the release of political prisoners from all the jails in the country; but he could not hope to come under this category. He was not classified as a political prisoner.

The Chief sent for Sriram. His tone was suddenly friendly: "I don't know what the Government order will be about you. But we have received a number of names for release this week. I am glad to do it, because it will reduce our pressure of work. However," he said, looking through the list, "Your name is not on it." Sriram's heart sank. He had a feeling that he was being kept in a cage when all the others were roaming the wide earth freely. He thought unhappily that someone was discriminating against him. It was a cruel and sadistic world. The Chief noted the pain in his face and said, "Evidently you have not been classified as a political prisoner. All those who have done what you have done are under the consideration of the government. If you like, you may send in a representation, with an undertaking, and I will forward it."

"What representation and what undertaking?" asked Sriram.

"You will have to give an undertaking to report your movements to the police for some time till all the papers are scrutinized and your classification is settled."

Sriram thought it over. "Is this a New India or are the British still here?"

The Chief answered, "I cannot tell you anything about it. That is politics. I am merely carrying on as per the rules."

In a moment it flashed across Sriram's mind that all the difficult, hazardous things he had done would be set at naught by this undertaking. If he met Bharati she'd probably say, "You sneak out of prison, do you? You have degraded your-self beyond description. Get out of my sight."

He told the Chief. "No. I can't give any such undertaking."

"All right, please yourself. Right, dismiss." The warders tugged his biceps and he turned and walked out of the room, depressed more than ever.

After all there came a day when he went into the office adjoining his Chief's room, a spacious office in which there were a number of racks. He was led in there by his usual warders without much ado; he handed a slip of paper to a uniformed man sitting at the table; there were a number of others standing around him, to each of which he was passing bundles of cloth. Sriram waited patiently till his turn came; the man took the slip from his hand, looked him up and down, and cried "Number six seven," at which one of the attendants ran up a ladder and brought out a bundle, and placed it on the table. The man scrutinized the bundle, looked at Sriram and asked, "Are these yours?" Sriram looked at the clothes; he had been made to take them off long, long ago and change into jail uniform. He was thrilled at the sight. He hugged them close to his breast and said, "Yes, these are mine."

"Wait," said the other, snatching them back from his hand, "Sign here." He held a sheet of paper; there were numerous sheets of papers to be signed. Sriram was irked by the number of hurdles he had to cross before going out of this hateful place. At last the man was satisfied. He handed him the bundle, his old close-collared coat, shirt, and *dhoti* in which he had been arrested ages ago at the cremation ground. "Change into your clothes now. You are no longer a prisoner." Sriram proceeded to strip his jail dress before everybody. Life here had toughened him. The man said, "You can go behind that shelf and undress." When Sriram emerged from behind a shelf loaded with old discolored bundles of papers and documents, he felt he was back in his old shape. He rolled up his striped shorts and jacket, and shoved them into a corner. The man said, "You are free, you are discharged." Sriram stood still, unable to decide which direction to take. "Go this way, the door opens out," said the man. Sriram saluted him vaguely, and muttered, "I am going," and opened the door; it gave onto a small yard which was closed with a barred gate at the other end; an armed sentry paced in front of it. Sriram's first instinct was to turn back at the sight of him, but he told himself, "I am no longer a prisoner," and walked on haughtily. The man opened the door at his approach. He said as Sriram passed, "Going out! Very good, try not to come back, unless you like this place very much."

"I hate it," said Sriram with feeling. "I never wish to see a prison again."

"That is the right spirit," said the man, "Keep it up." He was evidently used to uttering this formula to every outgoing prisoner. It was a sort of convocation address.

When the barred gate closed behind him Sriram could hardly believe that he was free. He felt weak and faint, and inexplicably unhappy. The memory of his cellmates who had become sullen and gloomy when it became known that he would be leaving, was painful. The bully had said, "You are a selfish sort. I don't like your type." The forger said, "If you can be released, why not we? Tell Mahatmaji that we want to come out."

Another one said, "If you become a big minister or some such thing, don't forget me."

The bully had added, "When I am released I will break into your house some night, and teach you good sense. I don't like selfish fellows like you."

The warders had trooped behind him for tips. There was a little money that had accumulated as his wages, which the Jail Accountant had handed over to him, and his old warders followed him muttering, "We have been together so long." "I would like you to remember us." "This is my child's birthday. Give me something to remember you by." "We cannot come beyond this block and please give anything you like." "We have looked after you all these months." Sriram gave a rupee to each of the crowd that followed him importuning, and that took away fifty percent of his earnings.

Part Five

H E WALKED on as in a dream. It was difficult for him to move about without a guard following him, and without being told where he should go. He found the evening light dazzled his eyes, the wide open spaces were oppressive. He turned back to cast a look at the building which he had occupied for years now. It looked in its slate-gray color an innocent enough building, but what a tyrannical world it had contained: a fellow could not do anything he wanted, even the calls of nature had to be answered as per regulations! The jail was outside the town limits at the Trunk Road end. He had never gone so far before; he had been living all along on the Trichy Trunk Road, not knowing where he was. He walked down the road towards the town, wondering where he should go now. A few busses passed him. He hoped people would not recognize him. There was a policeman sitting in one of the busses and Sriram turned instinctively away from the direct line of his vision. He walked on along the edge of the road. "This is an independent India into which I am walking now," he reflected. What was the sign that it was independent? He looked about him. The trees were as usual, the road was not in the least improved, and policemen still rode on the footboard of highway busses. He felt tired and hungry. He had not more than a few rupees left, after the warders had had their claim. He wished that some sort of transport was provided for prisoners let out of jail: it was very inconsiderate, even in a free India to have to face this! He hoped that some day they would make him a minister and then he would open a canteen, and place station wagons at the disposal of prisoners at the jail gate so that those that came out might not feel so lost.

It was dusk when he got into the Market Road. Nobody seemed to notice him. Here and there he saw buildings hung with the tricolor flags, the *Charka* in the middle. He saw that there was less traffic than formerly. Shops were lit and crowded as ever. He felt a pang of disappointment. He had a gnawing hunger inside him. There were still a few rupees in his pocket, hard-earned, literally earned by the sweat of his brow. He put his hand into his pocket and jingled the coins, and remembered the axe he had wielded, and all the undreamt of tasks that he had performed. He had a feeling of pride at the thought of all he had earned by his hard labor: no one could say that he was one who lived on the fat of the land. Even his granny could feel proud of his achievement and ability. He sat on the bench of a small park that had been formed at the traffic junction of New Extension and the Market Road. He sat there in order to think clearly how he ought to manage. There was no use trying to settle things while walking. This was a free country and no one was going to demand why he sat there and not somewhere else. It was difficult to get used to the idea; it was a luxurious idea worth brooding over. But he felt startled again and again as he realized in a habitual way that he was exposing himself to the public gaze too much, and that he might have to slip into his hiding swiftly. Sitting there on the cement bench beside a potted fern he told himself: "I'm free. No one can come after me now. No one will bother whether I have a clean-shaven face or a hairy one." He felt hurt at first that the pedestrians went by without noticing him and the traffic without pausing to say, "Hallo, hero!" But he soon realized the blessedness of being left alone after all the years of being hunted and looked for everywhere.

He realized that his first business was to eat something. He could do the clear thinking while sitting on a hotel chair instead of a park bench. He got up and moved off briskly down the road. The first hotel that showed itself in sparkling bulbs was Sri Krishna Vilas's. He turned in. Most of the tables were empty. It was long past the rush hour. He sat on a marbletopped table and waited for someone to come and ask what he wanted. A man sat at the exit on a raised seat with a cash box. The waiting boys were all in a group chattering among themselves. "They don't care," Sriram told himself. "I suppose I look like a gutter-rat. They will drive me out." He looked around him. He recognized one of the waiters: he used to come here often in other days. "Hey Mani!" he called, and the waiter turned. "Come here," he commanded.

The other came up. He recognized Sriram, and cried, "Why, it's you! Where have you been all these years, sir? It's a long time since we saw you."

"I was away on business. Give me something good to eat."

At the word *good* the boy puckered his face in worry. "There is nothing very good now, sir, what with the present difficulty of getting rice and any pure food. Our government do not do anything about it yet. Do you know how hard it is to get any frying oil? Most of it's adulterated stuff, I tell you." He started on a long narrative about the food situation in the country, the food shortage, the postwar confusion, and the various difficulties and hardships that people experienced. All this was a revelation: it was the first report that Sriram was getting of the contemporary world. But he had no patience to listen to too much of it. "What have you?" The boy cast a brief look at the shelf on which trays of eatables were on display and started, *"Kara sev, vadai,* and potato *bonda . . ."* Sriram said sharply, "I can see all that from here. I want to know if you have anything fresh inside, on the oven, something more solid." The thought of *idli*, soft and light and of *dosai*, were alluring. It seemed as if he had tasted them in a previous birth. While he spoke he was racked with the thought that he had probably lost the necessary idiom to get on with ordinary folk. Perhaps he only had the ability to talk to jailmates. He said, "Something very g—" he avoided the word *good* lest it should start the other off analyzing the world situation. He said, "I want something heavy, just made, I am very hungry."

"There's nothing inside, sir. This is closing hour, and the kitchen department is the first to shut up. While our proprietor wants *us* to work till ten, those who sit at the fireside—"

Sriram lost his patience. He didn't want to spend the rest of the evening listening to shoptalk. He said sharply, "All right, all right, get me something, anything to eat, now run and get me coffee, *good* coffee," and he felt sorry that he had again blundered into the word, for the boy began to say something about the difficulties of making good coffee: milk-supply difficulties, the sugar racket, and the general avarice of black marketeers of various kinds. Sriram didn't know what to do. He lost his patience completely, "Why do you tell me all that?"

"Because it is so."

"All right," he said callously, "I'm hungry. If you are going to give me anything look sharp. If you stand here and talk, I shall get up and go away."

"What shall I give you, sir?" the boy asked officially, for the first time giving an impression that he was on duty.

"Two sweets, one savory and a large quantity of hot coffee," commanded Sriram. This was the first time in many months he was able to order anyone about. He was surprised at his own voice, almost fearing that someone would say that he was to be put into solitary confinement. But it worked. The boy ran off with alacrity and interest.

He felt elated after his tiffin and after chewing a betel leaf and nut, he felt as if he were back in the times when there was no war, no political struggle of any kind. He was himself grandson of a grand old lady, with no worries in life, shuttling between a free reading room and market place and Kanni's shop, and living in a world with well-defined boundaries, with set activities, no surprises or worries, everything calculable and capable of anticipation.

He hurried on to Kabir Street. It was a fine homecoming. It was seven o'clock, but as usual children were playing in the streets, and the space in front of every house was washed and decorated with white flour. Why could he not have lived like these folk without worries of any kind or any extra adventures; there seemed to be a quiet charm in a life verging on stagnation and no change of any kind. The lights were on in most of the houses. He ran down the street with his eyes wide open. He stopped in front of his house. He looked through the doorway. Some strangers were moving about. He felt angry and cheated. What right had they to usurp his place? Some unknown children were chasing each other in the front hall under the lamp—that old lamp where the old lady had taught him so many things in life! He wanted to run up the steps and tell the children: "You can't run around here, I can stop you if I want to." They were probably knocking holes in the wall, banging the doors and shutters, leaving wreckage behind for him to occupy himself with when the time came.

He turned round to see Kanni and talk to him. But the shop had gone: the portrait of Maria Theresa was no longer there to brighten up the surroundings. In Kanni's place, a new cement structure rose without windows, probably a godown. He felt pained and cheated again. He walked up and down the road. None of his neighbors saw him. He saw a few of them in their houses sitting by the window reading an evening paper—comfortable folk. He felt like going up and talking to them, but they'd probably reprimand him for various lapses, and he also felt diffident about his ability to talk to anyone! He was obsessed with the thought that he had lost the idiom of communication with these people. The street remained very much unchanged since he saw it last—only Kanni's shop was gone, and there was no one of whom he could inquire.

Suddenly he felt that he had nowhere to go that night. In the prison at least, one had been assured of a place of retirement for the night.

The photographer's establishment was brightly lit, and threw on the road all the illumination the place had. It was a low-roofed shop with the usual glass front stuck with a variety of enlarged portraits of children, pretty girls, and important men.

There was no one in the front parlor with its *coir* carpet and a small stool with a decorative potted plant on it. There was no sign of anyone living there. Sriram stepped into the next room, which was also empty. He cleared his throat and made sounds with his feet in order to indicate his presence.

"Who is there?" came the call. It was the photographer's voice.

Sriram replied: "A jailbird." He felt happy that after all there was someone known to him to meet in this world.

The other came out of the innermost chamber and advanced, trying to find out the identity of the visitor. He had evidently been working close to a light and could not see clearly. When he came near enough, he cried, "You! When were you released? What a pity I didn't know! I was wondering what you had done with yourself. Where were you? They would not tell us where you were. If I had known you were coming out today, I'd have arranged a grand reception for you at the jail gate with flowers and garlands. The trouble is that things are still disorganized. But I blame no one. Ours is an infant state, still a baby, many things are still to be done, we must be happy that we are our own rulers and no foreign nation rules over us. We must be happy that things are being done and not spend the time finding fault with anyone."

"Rather, we must rejoice that it's our own people that are blundering, isn't that so?" Sriram asked, some of his irresponsible spirit returning. "Fancy Nehru and Patel and the rest sitting there where there were haughty Viceroys before. Didn't Churchill call Mahatmaji 'The Naked Fakir?' The 'Naked Fakir' is everything now, think of it—" He was excited. "There are bound to be mistakes, bound to be blunders everywhere, but we must not make much of them." He was wildly incoherent and happy.

"If you had been out of jail, you would have been garlanded and carried in a procession on Independence Day. What a pity, you missed it! It was a grand affair."

Jagadish seated Sriram on a large sofa, put a mighty album on his lap, took a seat by his side and turned its leaves. He remarked, "As a photographer, I am proud of this. Future generations can never blame me for being neglectful. I have done my best. Here is a complete history of our struggle and the final Independence Day Celebration." He had put various pictures of himself into the album, subscribing himself as a humble soldier. There were even photographs of the ruined temple, where Sriram had lived and worked. The photographer had entitled it: "One of the secret headquarters of the Independence Army." Sriram looked through the album, which in effect was a documentary of the independence movement.

Jagadish had even stuck in photographs of jails and their exteriors. He had pictures of barbed wire entanglements. It was a completely romantic picture. Nor could he be said to suffer from modesty in any way. He was the chief architect of Independent India, the chief operator in ejecting the British. He had included several pictures of Malgudi Street scenes. Flags flew from every doorway and shop, crowds were moving in procession with people singing and playing musical instruments. Flowers everywhere. Great masses of men moving down the roads. Jagadish looked at the scenes, with great pride. He felt he had striven to give people a good time and had succeeded. He said, "After all what do I get for all the trouble I took and the risks I ran? Are they going to make me the Minister of this and that? Not a chance, sir, there are others waiting for the privilege. Even if I stand for an election, who will know who I am? Will the parliamentary board choose me as their candidate? Not a chance, sir. That is the reason why I have held fast to my camera and studio all through my various activities. Nobody can take it away." There was a tone of regret in his voice which Sriram did not understand. "After all, as you said now, we are an infant nation," the word was very convincing, it had a homely and agreeable sound, nobody need worry what it meant or why it was mentioned.

"True, true," said the photographer, "I'm not complaining or grumbling. What I have done, I have done with the utmost satisfaction. I am not worried about it at all. What I say is I have got these photographs to record all that we have done, that's all."

There were hundreds of pictures to wade through. Sriram began to turn the leaves fast. He felt bored. They were monotonous to see. More and more processions. More and more people. Flags. Pictures carried in the procession of national leaders and others, and more and more people. There was a sameness about the whole thing; he simply could not stand any more of them. He briskly turned the leaves of the album and came to the last page of the sequence in which Jagadish was seen hoisting the flag at some public gathering. Sriram put away the album and asked, "How did you manage to photograph yourself?"

"Ah, a pertinent question, who could photograph the photographer? Guess how it was done. Do you imagine I attached a camera to my back to follow me and take the pictures?"

"Possibly, possibly," said Sriram losing interest in the whole question. He didn't want to look at any more pictures or hear about them. The sight of the Independence Day celebrations irritated him. He almost said, "If only I had known that people would reduce it all to this! I didn't go about inscribing 'Quit' and overturning trains just to provide a photographer with material for his album." He decided that he wouldn't look at any more pictures.

The photographer said, "I have three more albums. They present another phase of our struggle." He attempted to reach them down from a shelf. Sriram held his hand, saying, "No, not now. I have a headache. I won't look at any more pictures." He was terrified at the prospect of having to look through more crowds, flags, and assemblies. The photographer said: "Good photographs are a sure remedy for headache. That's what an American scientist has recently found

217

out." Sriram said defensively, "I will examine them again tomorrow."

"Very well. You know what my greatest regret is?" He paused to give him time to guess, and added, "That I haven't a cine-camera. If only I had had one I'd have shown you all the scenes you have missed as if you were seeing them before your eyes. That's the stuff. If I had charged as much as other photographers, I'd have had the biggest movie camera there is. But oh, this troublesome conscience with which some of us are burdened!"

Sriram felt disappointed with the man: he had looked so imposing as an underground worker: so precise and clear-headed and purposeful. Now he seemed woolly-headed and vague. The atmosphere of peace did not suit his nature. Sriram wondered for a moment why he had ever carried out his orders at all. He was disappointed that the other showed so little interest in his own jail existence. Sriram asked, "Did the police get you?"

"Me! Oh, no! How could they? They didn't know my whereabouts. It was possible for me to evade them completely. I lived, after you left, in that temple; didn't you see it as the first picture? Didn't you notice how I labeled it?" He again tried to reach out for the album. Sriram said hastily, "Yes, yes, quite right. It was very apt," although he could not clearly recollect what it was.

"Moreover," concluded the photographer, "there was no occasion for the police to get me. My grandmother did not start dying at a wrong moment. If it hadn't been for your grandmother, you would not have gone to jail at all."

Sriram said nothing in reply. This was a subject which he did not wish to brood over. He had a hope they might have something to talk about in common, some diversion from the photographs. He asked point-blank, "Where is Bharati? Did she come out of jail?"

"Oh, yes, I was wondering why you hadn't asked anything about her. I thought perhaps you had forgotten her!"

"No, never! Not even for a moment!" cried Sriram passionately. "Have you seen her?"

"Of course," said the photographer in a tone which made Sriram anxious and jealous. While he had been having social intercourse with homicides, she seemed to have come out of prison, been received and garlanded by the photographer and his friends, and probably they all had a good time. She must have wondered why he was not there! He hoped that the others had had at least the goodness to remind her that he was still in jail.

"Did you receive her at the prison?" he asked suddenly.

"We should have, but it was impossible to meet her. She was in one of the earliest batches to be released, and she immediately took the train that very evening for Noakhali."

"Noakhali? What is her business there? Where is it?" His geography was poor.

The photographer ignored the geographical question and said, "Are you aware of what has been going on in East Bengal? Hindus versus Muslims. They are killing each other. Are you not aware of anything?"

"No. How could I be?" said Sriram. "I was not kept in a municipal reading room or the public library. I'm not aware of anything or of what you are talking about."

"Whole villages have been burnt in intercommunal fights. Thousands of people have been killed, bereaved, dispossessed, demented, crushed."

"Who is doing what and why?"

"Don't ask all that. I am a man without any communal

notions and I don't like to talk about it. Somebody is killing somebody else. That is all I care to know. Life is at a standstill and Mahatmaji is there on a mission of peace. He is walking through villages, telling people not to run away, to be brave, to do this and that. He is actually making the lion and the lamb eat off the same plate. And Bharati seems to have had a call."

Sriram was seized with cold fears. This was a new turn of events for which he had not bargained at all. Noakhali, Calcutta, Bengal, what was the meaning of it? What did she mean by going so far away from him? Did she do it by design? Did she try to make good her escape before he could come out of prison? "What did she mean by going away?"

The photographer simply laughed out the question.

"Couldn't she have come and seen me in prison? She must have known I was in prison?"

"How?" asked the photographer.

"By inquiring, that is all, it is simple," said Sriram with feeling. He said, "Probably she has no thought of me. Perhaps she has forgotten me completely!"

Jagadish became serious on seeing his gloom. "Don't let all that disturb you so much. Were you thinking of her often?"

Sriram began to say something in reply, but could not find the words, spluttered, remained silent and began to sob. The photographer patted his back and said, "What has happened now that you feel so bad about it?" Sriram had nothing much to say in reply. He merely kept sobbing. The photographer said, "You are a fool! What have you done to keep in touch with her?"

"What do you mean? What could I do, chained and caged?"

"Now, I mean. What are you going to do about it now? Now you are not chained or caged. What are you going to do about it?"

"She is so far away, thousands of miles from me," Sriram wailed. The thought of Noakhali was very disturbing.

"But there is such a thing as a postal service. You don't have to employ a special runner to carry your mails. Why don't you write to her?"

"Will you see the letter addressed and despatched properly?"

"I promise. Give it to me. I will send it off."

This brought a ray of hope to Sriram. He suddenly asked, "What should I write to her?"

"H'm, that is a thing I can't tell you. Each man has his own style in these matters."

It was clear that his mind was in a complete fog. To think or plan clearly was beyond him. Prison life showed its damage only now.

The photographer took pity on him. He said, "Please rest a while, close your eyes and relax," He went to a small table and took out pen and a sheet of paper, and started writing. The traffic on the road outside had ceased.

"Don't you wish to close your shop?" Sriram asked.

"Don't let that bother you. I can look after myself. I'm not much good at writing this sort of stuff. Anyway, I will try. Meanwhile shut your eyes and switch off your thoughts, if you can." He sat and faithfully wrote a long letter which began:

"My darling, who keeps slipping away like this! I might as well be in jail. But in jail or out of it—there is only one thought in my mind, that's you. I have been thinking of you night and day, and not all the jail-regulations could prevent me from thinking of you. And today I come out of the prison and my good friend Jagadish (he is a very fine man, let me say) told me about you. The prison-bars kept me away from you so long, and now all the miles between here and there, but that is of no consequence. This distance is no distance for me. May I come and join you, because I will gasp and die like a stranded fish unless I see you and talk to you? Give me your answer in the quickest time possible."

Jagadish got so lost in writing the letter that he forgot what time he was taking, and Sriram began dozing in his seat and snoring gently. Jagadish looked at him, hesitated for a moment. He put the letter under a paperweight and wrote a covering note: "If approved this letter may be signed and sent first thing in the morning, though preferably it should be copied in your own hand." He got up and shut the front door of the shop. He switched off the light, and went into his living apartments, softly closing the door behind him.

Ten days of anxious, desperate waiting, and Sriram received a letter:

"Happy to hear from you. Come to Delhi. Birla House at New Delhi, if you can. Our programme is unsettled. We are going to Bihar with Bapu, where there is trouble. There is much to tell you. We shall be in Delhi on 14th January. After that come any time you like. We shall be happy to meet you.

BHARATI."

The Grand Trunk Express in the end arrived at New Delhi station. Sriram struggled to reach a window in order to have the first glimpse af Bharati. The men near the window would not let him near it. It was no use speaking to them: they seemed to live in a different world. He spoke Tamil and English, and they understood Hindi, Hindustani, Urdu or whatever it might be. He could now realize the significance of Bharati's insistence that he should learn Hindi. Just to please her he had looked through readers and primers, but that took him nowhere. He had been isolated for the last thirty-six hours. He had sat brooding; jail life had trained him to keep his own company. His greatest trial had been when two men appeared suddenly from somewhere when the train was in motion, and scrutinized all the people in the compartment; when they came to him, they stopped in front of him and asked a question. He could catch only the words "Mister" and "Hindu" with a lot of other things thrown in. They were rowdy-looking men. He said something in his broken Hindi, and Tamil and English, which seemed to made no impression on them. They came menacingly close to him, peering at his face; Sriram was getting ready to fight in self-defense. He sprang up and demanded in the language that came uppermost, "What do you mean, all of you staring at me like this?" As he rose one of the two pulled his ear-lobe for a close scrutiny, saw the puncture in it made in childhood, and let go, muttering, "Hindu." They lost interest and moved off. After they were gone, a great tension relaxed in the compartment. Someone started explaining, and after a good deal of effort in a variety of languages, Sriram understood that the intruders were men looking for Muslims in the compartment: if Muslims were found they would be thrown out of the moving train: an echo of the fighting going on in other parts of the country. Sriram lapsed into silence for the rest of the journey.

It was a most uncomfortable journey: he was crushed, could not find the space even to stretch his length or swing his arms: people came crowding in and sat on him. Sometimes he could not even extricate his legs. When he felt sleepy, he leaned his head back on the window or on the shoulder of a total stranger. When he felt hungry, he called up someone selling tea outside, and drank it. He could not get coffee. The people here seemed strange men who could swallow the very sweet *jilebi* and wash it down with bitter tea, the very first thing in the day: this only confirmed his feeling that he was in a strange, fantastic world. He yearned for coffee, his favorite, like a true South Indian, but coffee could not be had here. He had to content himself by dreaming of it as he used to do while in jail. In fact this seemed only an extension of prison life: this life in a crowded, congested compartment, with a lot of strangers. He felt more uncomfortable here than he had felt in the prison. There at least he could say something or hear something from others' lips, but here the human voice conveyed nothing but jabber. The compartment was full of people who smoked *bidi* and filled the air with it, spat on the floor without a second thought, and the closet was nearly always inaccessible. He managed by jumping out of the train when the train halted and rushing back to the train when it whistled.

At ten-thirty or eleven on some day or other the train came to New Delhi. *"Nav Dheheli,"* people in the compartment cried and bustled about. He tried to run to the window or door to catch a glimpse of Bharati. She had written promising to meet him at the station. He felt ashamed of his appearance: he combed back his hair with his fingers: it was disheveled and standing on end. He knew he was grimy, grisly, and unsightly. He wished he could tidy himself up before Bharati set eyes on him after all these years. He caught a glimpse of her through a number of heads and shoulders jammed at the window, and, in his anxiety he pushed and bumped into people rudely, and the train moved past before coming to a halt. He saw her standing, gazing earnestly at the window. For a brief second he caught a glimpse of her figure, and his heart sank. He wished he could improve his appearance before facing her. He wished he could skulk away with the crowd and see her later. He had great misgivings as to what she might think of him if she saw him in his present state. But even in that desperate state, he knew, by his experience in the train itself, that he could never ask his way again and go in search of her. She might be lost to him forever.

When he got down from the train, carrying a roll of bedding and a trunk, Bharati's searching eye picked him out in the crowd. She waved her arms and came running to him. She gripped his hands and said, "Oh, how good to see you again!" and in that tone of spontaneous affection, Sriram lost himself, forgot his own appearance and griminess, and acquired self-confidence. He looked her up and down, and cried, "You look like a North Indian, yourself. You look like a Punjabi. I hope you understand our language." She took charge of him immediately. She picked up his bedding and said, "You carry your trunk." He snatched the bedding from her hand, and took the load on his own shoulder. She said, "Don't be silly. You haven't four arms, remember." And she snatched back the bed from his hands. Sriram lost his bewilderment. The proximity of Bharati gave him a sense of homeliness. It was as if he were back in Malgudi with her. He didn't notice the strange surroundings, the strange avenues and buildings, the too broad roads, the exotic men and women, and the strange shops they were passing. He had no time to notice anything. His attention was concentrated on Bharati. She looked darker, and more tired, but her tresses were as black as ever. She looked tired, as if she had undernourished herself. He could not get over the novelty of meeting her again. He was always on the point of disbelieving what he saw and felt. Perhaps he was going through a fantastic dream. Perhaps he was dead. Or dreaming from his confinement. For the first time these many months and years he had a free and happy mind, a mind without friction and sorrow of any kind. No hankering for a future or a regret for a past. This was the first time in his life that he was completely at peace with himself, satisfied profoundly with existence itself. The very fact that one was breathing, feeling, and seeing, seemed sufficient matter for satisfaction now. She kept looking at him, and asked, "When did they release you?"

He gave a summary of his jail existence and a résumé of all that had happened to him since she saw him last. The *tonga* ran smoothly. The extreme sympathy with which she listened to his story pleased him greatly. It gave it a touch of extreme importance. As he spoke, he was impressed with his own doings. He was on the point of asking himself: "Am I one person who has done all this, or is it someone else?" He was filled with a sense of extreme heroism. "I never thought I could put up with all this sort of trouble. I was very keen that the man in the street—" he began and puffed with his own importance. The listener in the shape of Bharati gave his whole life a new meaning and a new dimension. When they arrived at a colony of huts somewhere in New Delhi, he was completely satisfied with all the things he had done in his life.

"This is my present headquarters," Bharati explained. She had taken him to her own hut. "Yes, this is my home." There was a spinning wheel at one corner, and her clothes hung on a rope tied across the doorway.

"After all she is going to be my wife, that's why she doesn't mind my staying with her," he reflected.

She said, "You will have your 'room' ready in about an hour, till then you may rest here. There is another block, where you may wash yourself. Make yourself comfortable."

As she was speaking a group of children came running in crying, *"Moi, Moi—"* and they said something that Sriram could not make out. They came and surrounded Bharati, and dragged her by her hand. She stopped and said something to them in their own language. They left her and went away.

"Who are they?" asked Sriram with a touch of jealousy.

"Children, that's all we know about them," she said.

"Where do they belong?"

"Here, at the moment," she said, and added, "They are refugee children. We don't know anything more about them. I will be back in about an hour. Make yourself comfortable." And she went away with the children.

She was gone a long while. By the time she had returned he had explored the surroundings. He had discovered the bathroom and the tap, and washed, and tidied himself. He went back to her hut and spent a long time combing back his hair and studying himself in the mirror in order to decide whether he was worthy of Bharati. Bharati's kindness had restored his confidence in himself. He had never hoped that she would treat him with such warmth and kindness. The years that had separated them did not seem to make the slightest difference. It was as if they had separated only an hour ago: all the moments of loneliness and hankering and boredom that had made life a hell for him within the last few years were gone as if they had not existed at all.

He saw one of her saris hanging up, a white one with yellow spots. It was of course made of *khadi*, hand spun; the rope sank under its weight. He pulled it down to take it in his hands and gauge its weight, reflecting, "She ought to wear finery, poor girl. I will give her everything." He took it in his hand and weighed it. "It seems to weigh twenty pounds." He stretched it and held it before his eyes, "It's like a metal sheet. She must feel stuffy under it. I can't see any light through it." He rolled it up and pressed it to his breast. It had a faint aroma of sandalwood which pleased him. "It has the fragrance of her own body," he reflected, closing his eyes.

As he sat there the door opened and Bharati stood before him. "What are you doing with my sari?" she asked in surprise. "One would think that you were trying to wear it," she said with a laugh. Sriram reddened, and put it hastily away.

"It does not try to ward me off," he said, "when I take it to my heart."

"Hush!" she cried. "Don't try to be silly. We are all very serious people here, remember. I see you have tidied yourself up. If you have any clothes for washing give them to me."

Sriram handed her a small roll that he had brought back from his bathroom. "They are terribly soiled," he murmured apologetically. She snatched the bundle from his hands and went out. He reflected, "She is almost my wife, she is doing what a wife would do, good girl! God bless her. If I tie a *thali* around her neck somehow, when she is asleep, things will be all right."

She returned in a moment saying, "Your clothes will come to you in the evening. Here in this camp everyone is expected to wash his or her own clothes and not employ others to do the job, but you are new and I have got a *dhobi* to wash for you as an exception. Are you hungry?"

"Extremely," he said. "I am longing for something which I can eat."

"I don't know what you mean by something," she said. "You can't expect all our South Indian stuff. It is months and months since I tasted anything like that. You will have to learn to eat *chappati,* and vegetable and curd and fruit and not ask for rice or *sambhar.*"

She led him to a shack where some people were eating,

and children were sitting with plates before them. There were two platters laid for her and Sriram, side by side. "This is how husbands and wives sit together," Sriram reflected as he sat beside her and tried to work his way through wheat *chappatis*. He longed for the taste of the pungent South Indian food and its sauces and vegetables, but he suppressed the thought. Jail life had trained him to eat anything offered him. "I am really still in a jail," he reflected.

She was extremely busy all through the day. She seemed to have numerous things to do. She was always attending on children, changing one's dress, combing another's hair, engaging another group in dance or play, and continuously talking to them; besides this, she had a great deal to say to a lot of miscellaneous men and women who came in search of her. Hers was a full-time occupation. She gave the children a wash, fed them, put them to sleep on mats in various sheds, drew their blankets over them, said something to each one of them, and finally came back to her own room, sat down on her cot, and stretched her arms. Sriram followed her about for hours but could not get in a word of his own. He tried to smile at the children, thinking that that might please Bharati, but she hardly noticed his presence when she was with the children. It infuriated him. After a time, he turned on his heels, and went back to his hut. It was furnished with a rope cot and a mat. The hut had no door. There was a common bath at the end of the alley, which he shared with a number of others. He had felt indignant when he was transferred here. It seemed to dash his hopes to the ground. "Did she put me in here in order to get rid of me?" he reflected. "Because I picked up her spotted sari. If I had not done it, she would probably have let me sleep in the same room. I have probably destroyed her trust." He reflected ruefully. "Trust! Who wants her trust! I only want her."

He had switched on the light and was sitting on his bed. The entrance darkened. The low roof of the hut made it stuffy, although it kept the place warm in winter. She came in bearing his clothes which he had given her for washing. Sitting in his hut, Sriram had been seized again with the feeling that he was still cooped up in a cell. "My jail seems to be on my back, all the time," he reflected. The fatigue of the journey had begun to affect him; the intense cold air, and the gloomy and novel surroundings depressed him, and made him feel unhappy—a gloom and unhappiness without any cause. The brief spurt of happiness he had experienced seemed chimerical.

Bharati put his clothes on his bed and said, "Are you comfortable?"

"Yes and no. I feel happy when you are with me, and miserable when you go away." She looked at him, startled. He said, "Won't you sit down here?" and he made a space for her. She sat down. He moved close to her, and laid his arm on her shoulder.

She said, "Not yet," and gently pushed away his arm. "What a strange man!" she cried. "You have not changed at all."

He sat away from her and asked, "Am I still an untouchable?"

She said, "Bapuji alone can decide."

"Have you spoken to him about it?"

"Yes, more than once, but he has not given an answer yet." She sat with bowed head when she said it, her voice was low. She looked subdued. There was an uneasy silence for a while and then he asked, "Why? Doesn't he want us to marry?"

"It may not be that," she said, "but he really did not have the time to give it a thought, there were other things to do."

It was a relief for him to know that Bapuji was not against the notion of their marrying, but it was not enough. He held his breath and listened without speaking. He had a fear that his slightest word might spoil everything. This was an occasion for speech in the most delicate of whispers. Anything more harsh might destroy the whole fabric. He wanted to be on his guard. He wanted to do nothing that might scare her and take her away from him, nothing that might make fruitless all the thousands of miles that he had come. So he refrained from speaking. He wanted to shout at her and demand if it was only for this that she had wanted him to come all that way, he wanted to tell her that he regretted ever having set eyes on her. He wanted to threaten her that he would seize her by force and carry her back to South India. "More than anything else," she said, "the thing that pains Mahatmaji now is the suffering of women. So many of them have been ruined, so many of them have lost their honor, their home, their children; the number of women who are missing cannot be counted. They have been abducted, carried away by ruffians, ravished or killed or perhaps have even destroyed themselves." She appeared to be on the point of breaking down at the thought. Sriram felt he must say something in sympathy. "Why do these things happen?" And he felt ashamed of the utter inanity of his question. She didn't notice his question, but just went on speaking.

"On the fifteenth of August when the whole country was jubilant, and gathered here to take part in the Independence Day festivities, do you know where Bapu was? In Calcutta where fresh riots had started. Bapu said his place was where people were suffering and not where they were celebrating. He said if a country cannot give security to women and children, it's not worth living in. He said it would be worth dying if it would make his philosophy better understood.

He walked through villages barefoot on his mission. We followed him. Each day we walked five miles through floods and fields, silently. He walked with bowed head, all through those swamps of East Bengal. We stopped for a day or two in each village. He spoke to those who had lost their homes, property, wives and children. He spoke kindly to those who had perpetrated crimes—he wept for them, and they swore never to do such things again. I have seen with my own eyes aggressive rowdy-looking men taking a vow of non-violence and a vow to protect the opposite faction—don't ask what community they were: what one community did in one part of the country brought suffering on the same community in another part of the country. I have seen what has happened both at Noakhali and Bihar, and then at Delhi. How can one choose? Human beings have done impossible things to other human beings. It's no use talking whether this community committed greater horrors, or the other one. Bapuji forbade us to refer to anyone in terms of religion as Muslim, Hindu or Sikh, but just as human beings. He said one day that he sometimes pitied those who committed acts of violence—he advised some women in a village that they should sooner take their lives with their own hands than surrender their honor—"

"You must have gone to many places," said Sriram, not having anything else to say.

"Yes, for about a year I have been with Mahatmaji. He was at first unwilling to take me to all those places but I troubled him again and again after I was released from jail. I don't know how many villages I have seen. We followed the Master through burning villages. Of course, anything might have happened to us anywhere. There were a few places where they showed their anger even against Mahatmaji. They held up placards threatening Bapu's life unless he turned back and left them. But in such places he stayed longer than in other places. And ultimately he held his ground."

"Were you at any time in danger?"

"Of what? Of being assaulted? Yes, sometimes, but Mahatmaji had advised women as a last resort to take their lives with their own hands, rather than surrender their honor. There was no sense of fear where Mahatmaji was. But—if any unexpected thing happened, I was always prepared to end my life."

"No, no," said Sriram, horrified.

"It seemed quite a natural thing to happen in those places, where one saw burning homes, children orphaned, and men killed and women carried away. I felt we were in some other country. My special charges were children wherever I saw them. I gathered them and brought them here. All those children you saw here, we don't know anything about them. They escaped death, somehow, that's where Providence has shown its presence. They are all gathered from various villages in Bengal and Bihar. We had more, but some were reclaimed in Calcutta itself. But the ones we have now with us, we don't know anything about them. If their parents are alive, they will know they are here and come for them: otherwise we will bring them up. We have collected toys and clothes for them. Don't ask whether they are Muslim children or Hindu children or who they are. It is no use asking that which we don't know. We have given them only the names of flowers and birds. Bapuji said once that even a number would be better than a name, if a name meant branding a man as of this religion or that. You see one child was called Malkus, that's a melody: a girl is known as Gulab, that is a rose. These children must grow up as only human beings." Sriram shivered a little, and Bharati said, "I'll give you some warm clothes and blankets out of what we have collected for refugees. For this purpose, we'll count you as a refugee, no harm in that." She laughed slightly. He was frightened of her. She seemed too magnificent to be his wife. "You now understand why I could not talk to Mahatmaji about our own affairs. It would have been sacrilegious. Even so, I mentioned you to him one day in a village in Bengal. He was about to say something, when someone dashed in crying that he had been stabbed, and then another time in Calcutta I was telling him about you, and he asked when you were coming out of jail; it was late at night. I had waited for our opportunity when there would be no one about, and suddenly some big men, ministers of the place and others, arrived for urgent consultations. I never got a chance again."

"Will he remember me?"

"He never forgets anyone. I felt that the time was not yet—Tomorrow, let us go together and see him at Birla House, and if there is an opportunity, we shall ask him together."

"If he says no?" asked the anxious lover, with a shudder.

Bharati rose saying: "I will send you the blankets in a minute."

Next afternoon, Sriram, before setting out for Birla House, tidied himself up, looked into a mirror, and suddenly decided that he was probably looking too smart for the occasion. He rumpled his hair a little. His mind was buzzing with numerous doubts. Bharati had gone ahead to arrange an interview with the Mahatma. She had left a guide behind to conduct him to Birla House. He picked out a *khaddar* shirt and vest, wrapped a shawl around his shoulder, satisfied himself that he looked unostentatious. His greatest fear was that Mahatmaji would be reduced to saying, "Marry you! Bharati marrying you! Begone, you presumptuous worm!"

Bharati took charge of him at the gate of Birla House. She said: "He is terribly busy, but he will see us both for a moment. He knows we wish to see him urgently." A lot of people were going in and out, people in *khadi* and white cap, foreign correspondents in European dress; motor cars were passing on the drive. Sriram was blind to his surroundings. He asked Bharati: "If he asks me about anything, what shall I say?"

"Say anything, he will not mind it, as long as you speak the truth."

Sriram was amazed at the ease with which she moved about the place. He was confirmed in his view that she was too good for him, that he was not right to expect her to become his wife. All kinds of people stopped to have a word with her. She spoke English, Tamil, Hindi, Urdu, and God knew what else. She spoke with great ease to men, women, young boys and old men of all nationalities. She had a smile or a word for everyone.

"What a lot of people you know!" Sriram said with admiration. She acknowledged the compliment with a smile that charmed him.

"Yes, but I don't know the names of most of them," she said. They went through the drive and the garden.

"What a mansion!" he cried. They had to speak mechanical trifles: both of them were preoccupied with one thought: the impending interview with the Mahatma. If he said "Yes," what should they do next? To Sriram it was entirely unbelievable. It meant that he needn't dwell in a separate hut, that he could touch her, take her, he would have rights over her person, and he could always be with her. He took her aside on the lawn. "Just a moment, Bharati," he whispered, "if Bapu permits us to marry, shall we go through with it immediately?"

Her breath blew on him warmly as she whispered: "Yes, without doubt."

"How could we do it immediately? How could we make the necessary arrangements?" he asked.

"What arrangements? Are we going to have pipes and drums and a dowry and feasts?" she asked.

"Don't we have to buy flowers at least? Where am I to buy them in this place? I don't know anyone. I don't know my way about. How can I ask the bride to undertake all this for me? If only it were Malgudi, instead of Delhi, you would have seen what I would do."

"Don't worry about all that. Bapu himself will tell us what to do."

They crossed a small stretch of ground on which already some people were sitting. There was a dais at one end. "This is where Bapu holds his evening prayers every day," she said.

She entered the main building through the back. They reached a small veranda, crossed a passage, and stopped just ten yards from a window. She hushed her voice and pointed through the window. "There he is!" There he sat with spectacles on his nose, with his legs folded under him. He was earnestly listening to the talk of two people sitting. "That's Nehru, that's Patel," the girl whispered. There were a number of others also in the room—very busy men. "We must not disturb them," she whispered, and flattened herself against the wall. Sriram followed her example. The men inside were talking in low whispers. Someone came out of the room and smiled at Bharati. Bharati told her something in Hindi. "She is Bapu's grandniece, she looks after him."

"Won't they mind our being here?" Sriram asked. "They seem to be talking over important things."

"But Bapu has asked me to wait here for him and take a chance. I'll peep in at the right moment and show my face at the window. He will call me in, or he may come out for a moment."

"I tremble at the thought of his coming out!" Sriram confided to her.

"This is the only way we can have a word with Bapu. He is always busy and surrounded by people."

"He is looking somewhat weak," Sriram ventured, peeping through the window for a moment.

"Yes, his last fast has completely fatigued him. Sometimes he lay there without moving, unconscious." She stopped talking as a couple of girls passed. Someone with a shorthand notebook and pencil hurried off. A liveried government-house servant went in bearing a glass of water.

Seeing all this, Sriram wanted to postpone his meeting with Gandhi. "Should we disturb him today? He may not be free."

"He is always busy. This is the way. He has told me to wait for him and meet him today. I just told him that you were here and he said, 'Bring him along *today*.' 'Sometime tomorrow, Bapuji, you are busy today,' I said, knowing that he was going to have important conferences with the Prime Minister and others. 'I *mean* today,' he emphasized. He even indicated the spot where we should wait. He said when he had a moment to spare he would see us."

"I know you are waiting there. Come in, come in with your friend," came Mahatmaji's voice. "You may come now, all the dreadfully serious business in life is over. Come, come, my daughter."

"That is Bapu," said Bharati, clutching Sriram's hand, and leading him. His heart palpitated. Just before stepping into the room, she whispered, "Be natural and truthful. And tell him about the marriage."

237

"Yes, yes," Sriram gulped. They stepped in.

The Mahatma was seated on the floor. He looked up from a paper. Bharati brought her palms together and saluted. Sriram said, "*Namaste,* Oh, Revered Master!"

The Mahatma returned their salutations with a smile. He indicated a place near him and said, "Come and be seated here. I have postponed meeting you too long. Now tell me about yourself. Bharati, I hope your children are flourishing: you are a mother to thirty already. What a blessing!"

"Yes, Bapu," she said. "They are all fine. There was a little one who was down with a cold, that little girl whom you named Anar."

"Oh, yes, I remember her, you know what *Anar* means, pomegranate bud; what a beauty! God reveals himself to us in the shape of children. I have collected a lot of fruit today, you know the fuss people make when I fast. They always seem to think that it must always be followed by a feast! Well, I have kept them for you. Take them to the little ones and let them enjoy the feast." He indicated in a corner a heap of bright oranges and apples.

"Yes, Bapu."

"And don't forget to take them the flowers, too." The Mahatma now turned to Sriram: "Now tell me about yourself." Sriram for a moment hesitated. "What have you been doing in your part of the world?"

"They kept me in prison till a week ago," he said.

"Why didn't they release you earlier?" Gandhi said.

"I was awarded an ordinary sentence," he said putting into it all the poignancy he felt at the thought.

"That's very good. What did you do?"

Sriram hesitated for a moment and remembered Bharati's injunction to be truthful. He said, "For some time I preached 'Quit India,' but later I was overturning trains and—"

Mahatmaji looked grave. "You have done many wrong things. It's no comfort to think that worse things have happened since."

"Bharati went away to jail, and there was no one who could tell me what to do; no one who could show me the right way."

"That is an excellent confession," Mahatmaji said with a smile. "Yes, the mistake was hers in leaving you behind."

"No," said Sriram: "The mistake was mine. I refused to go with her to the jail, when she told me about it."

"Indeed, is that so, Bharati?"

"Yes, Bapu, he said he was—"

"Very well, when all this stress is over, you will tell me in detail all you have done as a political worker, and we will decide what we should do." He laughed. "We will hear if there has been anything so serious as to warrant my going on a fast again. Do you know how well a fast can purify?"

"I will fast if you order me to," Sriram said.

"I hope you have done nothing to warrant it. We will go into the question later."

"If it is decided, I'll be prepared to go through a fast myself," Bharati added, her face all flushed and red.

"You!" said Mahatmaji, "For your friend!"

At this point, at the farthest end of the hall someone was moving. The Mahatma said: "There is my conscience-keeper dangling a watch, telling me it is time to get up." He held up five fingers and said, "Give us five minutes more." He turned to his visitors: "I'm sorry I have to leave you in five minutes. Already people must have assembled on the prayer ground. Don't you hear their voices?" Sriram was seized with anxiety at the thought of time running out. Every minute counted. Already, even as he was thinking, he was losing precious moments. Only three and a half minutes more. He

239

must speak before the watch was dangled again. He threw a side glance at Bharati in the hope that she might at least seize the precious hour. But she turned on him what seemed to him a look of silent appeal. The Mahatma kept looking at them with an amused look. Sriram suddenly heard himself saying, "We are waiting for your blessed permission to marry."

Mahatmaji looked from one to the other with joy. "Do you like each other so much?"

Sriram burst out, "I've waited for five years thinking of nothing else."

"What about you, Bharati, you are saying nothing."

Bharati bowed her head and flushed and fidgeted.

"Ah, that is a sign of a dutiful bride," said the Mahatma and asked, "Does this silence mean yes?" Sriram looked at her with bated breath. Mahatmaji observed her for a moment and said, "She'd be a very unbecoming bride, who spoke her mind aloud! Good, good, God bless you. When is the happy occasion, tomorrow?"

"Yes, if you bless us so."

"Very well. Tomorrow morning, the first thing I will do is that. I will be your priest, if you don't mind. I've been a very neglectful father; I'll come and present the bride. Tomorrow the very first thing; other engagements only after that. I already have here all the fruits and flowers ready, and so after all you can't say I have been very neglectful."

When the man with the watch appeared again, the Mahatma said, "I'm ready for you." He rose to his feet. Sriram and Bharati also got up. The Mahatma said, "You have already a home with thirty children. May you be their father and mother!" He went into an antechamber and came out after a minute. Bharati waited at the door for him. He passed her with his eyes on the floor. Bharati followed him out with Sriram trailing behind her. Mahatmaji suddenly stopped, turned round and said: "Bharati, I have a feeling that I may not attend your wedding tomorrow morning."

"Why? Why, Bapu?" she asked.

"I don't know." His voice trailed away: "I seem to have been too rash in promising to officiate as your priest."

"Bapu, without you—"

"Tut, tut," said Gandhi. "You don't have to say all that. I want to be there very much, but I don't know. If God wills it, I shall come. Otherwise know my blessing is always on you both. Anyway, you are not to put off your marriage for any reason, remember," he said, with a new command in his voice, and Bharati replied, "Yes, Bapu." The Mahatma patted her back, threw a smile at Sriram, and hurried down the passage. He walked leaning on the shoulder of his grand-daughter. Sriram and Bharati followed, their heads full of their plans. Mahatmaji took out his watch and said, "I hate to be late—"

As they stepped onto the lawn, Bharati said to Sriram, "Let us attend the prayer today. There is a place for the two of us." They stepped aside. As the Mahatmaji approached the dais, the entire assembly got up. At this moment a man pushed himself ahead of the assembly, brushing against Bharati, and Sriram cried petulantly, "Why do you push like that?" Unheeding the man went forward. "I'm sorry to be late today," murmured the Mahatma. The man stood before the Mahatma and brought his palms together in a reverential salute. Mahatma Gandhi returned it. The man tried to step forward again. Mahatmaji's granddaughter said, "Take your seat," and tried to push him into line. The man nearly knocked the girl down, and took a revolver out of his pocket. As the Mahatma was about to step on the dais, the man took aim and fired. Two more shots rang out. The Mahatma fell on the dais. He was dead in a few seconds.